The Martlet is a Wanderer

Betwixt & Between Book I

A companion novel to the
Stormclouds/Harbingers fantasy series

Jane M. Wiseman

Shrike Publications
Albuquerque, New Mexico

Shrike Publications
Albuquerque, New Mexico
www.janemwiseman.com

Publisher's Note: This is a work of fiction. Names, characters, places, and incidents are a product of the author's imagination. Locales and public names are sometimes used for atmospheric purposes. Any resemblance to actual people, living or dead, or to businesses, companies, events, institutions, or locales is completely coincidental.

Book Layout © 2017 BookDesignTemplates.com

The Martlet is a Wanderer/ Jane M. Wiseman . -- 1st ed.
ISBN 978-1-7332998-7-9

For Will and Wallace

Noun, Heraldry

MARTLET: A bird icon like a swallow without feet, borne as a charge or mark of cadency for a fourth son.

THE MARTLET. . . never appears to alight on the ground as other birds do. . .
> --John Vinycomb, Fictitious and Symbolic Creatures in Art

This guest of summer, The temple-haunting martlet.
> --William Shakespeare, Macbeth I.vi.

TRIGGER WARNING: This novel contains depictions of sexual abuse. If such references and scenes distress you, please take care of yourself.

THE KNOWN WORLD

1 The Sceptered Isle
2 The Western Isle
3 The Eastern Baronies
4 The Ice-realm
5 The Southern Primacy
6 The Fire Isle
7 The Lyre Lands
8 The Cold Lands
9 The Burnt Lands
10 The Realm of the Asp
11 The Mountain Fastnesses
12 The Trade Road Fortifications

TO THE EAST:
• The Silk Lands
• The Forgotten Kingdom

THE GREAT SEA

THE UNKNOWN LANDS

The Stormclouds/Harbingers Fantasy Novels

Stormclouds: The Prequel Series

Book I, *A Gyrfalcon for a King*
Book II, *The Call of the Shrike*
Book III, *Stormbird*

The Harbingers Series

Book I, *Blackbird Rising*
Book II, *Halcyon*
Book III, *Firebird*
Book IV, *Ghost Bird*

Betwixt & Between: The Companion Series

Book I, *The Martlet is a Wanderer*
Book II, *The Nightingale Holds Up the Sky*

Stand-alone novel set in the Stormclouds/Harbingers fantasy world:
Dark Ones Take It: being the origin story of Caedon and his brother Maeldoi

All novels in the series available on www.amazon.com in paperback and for Kindle.

Contents

CHAPTER ONE

Silence

The man wasn't sure where he was or even exactly what he was. He was positive he did not know who he was, but that question came later.

He only knew that he was covered in some kind of filmy material, and that he was in some kind of long narrow box made of sweet-smelling wood. And that the world was rocking back and forth, first gently, then more and more urgently.

It made him feel sick.

Now, through the filmy material covering his face, he saw the outline of a woman bending over him, murmuring something.

He wasn't sure what she was saying. It sounded rhythmic, like chanting.

He tried to raise his arms to cast the cloth away from him, but for some reason his arms wouldn't move. He tried to speak, but no word came from his lips.

This woman had in her left hand some kind of light, maybe a rush light. She was raising the light and coming nearer. The light diminished and he heard scraping sounds as the light bobbed about overhead; she was fixing it into a bracket, perhaps. She returned. Now her left hand hovered just above his face, as if she were about to draw the filmy material back. She was lifting something, long and narrow, in her right hand. Even through the filmy material, he could see that this object glinted in the rushlight. Something made of metal. Maybe a knife.

He hoped she would take the filmy material away. Maybe she was about to cut it away, with the knife. He was feeling suffocated in the layers of cloth, and he suddenly realized he was very thirsty.

But then an obscure banging became a loud banging, and the rocking motion became a bounding, twisting, vicious careening.

The woman screamed. The torch must have fallen from its bracket, because the world around him plunged into darkness. He heard a clatter as something dropped on the floor—*the knife*—and a scrabbling sound, and a shouting. A door crashing open, quite close by. Another light, but dim and further away.

"Mistress, come with us. Up on deck. We're feared we may break up. You must come!" An urgent male voice.

The door clapped to, and this dimmer light disappeared as well. In the darkness, he felt the emptiness of the rocking, bucking room that contained him. He was alone.

With a mighty effort, he did manage to raise an arm. As the heaving and swerving of the room increased a hundred-fold, he fought in a panic out of the folds of cloth. Grasping the sides of the narrow box in which he lay, he hauled himself upright. But before he could try to clamber out (and he had his doubts whether he'd be able to do that, his limbs were so weak), a tremendous crash threw the box sideways, with him in it. The box upended on the floor below. Lying half-stunned with the kindling of broken shards of boards shattered around him, he realized the box had been set up on a kind of frame, and it had tipped over and spilled him out onto the planking of the room's floor.

Now, though, the hurtling of the ship quieted. That, he realized, was where he must be. Not in a room. Not on a floor, but a deck, in a ship's cabin. The ship rode more steadily.

He crawled from the wreckage of the box, scraping himself on splintered wood, and then he fought his way from the cloth tangled about him. Putting out a hand in the dark, he found a stable strut of some type, and after many attempts, he hauled himself upright, using it as a support.

He wondered if the woman, or the men who had summoned her, would come back. He hoped they would. He was full of questions now. How was he here? Where was he? Why? Too many questions to take in, just at the moment, as he stood unsteadily, holding onto the strut, his head swimming.

From far away, he heard voices.

I must get out there, he thought. *I must let them know I'm here. They'll help me.*

He began feeling his way through the dark toward the place where he thought the door of the cabin might be. The motion of the ship was still heaving, and his head was still swimming, so he grabbed on to handhold after handhold—the strut, the ladder back of a chair, some other solid object—and made sure not to let go of one until he had securely grasped the next.

Now he saw the door. A dim line of light from underneath it showed him where it was, and let him know that outside the door he'd be able to tell more about his surroundings.

He got to the door and pushed at it. It opened out easily into a narrow corridor where he could support himself with both hands on the closely-opposing walls. At the end of the corridor, rushlight flickered. He knew he must be on the ship's lower deck. Probably a fairly large cog, the kind used for shipping.

He stopped to listen. He kept hearing the voices. They weren't near. He must make his way in their direction.

As he lurched along, he saw he was nearly naked. A brief white cloth was drawn about his loins. He leaned to catch his breath against one of the heaving corridor walls, and looked down at himself. His rib cage was bandaged tight. He felt the bandaged area and winced. There was a wound there. Underneath the bandage he could feel the edge of some long straight gash down the middle of his torso.

Around his neck was a thong, and from it dangled a small object.

He put his hand to his head. It pounded, as if a tight band were being screwed tighter around his skull.

I've been injured, he thought. The woman bending over him must have been tending to his wounds.

But how had he been injured, and when? Judging from the seepage into the bandage, it might have been days ago. At least a day ago. A few days. That's what he decided.

He had the eerie notion that the bandage was keeping his body from falling apart into two halves. That the long straight cut down his torso had been made to slice him apart.

He managed to stagger to the end of the corridor where he heard voices just at the place it teed into another. He made his way as hurriedly as he could toward the voices.

Two men. As he approached them, they turned, and their eyes widened.

"What's this, then?" one of them said.

"Good sweet Lady's tits, did the hold burst open too?" said the other, weary, exasperated. He looked to be a sailor. He seized the man, bandaged, bloody, nearly naked, by the elbow. "Come with me, fellow. Back to where you belong."

Startled, the man tried to yank back out of the sailor's grasp, but the sailor was strong and the man was weak. This sailor pushed the man reeling ahead of him down another corridor, curved with the hull of the ship. The two of them pulled up short before a square hole in the planking of the deck.

"Pirtle Jailer," the sailor holding the man called out.

A head popped up from the hole.

"You're missing one of your prisoners," said the sailor. He gave the man a shove, sending him stumbling toward this other one called Pirtle. The man clung to Pirtle as the ship made a lurch, but Pirtle hustled him down a ladder into the hole. Then fended him off.

Confounded, the man looked back up over his shoulder at the sailor who had dragged him there, gaping down at him from the top of the ladder. The man opened his mouth to exclaim— to insist— to say—

To say what? He wasn't sure what to say. *I'm not a prisoner?* But what if he were? That's when he realized. He didn't know what he was. He didn't know who he was.

By the time these thoughts had swarmed like bees into and out of his head in a confused buzzing, the man named Pirtle had thrust him roughly into the stinking dark and had withdrawn up the ladder, slamming the trap door to the square hole shut behind him.

A groaning came from all around.

As his eyes adjusted to the dimness, he made out huddled bodies. Scores of them. Prisoners, it seemed. And he was one of them. What had he done, he wondered. And why hadn't he been down here before? What had he been doing up above? What had he been doing in that box?

Before he could think much about these disturbing notions, he felt himself lapsing back into the dark he had come out of not too long before. Not the physical dark of the fetid space into which he had been cast. A darkness lapping at him from inside his head, taking him off to some unknown place of oblivion.

How much later before he came back to himself again? It was hard to tell, but a watery green light was filtering into the room, so the world underneath the Spheres had moved from darkness into daylight. Now he could make out the tumble of bodies, largely naked, mostly male, that lay in the room.

The hold, he told himself. Not a room. The hold of a ship. A swimming, swarming feeling assailed him. But then he understood the rocking and swerving that were causing his gorge to rise were coming from his surroundings, from outside him, not inside.

The bounding motion made him retch, and the stench. Most overwhelming of all, the thirst. He tried to call out for water, but only a dismal croak came from his mouth.

"Child keep you, I thought you were one of the dead ones," said a voice. "You certainly were sweet-smelling when they pushed you down here. Someone rubbed you all over with spices, like. Less sweet-smelling now."

The man looked toward the voice. A large powerful fellow, one of the prisoners, lay near by. This big man raised himself up on an elbow. "Name's Kipp. And you are?"

He opened his mouth to reply but closed it again. He knew he couldn't say his name. He didn't know it. But he wanted to tell this man Kipp, *I don't know it*. Maybe somehow Kipp could help him find out what it was. He opened his mouth again to speak, to ask for Kipp's help, and he found he didn't know how. *Strange*, he thought. *I don't know how.*

Now this man Kipp changed to the speech of the Baronies and asked again.

Another prisoner had gotten up and had moved over to them to crouch down and look into the man's eyes. "Think he fought for their side? Are you crazy, man? Why would he be in here with us if he fought for the barons."

The prisoner named Kipp shrugged. "Worth a try. He could be a deserter."

"Could be," said the other one. He peered harder into the man's face. "Tell you one thing," he said to Kipp. "He's the Sea Child's for certain."

"Looks like it," said Kipp. They were speaking of the man as if he were some inanimate object. "But if he is, what's this, then?" This man, the one called Kipp, reached over and tugged at the leather thong about the man's neck.

He heard himself making an inarticulate soft sound of distress. He didn't want these others touching it.

Kipp dropped it and regarded him with interest. "Some sort of amulet. A bird."

"Blackbird," said the other prisoner. "Ours."

"Not a blackbird. Look at it." Kipp reached out his hand again, and the man shrank back. "Don't worry," he said with a kind look. "I promise not to touch it. But look at it," he said to the other prisoner.

"Not a blackbird," said the other one, grudgingly, peering at it in the dim light. "Like a blackbird, sort of."

"But different," Kipp insisted.

"Different," the other one agreed. "Sea Child eyes for certain, though."

"Whoever and whatever he is," said Kipp, "I think he can't speak."

"Master Silence, is it?" said the other man.

"Don't mock him. Who knows what he has seen?" said Kipp.

But from then on, the man's name was Silence.

Silence fingered the amulet on the thong about his neck. He didn't know what it was, either. Just that he didn't want anyone touching it.

For the few remaining days of their voyage, Kipp appointed himself Silence's protector.

The next time Pirtle came through with pieces of bread, Kipp made sure Silence got one as the others in the hold pushed and shoved to grab their share.

Kipp made sure to go to the water butt with the ladle and come back with water for Silence, again and again, until Silence had drunk his fill.

He sat by sympathetically as the bad water and the wormy bread ravaged Silence's starved skinny body, leading even the foulest of the rest of the prisoners to edge away from him in disgust.

If I had ever been sweet-smelling, thought Silence, *I'm not now.*

Kipp helped Silence take the bandage off his wound as the cloth became dirtier and dirtier.

"Any protection that bandage gave you has long been lost," he told Silence. Then he examined Silence's wound. "You're lucky, man. It has healed up nicely, no festering. You must have had a good healer. If it had started to fester, you would have gone fast down here." He considered it for a while. "It's an odd wound, though. What weapon and what kind of thrust would make a long straight wound like that one?" After a while, he asked, "Do you know who you are, and who you fought for?"

Silence looked at him in confusion. Had he fought? He must have. How else explain the wounds.

One of the others, overhearing, laughed. "That dummy lost his speaking, and he lost his mind with it, looks like," he said.

"He's not stupid," said Kipp. "He may not be able to speak, but he knows things as well as we do. Ordinary things. I think he may have been knocked in the head, though," he agreed after a moment, "and his memory knocked out of it." Kipp considered Silence carefully and gave him an encouraging smile. "He doesn't know his name, I don't think. Not just that he cannot speak it. He doesn't know it."

Silence looked at him and at the others. He shook his head.

"You see?" said Kipp. "He knows what I'm asking him. He may not know who he is, but he knows ordinary things. He does. We're on a ship, aren't we?" he said to Silence.

Silence nodded.

"You see?" said Kipp.

"You told him we were on a ship," the other man argued. "You just did," he insisted. "He's a dummy. He's no use. They'll kill him when we get to port."

"He'll be very useful to some master," said Kipp. "They won't kill him. They'll get good coin for him. You watch."

But Silence saw Kipp wasn't very certain about what he was saying. Silence saw he was saying it to be reassuring and kind.

He summoned up a smile for Kipp. He rubbed his two fingers together, miming the fingering of a gold piece.

Kipp laughed, delighted, and nudged Silence.

Silence laughed too.

"You see?" said Kipp. "He can laugh." Kipp peered through the dimness at Silence. "He has good teeth, too. Maybe he's a gentle."

"Nah," said the other one. "If he was some gentle, do you think he'd be down here with us?"

Will they? Silence was thinking, ignoring all the rest of it. *Will they kill me? And who are they, and why would they want to?*

Later that first day, Kipp approached Silence hesitantly. "Silence. I think you must have had a head wound. May I look?"

Silence nodded and inclined his head.

Kipp probed his skull with his hands. "Yes. You have another scar here. A ragged one. Someone struck you over the head. Probably a mace or some kind of club. Your hair has grown summat over it, though. It must have happened several fortnights ago. Maybe a turning of the moon. It's not noticeable. Do you have headaches?"

Silence nodded. He did. It was odd, though. Yes, he had had headaches since he opened his eyes in the strange box. But before that. *Well,* he thought. *There was no before.* Only the day or so since he opened his eyes to see that woman standing over him. As far as he knew, that was the entirety of his life.

Yet it couldn't have been. Kipp was right. He knew ordinary things: that they were on a ship, that they were prisoners being taken somewhere. He knew what war was, and he knew from listening to the others that he must have fought in a war, even though he couldn't remember doing so.

It was as if he were a new-born babe, but born as a man fully grown.

"Give it time, man. It may be you'll start to remember things," said Kipp.

Around the third day, by Silence's count, the third day since he had opened his eyes on this strange world he inhabited now,

Kipp and the others decided from the motion of the ship that they were probably coming into port.

"It's taken us a while, if we're going where I think we're going. My guess is we were blown all the way down the Narrows by that storm. You stick close beside me, when we make landfall." Now Silence saw real fear cross Kipp's face. "Can you stand, man? Because if you can't—"

There was a noise at the hatch. Someone lifted it and a shaft of light illuminated the hold where the prisoners were kept.

Silence blinked in the unaccustomed brightness. Once a day the hatch would be lifted as Pirtle came down with his basket of bread and bucket of water, but that was at night.

"Try standing," said Kipp urgently. "I'll help."

Silence was sitting against a post, so he circled his arms about it and struggled to pull himself upright.

Kipp put a hand under his elbow. Between the two of them, they got Silence to his feet. All of the prisoners were clambering to their feet now, all who could.

The motion of the ship changed. There came a shudder that caused Silence nearly to fall again, but Kipp steadied him.

"We've dropped anchor, I'm thinking," said Kipp.

Before Kipp could speak further, armed men had come down the ladder and were prodding the prisoners into a line against the far wall of the hold. The prisoners had to stand huddled together and bent over, the ceiling was curved so low there. Silence was glad of it. The prisoners were packed too tightly for him to fall down very easily, even if his knees buckled, as they threatened to do.

The armed men were moving swiftly from person to person among the prisoners who had not gotten to their feet, dispatching them with quick thrusts of their swords or calling out to Pirtle that this prisoner or that one was already dead.

Silence turned his eyes on Kipp. Kipp pressed his shoulder. "You see," he whispered.

Silence nodded and pressed Kipp's hand back, in thanks. If not for Kipp, he'd be dead. He wouldn't have been able to get to his feet fast enough.

The prisoners were herded up the ladder from the hold and out onto the deck, then unceremoniously dumped into the sea to wade their way to shore. Silence saw how most seemed terrified. But he was not. The deck was low, the drop not so far, and the sea felt delicious. *So,* he thought. *It must be true. I'm the Sea Child's.* Most others feared the sea. Not the children of the Child of Sea.

He found Kipp was right. Silence did know things. He knew about the Children, and he knew about the Sea Child. Whether they were actually his gods or not—that he did not know. Just that he wasn't afraid of water. He thought briefly about trying to swim away, but he was weak, and bowmen were training their arrows from the ship's deck down on the prisoners. On shore, armed men were waiting for them.

The sea was refreshing. He stayed in the water as long as he could, and plunged under, rinsing his hair of the dirt and debris that clotted it. His wounds stung from the salt water, but he thought that was maybe a good thing.

One of the armed men on shore was gesturing to him and shouting at him, and he saw Kipp was looking anxious, so he made himself come out.

When he emerged, he felt cleansed of the filth of the ship's hold. In a strange way, he felt he'd been made new. But only, he saw right away, to fortify himself against the great difficulties to come.

Once ashore, he pulled the sodden cloth more closely about his loins and pressed near to the others while the ship's important passengers were helped to land in small boats, far away from the stench and squalor of the prisoners.

Silence saw a woman disembark, the only woman he could see among the passengers. Small. Dark-haired. *If I could get to her and ask her, maybe I'd find out who I am,* he thought. She must be the woman he'd seen so strangely bending over him when he was in the box with the cloth over his face.

But he couldn't get to her. He saw at once there'd be no way he could.

Armed men set to guard them went now from prisoner to prisoner with leather collars, fastening them around the prisoners' necks. Silence bent his neck meekly to let a collar be put on him. Beside him, Kipp was doing the same. But Kipp was seething with rage.

"They can do this to me," he whispered to Silence, "but they can't take away the freedom that's in here." He thumped his chest. "I found that out when I threw in my lot with The Rising." When Silence looked blank, he said, "You mean you've never heard of The Rising?"

Silence shook his head no.

"Wonder how you did get wounded, then," said Kipp. "But maybe you fought with them and don't remember it. That blow to the head. It's the only explanation."

Kipp stopped talking. Some man was moving amongst the prisoners now. By his clothing, Silence thought he must be important. This important man pointed the prisoners out one by one and made statements about them to a scribe who was writing out some list as the important man spoke.

He stepped to Silence and grabbed Silence by the jaw. He peered into Silence's eyes and poked around his torso. "Nice-looking fellow," he said to the scribe, who didn't write this down. "Half-starved. A wound here down the torso. It will make a nasty scar. Look how well it has healed, though. What's your name?" he asked Silence. He spoke in the language of the Baronies.

Silence opened his mouth to speak, but nothing came out.

"He can't speak, lord," said one of the other prisoners. "He's a dummy. Blow to the head. Simple-minded."

"He's not." Kipp spoke up. "He can't speak, but he's not simple. He's perfectly capable."

"Be quiet, there," said the important man. He said it again in the language of the Sceptered Isle. He looked Silence up and down. "What's this?" He reached for Silence's amulet, and Silence drew sharply back away from him.

The important man slapped Silence across the face.

Silence stood with his head bowed, trying to drive down his rage. He saw it right away. The important man and the armed men had all the power. He had none.

"Lord," said Kipp, pointing to Silence's amulet, "It's something dedicated to the fellow's god."

"Didn't I tell you to be quiet?" said the important man. But he stood a little aside from Silence and examined the amulet without touching it, or Silence. "Doesn't look very valuable," he said.

One of the guards was making a small warding motion with his left hand.

The important man looked a bit nervous himself. "I don't know what god this object might belong to, but it's not gold, I don't think. Let the fellow keep it," he declared. Now that he knew what it was, or thought he did, the important man didn't seem to want to touch it, or so it seemed to Silence. The reverse, in fact.

"What shall I write down, lord?" said the scribe at his elbow.

"About this man? A pretty fellow. Can't speak, so what good is he? But he might be good in the brothel. There. That's where he'll go. Write that down. There's the scar, of course. But look at that face. And he's finely made."

Silence felt a flush rise to his cheeks.

"Look, he's blushing," said the important man to the scribe. "A very pretty fellow. He'll be popular, in there, scarred or not."

Beside him, he heard Kipp begin to make a small protesting noise.

"This one," said the important man, rounding on Kipp. "Labor in the fields." He strode on.

Silence looked up into Kipp's face. He knew his distress must be plain for Kipp to see.

"You must bear it, man," said Kipp. "Promise me you will. Do not despair. Tyranny can't last forever."

Silence stared numbly at Kipp. *No*, he thought, *maybe not forever. But it can last a long time.*

One of the other prisoners nudged Kipp. "Off to the fields with the likes of us."

"Huh," said Kipp. "I was born to it. Then I became a soldier. Now I'll go back to breaking up clods of dirt with the plow."

"I wouldn't mind the dummy's life," said the other man. "He won't have to work hard."

"I'd mind it," said Kipp. "And take a look at Silence. He minds it. Too bad I don't have the running of the world. I'd have the two of you switch places, since you want his life so badly. Bet you'd be good at it, brothel work."

The other man made a belligerent suggestion about Kipp's mother and brothel work, adding some unexpected anatomical detail involving her. Kipp responded in kind. The other man rushed at Kipp, but Kipp put out a big hand and easily fended him off. Then the guards came in with their clubs and began knocking heads. In the melee, Silence was separated from Kipp.

A well-dressed man came up to Silence as he stood bewildered on the shore. This man bound Silence's hands and began leading him away. Silence looked over his shoulder at Kipp, where he was being herded with most of the others to an area further down the shore.

His own minder stopped to bind and lead after him, along with Silence, several young women who were trying vainly to hide their near-nakedness from the gawking guards and the few townspeople who had come down to the shoreline.

And so Silence's new life began.

CHAPTER TWO

Buyers and Sellers

S ilence hated life in the brothel. He hated the brand they marked him with, on the wrist. The place where the hot iron marked his flesh burned and stung for a fortnight, and every time he looked down at it, he was reminded of what he now was. *Not that I have any former life to compare it to*, he said to himself.

He hated too what they made him do in the brothel. He couldn't stop what men paid to do to him. He endured it. He tried not to think too hard about what was happening to him, but he began to think harder about who he was.

Especially he began to think about how he could get away.

In the brothel, everyone called him Silence. He wasn't sure how they knew that was his name—the only name he remembered having. Perhaps the young women taken with him gave this name to his owners.

He lived up to his name. Sometimes he made a noise. But he didn't speak. The rare times he was alone, he practiced trying to speak, at least at first, and found he couldn't. The words stuck in his throat and didn't make it out into the world past his lips. So after a while, he stopped trying.

He had arrived with almost nothing in the strange world where he found himself. Just the piece of cloth around his loins and the amulet around his neck.

The piece of cloth, filthy rag that it was, had long been taken away and other clothing given him, a loose pair of trousers and an old cloak to wrap himself in when he slept. The master made him wear a tunic, too, so his scar and its stark strangeness wouldn't put off any customer.

But the amulet stayed around his neck, hanging by its thong. After that first attempt, no one tried to take it from him. Everyone seemed to agree that it had something to do with some god he worshipped, some maybe frightening unknown god, and left it to him.

Silence didn't know what god he worshipped, unless maybe it was the Sea Child, as Kipp and the others had suggested. He supposed that was because of his eyes. Everyone said so. He had looked into a bronze mirror once, a valuable thing owned by the master's highest-earning whore, and had seen a wavering reflection of his face. His eyes were gray. Those of the Sea Child had such eyes.

"Look at yourself, pretty fellow," this woman had said, offering him the mirror to hold and peer into. "You should see why those men want you."

He had seen his eyes then. If he happened to be desirable to the men who bought him, he wished it were not so. He wished sometimes he could destroy the thing in him they seemed to want, and now, looking into the mirror, he shuddered a little.

As for his amulet, it remained a mystery to him. He knew he wanted it always touching him, and he knew he wanted no one else to touch it. That was all he knew.

Sometimes he picked his amulet up from the hollow just above his breastbone where it hung, and stared at it. It was made of some dark metal, iron, probably. It was the shape of a bird. Not a blackbird. Its wings swept over its back. It had a little beak, an indentation of an eye, and no feet, just small carved bundles of feathers where feet should be.

If it were not the emblem of some god, what was it then? He had no answer to that question. He knew only that he needed it there around his neck. He needed to protect it from anyone who tried to take it from him or even touch it.

He was completely obedient to his masters, except for that, and they all liked him, how quiet he was, how graceful, how wide and darkly lashed his gray eyes were, how dark the hair held back off his face by a thong, how fine the ivory of his skin, his slender limbs, so they overlooked it.

He knew these things because he heard everyone talking of them. The master discussing them with a man who was deciding to buy him for an hour or a night. The bondsmaidens admiring and petting him as they went about their business straightening up and taking his things to be washed. The man in the bath shed where he went to cleanse his body. The women whores in the brothel, who all made much of him as if he were their mascot, maybe because he was one of the few men kept there, and the only one who was polite to them.

"Pretty Silence," they said to him. "Come over here and help me braid my hair. Come over here and tell me if I'm in looks for the banquet tonight. Come over here and tell me how you like my new scent." Silence might be kept in the brothel to serve men, but the whores knew he loved women. He didn't dare touch any of them, though, and they didn't dare touch him.

Not that he wanted to, or wanted them to, except in an animal, mindless seeking for comfort that sometimes came over him. Especially the times when the terrible headaches attacked. They didn't come often, but when they did, they were savage, and as he came out of them, he longed for some tenderness that he knew he wouldn't receive.

Silence liked the women well enough. But something kept him away from the intrigues that were always roiling the brothel—jealousies, hurt feelings, gossip, destruction of reputations.

There was a woman he loved, and he wanted only her. Hers was the touch he longed for. He didn't know how he knew this, or even if there were such a woman in the world, or in his past. But he knew it.

One matter struck him as odd, the more seasons he passed there and the longer he thought about it. Because he did not speak, everyone around him seemed to think he did not hear. Well, of course they knew he could hear. They gave commands, and he obeyed them. They asked him questions, and he replied with nods and gestures. But it was if he were a piece of furniture in the room, or some implement for them to use when they needed or wanted it and to forget it was there when they didn't.

The people around him all spoke in the language of the Baronies, so he knew he must be in that realm.

But he also knew he had understood the language of Kipp and his fellow prisoners perfectly well, and they spoke the language of another realm, the Sceptered Isle, the realm across the Narrows from the Baronies.

He wondered which place was the one where he really belonged. He gradually came to understand that a war had been fought between a powerful noble of the Baronies and a monarch in the Sceptered Isle, and the Baronies noble had won. He began to think he must have fought as a soldier for the forces of this monarch in the Sceptered Isle. That was the easiest way to explain his wounds, and the easiest way to understand how he came to be a prisoner and a bondslave in the Baronies.

He wasn't sure at all what Kipp had meant about The Rising. Kipp had asked him if he fought for The Rising. Silence didn't know what The Rising was and couldn't ask anyone. It must have had something to do with that war, he decided.

He wanted to ask something else, too. He wanted to know where Kipp had gone. He couldn't ask it, and he realized that even if he could, it was unlikely anyone at the brothel would know the answer.

Underneath his silence, he thought always of how he would get away.

For the most part, he could put aside the things they made him do at the brothel and live in a place in his head where these things didn't exist. But just being able to cut these experiences out and enclose them in some box inside him—that was not enough. It let him survive, but it wasn't enough protection to allow him to live in the world as a person underneath the Spheres. It gave him just enough protection to live as a sort of animal.

Then there were experiences it was not so easy to put into the box, even for survival's sake.

One person who came to buy his services was a man who loved to inflict pain, and Silence was his favorite object. *Probably because I can't say anything back to him,* Silence thought. *He can goad me, and goad me, and I can't answer back.*

Silence could push other experiences at the brothel aside into that small box and pretend these experiences were happening to someone else, somewhere else. But not the things this man did.

Silence discovered he could scream. If this man inflicted enough pain on him, he did, whether he wanted to or not. The man seemed to enjoy forcing Silence to that point. Silence tried not to scream, because he didn't want to give the man the satisfaction, and the man saw that, and then he was able to accomplish it by a number of wicked means at his disposal.

At the brothel, though, he could go only so far with his torments.

In the aftermath of one of these sessions, Silence was brooding in the courtyard of the brothel, where a serene pool reflected the sky. It was the only place in the brothel where he felt at home, even a little. Because of the pool, he thought. Being by water always calmed him.

He was waiting there for the master of the brothel to tell him what he must do next.

Alphonsine, one of the female whores, came out to the little pool too. "I saw you out here, Silence. I knew I'd find you here. It's your favorite place, isn't it." She hurried on. "I wanted to talk to you."

Silence looked up at her with a smile and patted the bench where he sat.

Alphonsine sat down and took one of his hands in hers. "Did that plague-sore of a man hurt you?"

Silence nodded with a rueful grin.

"Show me," she said.

He turned his back to her. She uncorked a little bottle of ointment and began rubbing it gently over the weals.

"Sometimes he asks for me, you know," she told him.

Silence looked over his shoulder at her in alarm.

"Yes," she said. "But more often now, he asks for you." She swiveled him around again on the bench and sat for a moment stroking his hand. "You probably know how relieved I feel, when he doesn't ask for me. But then I feel terrible, because I know I'm wishing my pain on you, Silence, and you of all people don't deserve it."

He pressed her hand back and resumed his moody gazing at the water.

She ran her hands along his torso. "This wound of yours has healed up completely. The scar is beginning to fade. Soon it won't even bother anyone."

It doesn't bother me, thought Silence. Only in one way did it bother him. The sight of it aroused the man who loved to inflict pain.

"Silence, you know my room is just next to yours," said Alphonsine, dropping her hands into her lap.

He looked at her warily.

"No, silly, I'm not propositioning you. I just want to tell you something you may not know about yourself."

Silence waited.

"Silence. You can talk. You talk in your sleep."

Silence gave himself a little shake. He looked at her hard, incredulous.

"You don't say much, but you talk, Silence. You do. So I know you can do it. No, don't worry. I don't think you're faking it. If you think about it, you can't talk. But when you're not thinking about it, you can."

Silence tried mightily to say something. He couldn't.

"You see? You're trying, so you can't."

He nodded miserably. Then he gave her a quizzical look.

"I can see what you're thinking. You want to know what you say. You were in love, Silence. You talk about a woman."

Silence closed his eyes, trembling.

"You never say her name. You call her many endearments. I think you might be married, Silence. Or were. So there. I thought you should know this. You should know it in case the master ever overhears, or hears about it, and accuses you of faking. And you should know it for yourself, too. Am I right that you have forgotten many things?"

He nodded.

"A cousin of mine underwent terrible things in wartime, and he couldn't speak either, or remember anything. But his mother used to tell us that when he was dreaming, he was back as he was, and he would speak the names of people he once knew. That's how I know you're not faking. As if anyone could. What they put you through."

He saw her eyes glittered with tears, and he pressed her hand again.

She leaned over and kissed him on the cheek, and then she ran from the courtyard.

Someone I love is out there somewhere, underneath the Spheres, he said to himself. *Someone I hold very dear. Someone who loved me. Maybe a wife.*

Maybe she was dead. Maybe she was not dead, but thought he was, and had moved on to a new life. That was likely, he thought.

In his fantasies, he began imagining that he had sustained his wounds protecting her. He laughed at himself for such thoughts, but he kept thinking them, and kept getting comfort from them.

Even these comforting thoughts, that someone who loved him might be out there somewhere in the world, that he himself had deeply loved, and also, remarkable to him, that he really could talk—even all these could not console him for the thing that happened to him next.

His master decided to sell him.

CHAPTER THREE

A Discovery

The man who loved inflicting pain on Silence wanted to buy him, so he could do exactly as he wished with Silence.

No one would tell Silence about this for days. He knew something was going on. No one would look at him, and when they did, their manner around him was strange. Finally he cornered Alphonsine and searched her face with his eyes.

"Don't ask me," Alphonsine said, her voice and eyes miserable. "They don't want you to know. They think you'll be too upset and make trouble."

He seized her arm firmly and stared at her.

"They're selling you. To that man." She didn't have to say which man. Silence knew.

He nodded at her and gave her hand a squeeze. Then he got himself to the courtyard in a state of despair. But he had his duties to perform, so it wasn't until late in the night that he could finally give in to the despair that was like to finish him.

It wouldn't, he thought bitterly. He'd just have to endure it. He remembered what Kipp had told him. *Just endure it.* Kipp probably hadn't imagined this, he thought.

One of the terrible headaches descended on him then. Finally it faded and he got a little sleep.

The master came to him the very next day. "Last night, you cried out in your sleep," he said with a severe look. "Everyone heard."

Silence thought to himself, *if I could only speak and tell this man what I'm thinking.* He tried and couldn't. He knew his despair had probably driven him to crying out.

"Have you been telling me pretty stories all along, pretty man?" said the master, a savage glint in his eye. "No matter. I'm selling you. Go to the street door. Your new master is there to take you away with him." He gave Silence a shove in that direction.

He didn't tell Silence to gather his things. Silence had no things to gather. He owned nothing, just the amulet around his neck. The old master didn't demand his trousers back, at least, so Silence wasn't handed over naked to the new one. But he left his cloak and his tunic and his mended and washed second pair of trousers back in his room. He didn't have time to say goodbye to anyone, and really, what would he have done? Just look at them all, press their hands. He wished he could at least have given Alphonsine some kind of farewell, but it might have gotten her in trouble.

The new master led him to a cart and thrust him into it. The new master lived in a fine manor a few leagues away, and soon Silence found himself in a tiny back room in this manor.

A serving maid came in with a neatly folded pile of clothing. "Master says you're to wear these, and to come to board in a candle-measure's time," she said, dropping the clothes on the end of his bed and whisking away.

The clothes were fine things. Soft linen, banded in embroidery. An embroidered band to hold his hair back. As Silence put these things on, he realized he knew something. *I've worn clothes as fine as these before. Finer, even.*

Since he wasn't sure how long to wait, having no candle, he let himself out into the corridor and wandered around the manor until he reached the great hall, where servants were setting up the board on trestles for the evening meal and lighting the hearth fire.

He sat down at the hearth fire to wait.

He saw his life was about to get much better, and also much, much worse.

And so it did. When his master was in the mood for him, Silence had to endure a lot of pain. Then a long period of healing. Then the cycle would begin again. *Strange*, he thought to himself. *This movement from some vile experience to lying for a sen' night or more in the hands of a healer seems somehow familiar.* But until he fell into the possession of this new master, there had been no marks on his body that might suggest such a thing, so he didn't know where the familiarity came from.

Usually these grim sessions with his master would take place by rushlight in a special room in the manor. Everything there was dim, as dark as nightmare.

Maybe most frightening of all, although Silence couldn't exactly say why, because the pain wouldn't be any worse than what the man was already inflicting on him, was this master's promise to give him a new mark of slavery.

"My man is clever with the branding iron," he told Silence. "He can change that mark of the brothel on you. I'm going to see that done. You're no brothel slave. You're mine."

He hadn't arranged to do this thing to Silence yet. Silence dreaded the day.

One sunny morning in midsummer, his master decided he'd try out a new little whip tipped with iron on all of its many tails, and he decided to do it out in the garden. Out in the daylight so, he said, he could see the bright stripes of blood on Silence's skin.

"Master says you're to go to the garden," said the same serving woman to Silence. By then, he knew her pretty well, and he could tell by her expression that he was in for it.

He nodded curtly.

"Master says you're to wear only these," she said, handing him a pair of trousers. They were coarse things.

No bloodstains to mar anything nice and give the laundress a lot of trouble, thought Silence bleakly.

"Come here, Silence," said his master when Silence let himself into the garden.

Silence went to the man, glancing quickly down at the whip he held and then back to his master's face.

"I'm going to tie you to that tree," said his master, pointing. Silence could see how aroused he was.

Silence walked over to the tree. He blinked. In the strong sun, he could feel one of his headaches coming on. He felt sick and dizzy.

"Turn facing it," his master ordered.

Silence did this.

"Arms up."

Silence lifted them. He felt his master's breath on his neck and had to stop himself from cringing away, because cringing always got the man roused. He waited for his master to tie his arms to something or bind them. Nothing happened. After a long time, he risked looking over his shoulder.

The master was sitting on the garden bench before the tree, aghast.

Silence wanted to ask if he could lower his arms, which were beginning to burn with the effort of holding them up, but of course he couldn't. Finally he lowered them anyway. *What does it matter?* he asked himself. *That man is about to lay into me with that whip, no matter what I do.*

Finally the master spoke. His voice was weak. "Come here, Silence."

Silence stepped away from the tree and came over to the bench where the master sat.

"Raise your left arm."

Silence did it.

The master stood up and moved to Silence, fingering his arm.

Silence tried not to wince away from him. This must be some new game the man was playing.

The master poked a spot in Silence's left armpit.

"You belong to someone else," he said finally. His hands trembled.

Silence looked at him in confusion.

"Go off to your room. I'll arrange that you be given back as soon as I possibly can."

Back to the brothel? wondered Silence.

He never saw the master again. The man stayed well away from him.

In under a sen'night, Silence found himself in the same cart that had driven him away from the brothel. This time he was well-dressed in new clothes, with a new cloak. The journey took all day, so Silence knew they weren't going to the brothel.

Late in the day, the cart pulled into an inn yard where a much more magnificent cart waited.

The driver of his own cart opened the cart's door and handed him out.

A very wealthy-looking man, pale, dark haired, stepped from the other cart and came to them.

The driver bowed respectfully. "Is this the man, lord?" he said. He pulled deferentially on his forelock.

The wealthy man looked Silence up and down. He began shaking his head.

"No?" said the driver, startled.

"Yes, it's the man," said the wealthy lord with a profound sigh. "You may go. I have him now. What have they been calling you?" he said to Silence. Silence opened his mouth and felt the familiar hopelessness. But the wealthy lord spoke past him to the driver. "What do they call him?"

"Silence, my lord."

"Silence?" The wealthy man gave a bark of laughter.

"Seeing as he can't speak," said the driver.

"Oh," said the wealthy man. He stood beside Silence as the driver climbed back up onto the seat of Silence's former master's cart, and drove off in it.

At last this wealthy lord turned to Silence. He put out a hand to him. He began feeling Silence all over, his hair, his arms, running his fingers down Silence's cheeks. Silence stood there letting him. This was his new master now, or so it seemed.

The man had very strange eyes, Silence noticed. They were an odd shade of amber. They had filled with tears.

"Raoul, what have they done to you?" said this man at last, picking up Silence's wrist, the one with the brand, and staring at it. Silence saw he had to choke the words out. He led Silence to the cart and handed him into it. Then he got in and sat opposite Silence. He called out to his own driver, and the cart jolted away.

Silence looked uneasily away from the man.

"Don't you know me, Raoul?"

Silence shook his head no, emphatically. But he was starting to feel very strange. In part of himself, he was starting to feel that yes, he did know this man.

That part of himself was afraid.

In all of the confusion of feelings that assailed him, something else came hurtling down on him. His own name. It was Raoul, and this man knew it.

CHAPTER FOUR

Here Comes a Mighty One

A fter that first strange meeting with this noble lord who seemed to know his name, Silence—or was it Raoul?—was put into rooms in a manor larger and more richly appointed than the one of his former master, and he was left there. Servants attended him. He was bathed, fed, dressed. No one came to see him or to force him to do any horrifying thing. No one put hands on him except the man in the bathing shed, and when he saw Silence didn't like to be touched, he mostly kept hands off and handed Silence the sponge.

Silence really, really didn't want anyone touching him.

Days went by, then maybe a sen'night. He was beginning to think he'd been put in some sort of luxurious solitary confinement, even his meals brought to him there, when a serving maid came to his door carrying much richer clothing than before.

"Master says you're to wear these. Master will be here shortly to see you."

Silence steeled himself for whatever this man might do to him.

He sat on a bench before the hearth fire of his rooms and waited.

The same man as before walked into the room.

Silence rose to his feet and bowed. *Should I kneel?* he wondered.

The man came to Silence and led him back to the bench and sat him down there.

"You're looking well now, Rafe," he said.

Silence was startled. The man had called him Raoul. Now Rafe. Did he even have a name? Maybe this man just called him whatever came to mind.

The man laughed a little. "You can't speak, is that true?"

Silence nodded.

"And you remember nothing of your former life."

Silence nodded again.

"You can hear just fine, thank the gods, whoever they are. And I see those men who took you at least left you that amulet of yours. I'm glad to see it."

Silence put his hand to it and held it firmly. But the man didn't seem ready to snatch it away or touch it, so after a moment he let his hand drop.

"I see I've already confused you. Your name is Raoul. That's your name." He waited for this to sink in. "But everyone calls you Rafe. It's complicated why."

Silence made a small soft sound. Now he saw.

"And I'm Caedon." The man looked close into Silence's eyes when he said this.

Silence nodded. Caedon. He understood.

"That means nothing to you." This man Caedon's expression was unsettling.

Silence shrugged. It did mean something, actually, but Silence couldn't say how or why, or what the dim feelings surrounding this name might mean to him.

"I'm a lord. Actually—" and here the man named Caedon gave a little laugh, and the amber of his eyes gleamed. "Now that I've won a few battles, I think I can call myself a king."

Silence sat thinking this over. The battles. His wounds. Somehow these things were connected. Had he fought for or against this man?

"The Rising is done for," said Caedon.

There was that word again, Rising. Kipp had spoken of it. Silence realized Caedon was examining him narrowly for some reaction. He shrugged again.

"It's done for," said Caedon, taking Silence's hand and squeezing it hard, digging his nails into Silence's wrist where the brand was, forcing his eyes to Caedon's. "Avery is dead. Conal is dead. It's over."

The man seemed to need some response. Silence nodded warily.

"These names mean nothing to you?"

Silence shook his head no.

"What if I told you Diera is dead?"

Silence sat quietly, but his heart had seized him. That was a name that seemed to mean something. He wasn't sure what. He looked up at Caedon. He knew his eyes were pleading. *Tell me who this is*, he begged. *Tell me why I am feeling this way.*

"Ah," said Caedon. "That does touch you."

Silence nodded.

"She's not dead," he said after a long pause during which he looked searchingly into Silence's eyes.

Silence nodded. Whoever this woman was, she wasn't dead. He realized Caedon had maybe told him she was in order to gauge his reaction. He realized he was undergoing a sort of trial.

Caedon put his hand on Silence now.

Silence knew he had to let him.

Caedon turned Silence's head from side to side and probed Silence's skull with his fingers. "You have that scar on your torso and that's..." Caedon paused. "That's a different kind of scar. But here is another scar. Head wound," he said at last.

Silence nodded.

"Here's what happened to you," this man Caedon said tersely. "Some men dragged you down from the driver's seat of Diera's cart. You fought. Foolish. You must have seen you were outnumbered. If you had just given up, the way a sensible person might have." Caedon grimaced. "Then another man came at you with a big club. I remember the moment. It ended your foolish resistance. It should have killed you."

This man knows what happened to me. He was there, thought Silence.

"That blow should have killed you," Caedon went on, "but not if I could get you to a healer quickly enough."

He does know. He was trying to save me. I must have fought on his side, thought Silence. *This man is a noble, maybe even a king, and he valued my life enough to try to save me. So what does that make me?* he wondered.

Silence pulled his tunic up so Caedon could see the scar on his torso and looked a question at him.

"That. That's different. A cut made later on." Caedon got up off the bench and moved restlessly around the room, leaving Silence to wonder what he might mean. Caedon went to a small table. He took a few objects from a box on it and brought them back to the hearth and placed them on the bench between himself and Silence.

"You have no memory of the events I'm talking about. The Rising. Avery and Conal. Little enough," he said.

Silence nodded.

"Maybe some feelings you can't name."

Silence nodded.

"But as for ordinary things, you know them perfectly well."

Silence shrugged. He decided Caedon wasn't going to tell him about the other wound, the long straight cut down his torso.

Instead, Caedon went through a demeaning sort of test, moving around the room pointing at ordinary objects, the bed, a rushlight in a bracket, the hearth, naming them rightly (Silence nodded) or wrongly (Silence smiled and shook his head no).

"Good," said Caedon. "What about these?" He indicated the objects he had brought from the table to the bench.

They were a quill, an inkstone, and a piece of parchment.

Silence looked down at them, then back into Caedon's face. He began to laugh. He nodded.

"Try to write something," said Caedon.

Silence took the quill. He knew this. He knew how to write. He wrote, "I do not know who I am" on the parchment and handed it to Caedon.

"Nine Spheres," said Caedon. "You don't know who you are, you can't speak, but you remember how to write in the language of the Old Ones." After a moment, he said, "I'm the one who taught it to you."

Silence felt a burst of happiness. There had been no quills, no ink, no parchment in the brothel or at the house of his next master. He didn't know to think about them, and so he never asked for them. But now that they'd been presented to him, he knew them, knew what they were, knew how to use them. He saw he could say what was in his mind on this parchment to anyone who knew how to read it.

And there was another thing that came on him in a rush of emotion. A fantasy that had kept him many times from despair. The fantasy that somewhere he had people who knew him and cared about him. That they'd come looking for him, and find him, and free him. That fantasy had suddenly become real.

"You don't remember that you betrayed me," said Caedon. The words came out of him in a low snarl.

Oh, thought Silence. *So I fought against him, not with him. And now he has me.* The fantasy fell in brittle shards about him.

On the parchment he wrote, "Was I part of this Rising you speak of?"

Caedon didn't reply. He snatched up the parchments, ripped them in two, and threw them on the fire.

I must have been, thought Silence. *Kipp thought so. Maybe this man Caedon bought me in order to bring me to justice. Now he'll kill me.*

"I should have you killed," said Caedon, echoing his thoughts.

Silence bowed his head.

"Why do I always hesitate, when I know that's what I should do?"

Silence realized Caedon was asking himself this question.

"Always," Caedon berated himself. "Time after time. I know I must act, and then I don't." Caedon looked sidelong at Silence. "We are brothers, you and I. Brothers of a sort."

Silence didn't know what that might mean. He didn't think Caedon meant he was his actual brother. Caedon looked to be a little older than he was, and he too had dark hair. Silence regarded him dubiously. Maybe this man was his older brother. But the amber of his eyes set him distinctly apart from Silence. And there was something else. It didn't feel right. *This man is not my brother*, he thought.

Caedon's eyes turned hard. "My name means nothing to you. But when I spoke hers—" Silence saw Caedon was struggling with some violent emotion. "It's hard to kill your own brother, even if you know it's necessary. And you—" Caedon gave a bitter laugh. "You don't even know why it is necessary. You don't remember. Where's the savor of revenge in that."

Silence picked up the quill. He wrote, "Maybe one day I will remember, and you can take your revenge then."

"Or maybe I'll just do it now," said Caedon, menace in his voice.

Silence shrugged and nodded. Everything felt so odd. It was as if he and Caedon were discussing the fate of someone else.

"Instead, I'll have to take you to Gilles."

Silence looked a question at Caedon.

"You don't know who Gilles is?"

Silence shook his head no.

"Gilles de Rais, the most important noble in the Baronies?"

Oh, thought Silence. *That Gilles.* Of course he had heard of that Gilles. That Gilles was the one who owned the ship that had carried him to the Baronies, and the one who had profited when his prisoners became slaves.

Yes, he nodded at Caedon.

"But let me guess. You don't know why I must bring you to Gilles. Why Gilles will want to see you."

No, Silence indicated.

"You're his property," said Caedon. "That's how that despicable man knew to bring you to me. He saw Gilles's mark on you."

Silence nodded slowly. That explained a lot. He pulled up his tunic, raised his left arm, and twisted around to see under his own armpit.

"You probably won't be able to see it. Let me show you," said Caedon. He went from the room, leaving Silence to marvel alone on the bench.

"Here," said Caedon, coming back with a mirror. "That's right. Raise the left arm. Now look." Caedon angled the mirror so Silence could see. A small mark, shaped like a teardrop or maybe— *It's red*, Silence thought—like a drop of blood. *So*, Silence thought. *This man Caedon has not brought me here to free me from slavery. It's just as the other master told me. I belong to someone else. I'm someone else's slave. But in that case,* he thought, *how is it Caedon calls me brother?* Caedon was no slave. That was clear to Silence. Caedon was maybe a king.

"Gilles is supposed to be back now. We'll go to him. Gilles may be able to pry your mind open," said Caedon. "If anyone can do it, Gilles can." Caedon rose. "Come," he said.

Silence rose too. He followed Caedon out of his rooms and into a corridor and down it to a set of great doors. When he stepped outside, he saw the same cart Caedon had used to take him away from the former master's custody.

"Get in," said Caedon.

They jolted away. They were on the road for a number of leagues. Caedon said nothing, just gazed out moodily from the flaps of the covered cart.

Silence looked out, too. It was pretty, hilly countryside. In the distance, peaks of mountains lay blue on the horizon. It was good to be out in the light and air, out of a house. Silence had been pent up for a long time.

They wound up the motte of a big pile of a stone castle and they drew into its outer bailey.

Caedon climbed out of the cart and motioned Silence to follow. In the crisp air of late afternoon, Caedon addressed the man, a steward, it seemed, who came out to greet them.

"Is it true that His Most High Majesty is in residence now?"

"Yes, Your Lordship, and he is expecting you."

"This will be interesting," Caedon murmured. "What will he see, when he looks inside you?" As they followed the steward rapidly through a warren of small rooms and corridors, Caedon explained in low tones about Gilles. "He travels the planes. He has been on another plane, so his attention may not have been directed here, to me. Or to you."

This explanation made little sense to Silence.

"But now he's here, and he knows we are coming, so by now he knows all about it. Or maybe not." Caedon looked around at Silence, considering. "Maybe inside, you're sort of a blank. So what would he have seen, if he had looked there."

Silence had no opinion about it.

The steward ushered them into a high, vaulted, echoing stone chamber with a massive carved seat set on a dais at one end. The seat was empty.

Silence felt a chill of recognition. He knew that at some point, he had been in this chamber, and when he had been here, he had experienced terrible pain.

"This means something, does it?" whispered Caedon. "It should. You were nearly killed here. Gilles nearly killed you."

Caedon knelt in front of the empty chair, so Silence did, too.

"Nearly killed you right here where we are kneeling." Caedon was continuing to whisper. "But now you're only a blank." Caedon reached over and knocked with his knuckles against Silence's skull.

Silence shrugged away from him. *In some ways, he's right, I'm a blank*, he thought. *But in other ways, I'm not.*

"That being so, what could he see there? That would explain why he didn't know about you until I took you. He learned about you by looking into me," Caedon said, "You. Why would he have even looked? We thought you were dead. We all thought you were dead."

What in the Nine is he talking about, thought Silence.

"The cart carrying Diera came out from the drawbridge, and you were the driver. I should have realized. I should have given orders it was not to be you," said Caedon. His voice had turned savage.

"And then you did what you'd conspired to do, may the gods curse you. One of my men brought you down. I was watching. I had hopes maybe I could save you. Isn't that a stupid thing to admit. I had hopes you were alive." Caedon drew a ragged breath. "Then the entire cart turned over, and she was standing in the shattered thing sobbing and holding you, the silly woman, and it was clear you were dead."

Silence felt a strange stirring at Caedon's words. He wasn't remembering, not exactly, but a deep-sunken emotion was rising slowly to the surface, like some enormous, many-tentacled sea creature.

"So then, as you know—well, no, you don't know, but anyway—Gilles has interesting things he likes to do with the dead. We shipped your body off across the Narrows to him. Yet somehow, when the ship came to port, you weren't there."

Silence squeezed his eyes closed. He opened them again and stared up at the ceiling. He started to laugh. A rasping sound came out of him that he recognized as laughter.

"Shut up, you addlepate," Caedon hissed.

Silence couldn't stop. The box, the cloth enveloping him, the ship. The storm that had tipped the box over and him out of it. He had been in his coffin, in his shroud. Just not as dead as they thought he was. And then those sailors thought—

Silence stuffed a fist into his mouth to stop the laughter, and found he couldn't.

Abruptly, he found he could.

Something in the quality of the air changed. It was as if a sharp sword had sliced down cleanly, dividing the atmosphere of the room, a minim of time before, from the charged, terrifying atmosphere now, an instant later.

Into his memory floated a shred of song. He couldn't have said where it came from, not if someone held a knife to his throat and demanded he try.

Here comes a mighty one. Let it begin.
Open up your heart and let me in.

A blinding light bloomed over the high carved seat where he and Caedon knelt. Silence threw up his arm to shield himself from it. He cast himself on the stones of the floor, shuddering with a fear so profound he thought it might end him. Beside him, he was dimly aware Caedon was doing the same.

CHAPTER FIVE

A Reckoning

Silence darted a glance quickly upward to the high carved seat, then flinched and looked back to the stones of the floor.

The man sitting there was a dominating presence. He had seemingly appeared there out of nowhere. His eyes were piercing and dark. His face, close-shaved, was saturnine and narrow.

After a long time, the man rose from his seat. Silence didn't dare to look, but he heard the rustling of the man's robes. Gilles de Rais, the most powerful nobleman in the Baronies, a king in every sense that meant anything. Even Silence knew this.

The footfalls of the man, soft, his feet velvet-clad, came near. Silence began to tremble.

"Rise, my dearest boy," Gilles was murmuring to Caedon. He heard Caedon get to his feet beside him, but Silence didn't dare to move. "What treasure have you brought me?"

To Silence, he said, "Up on your knees." Silence rose from the stones.

"So," said Gilles again to Caedon. "What's this?"

"I'm sure you know, Most High Lord," said Caedon.

"But I want you to explain it to me. It's a most puzzling thing. You were bringing me something dead, but here I see something alive." Gilles leaned down and placed a light hand on the top of Silence's head, where some heat in it burned alarmingly until he withdrew it. "I want to hear the explanation from your lips, Caedon. My dearest boy." He was almost crooning now.

"I'll try to explain."

"Don't try. No trying," said Gilles. His voice turned from tender to hard. "Explain."

Silence heard stark terror in Caedon's voice. "It's Rafe I've brought you, Most High One."

"Yes. So I see. But when I gaze within, I see only shreds and pieces of Rafe. How is this? And how is he not dead?"

"We thought he was dead. He seemed dead. We packed up the body and sent it across to you, and we sent Vigilia with him."

"Vigilia," said Gilles. "Ah. Yes. Labinia's sister, from the Great City."

"Equally accomplished."

"Yes. After Labinia was killed. By Rafe, do you think?"

"By John," said Caedon. His voice quaked.

"So you sent Rafe's body across the Narrows in one of my ships, and Vigilia went along to tend to it."

"Yes. She rubbed it with spices to prevent putrefaction. She knew you'd want the corpse fresh, Mighty Lord. And then she made the cut. But before she could—"

"So you think I should not blame her? She failed to notice something very important. That this one—" Here Silence felt the prodding of a velvet-encased toe— "was not exactly dead." Now he prodded Silence again. "Stand up, Rafe," he said.

For a moment, Silence stayed kneeling. *Rafe*, he thought blankly. *He means me.* He got to his feet.

"Tell me, Rafe. How is it you aren't dead?"

Silence lifted his eyes to Gilles's, then quickly dropped them. He shrugged. But a chill was settling about him. The cut down his torso was not made by an enemy in the heat and chaos of battle. It was made deliberately, and then they planned to do something vile to him.

"Tell me, Rafe."

Silence struggled to speak and gave up. He shrugged again.

"No, Rafe. I want you to tell me. None of this shrugging."

"He can't speak, lord," said Caedon hastily. "The blow to the head—"

"Be quiet," said Gilles, turning sharply on him. Then he swiveled back to Silence. "Speak, Rafe."

Silence looked up at him miserably. He tried. He couldn't.

"Rafe," said Gilles in a low, penetrating voice. "Rafe, I adjure you."

"I wasn't dead," Silence heard himself saying. His voice sounded strange in his own ears. "I woke up and thought I had been dreaming. I was in a box. In some kind of cloth. I suppose I must have been in a coffin. In a shroud. Then high seas knocked the coffin over, and I fell out of it, and some sailors thought I must be one of your prisoners, so they put me in the hold, and then later they sold me for a slave."

"You see?" said Gilles to Caedon. "He can speak."

"He's been faking?" Caedon's voice was dubious.

"No. He hasn't been faking. This is a well-known phenomenon, Caedon. Psychogenic mutism. As you've seen, he hears perfectly well. He can read and write. He's as intelligent as he ever was. He speaks during sleep perhaps."

"So they say."

From Caedon's tone, Silence could tell he was as much baffled by Gilles's strange words as Silence was. *Words of power,* Silence realized, shuddering. This man must be some powerful mage.

With that thought, memories began to bloom inside Silence. Memories he wanted to shove far away from himself, but couldn't. One in particular, a terrifying memory. He couldn't see. He couldn't speak or move. And then some sharp thing sliced him open, and he couldn't scream. But he could feel every moment of the pain.

Beyond that memory, and a few vaguer ones almost as frightening, this man Gilles was commanding him to speak, and Silence was doing it. Gilles was somehow making him do it.

He shook his head, to clear it. He felt one of his headaches begin to tighten around his brows, an iron band.

"The head wound didn't cause his loss of speech. When someone experiences head trauma, and the speech centers are affected, the results are very different," said Gilles at last. "Disarthria. Dispraxia." Gilles made a dismissive gesture. "We don't see that here. Some traumatic experience did this to Rafe."

"It's all in his head," said Caedon.

"No. So many think that, of these types of injuries. It's not something he's imagining. Charcot knew. It's a functional disorder." Now Gilles looked quizzically over at Silence. "What's wrong?"

Silence squeezed his eyes shut.

"I'm guessing you have terrible headaches. Is that it?"

Silence nodded.

"All part of the clinical picture. So, Caedon," said Gilles. "Here we see it. Trauma. Psychological and physical trauma."

Silence and Caedon glanced at each other. Silence could see how confused Caedon was, as confused as Silence himself felt.

"He witnessed the deaths of people he loved," Gilles explained.

Silence put his hands gingerly to his forehead. The headache was receding. With gratitude, he realized it wasn't going to be one of the big ones.

"Avery. Conal. He probably thought Diera was about to die, and Wat," Gilles was saying to Caedon. "By then, remember, he had already been through a lot. Witnessing John's death first hand. John's brutal death." He directed a meaning look at Caedon, and Silence saw Caedon cringe. "And while he didn't witness the death of the young earl, he was close to Earl Drustan as well. That's a lot to take in. On top of that, his experiences at your hands, Caedon. You near-totally depleted him, and much too fast. You brought him far too close to the edge. So. Psychogenic mutism. That's my best guess." Now Gilles looked over at Silence. "What do you think? Do you have any opinion?"

Silence thought, *I'm not sure what all those words mean, but if he's asking me if I can speak, I just proved it.* He opened his mouth and nothing came out.

Gilles rolled his eyes. He gave himself a little shake. "Rafe, I adjure you," he said in that terrifying quiet voice again.

"I don't know. I don't know what you're talking about, and I don't know these people you're talking about," said Silence.

"The mutism isn't due to the head trauma, but I think this memory loss of Rafe's probably is," said Gilles to Caedon. "That and the headaches. So we have a mixed bag here," said Gilles. It seemed to Silence he had stopped talking to Caedon and had switched to talking to himself. "The head trauma and resulting loss of memory make the mutism worse. He has these terrible feelings but then nothing to connect them to."

Silence considered that. It sounded right, in spite of the strange words. *I do have terrible feelings*, he thought. *And I don't have anything to connect them to.*

"Now what do we do with him." Gilles stood silent for a few moments. "I could just salvage what I can of him, and make it quick. There's that. Or I could send him to my own plane. He would receive good treatment there. Nobody here knows the first thing about these matters, all these savage ignorant people." Again it seemed Gilles was talking to himself as much as he was talking to Silence and Caedon. He blew out his cheeks. "Dee would know what to do, or his colleagues would." Then his lips drew back in a snarl. "I'll never ask that man for help. Never. Not even for this."

"Let me try to help him, Mighty Lord," said Caedon.

"You'd like that, would you." Gilles rounded on Caedon in a fury. "Yet a lot of the psychological trauma he has suffered, and the physical trauma as well, have come at your hands, Caedon. I love this boy. I love you, Rafe." He said this last thing directly to Silence. Silence found it profoundly unsettling. "And you have damaged him," Gilles said to Caedon. "I ordered you to manage the lad, not destroy him. What was it, jealousy?"

"No!" Caedon cried out. "Never, lord. I love Rafe too."

"Funny way of showing it."

Caedon threw himself at Gilles's feet. "Punish me, Mighty Lord," he cried out.

"Oh, I plan to. Count on it."

Caedon lay shivering on the stones.

"I need you healthy and whole, Rafe," said Gilles to Silence. "I was overjoyed to learn you were not dead, although of course I could have made use of you dead, and that would have given me quite a bit of pleasure. Still can," he murmured to himself.

Now it was Silence's turn to shiver.

"Stand up, Caedon. Quit groveling down there."

Caedon got fearfully to his feet.

Gilles seemed to have made some decision. "Rafe must be made healthy and whole. You will see to this, Caedon. I don't have time for it." To himself he said, "Rest. It may just take rest."

"Yes, Mighty Lord. I'll see to it right away."

"Not right away," Gilles barked at him. Caedon shrank back. "You and I have a reckoning to come to, first. Do we not?"

"Yes, Mighty Lord."

"See me tomorrow, and make yourself ready."

"Yes, Mighty Lord."

"In the intervening hours you have, make sure to arrange for Rafe during the season or more you'll be unable to tend to him. A good long rest may do wonders for him. Good food. Things to read."

"Yes, Mighty Lord." Then Caedon whispered miserably, "A season or more."

Gilles ignored him. "How long has it been since you swung a sword, Rafe?"

Hours, Silence was thinking. *What are hours*. But then he realized Gilles had asked him a question and he needed to make some answer. Silence shrugged. Had he ever swung a sword? But then he realized, yes, yes he had. Thinking about it triggered something, some feeling deep in the muscles of his arms and shoulders. In the set of his hips. He did know how to swing a sword. He had swung one. He had done it well.

"Probably not for a long time," said Gilles, answering the question himself and scrutinizing Silence. "Maybe not since you left boyhood. See to it you train Rafe and bring him back to his former level of skill," he said to Caedon. "You had seen to it he was trained in Tam Fort. By Conal," he emphasized, his voice heavy with irony. "He trained him, all right. In more ways than the sword. That's how he fell in with those rebels, through your neglect. Then you let his skills deteriorate. You set him to stand watch over a silly girl. And all those other things you did to him. You made him masquerade as a servant. Some servile thing like that. Rafe is not servile. I didn't choose him because he was servile. This displeases me. You displease me."

"Yes, Mighty Lord." Caedon blanched.

It was curious, thought Silence, how so pale a man could look suddenly paler still.

"How about his letters?"

"They're fine, Mighty Lord. I checked."

"I'm glad to hear it. So concentrate on the arms training. Set him up with some arms master, the best you can find, before you come to me tomorrow."

"Yes, Mighty Lord."

"Then, when you have recovered sufficiently, take over his training yourself."

"I thank you, Mighty One. I thank you for this mark of confidence, entrusting his training to me."

Gilles made an irritated noise. "Who better? That's the way it should have gone, all along. Get it done."

"Yes, Mighty Lord."

To Silence, Gilles said, "I know this is hard. Maybe it's impossible. But every day, I want you to practice speaking. You see you can do it."

Silence nodded.

"Will you promise to practice? If practice and will-power don't work, there are things I can do about this problem of yours later on."

Silence nodded. He decided he didn't want to know about the things Gilles said he could do to solve his problem. He decided he'd make a mighty effort to do it on his own.

To Caedon, Gilles said, "I want Rafe healthy. I want him strong. I want people to call him by his proper name and stop calling him Silence, the idle-witted things. I want to be able to feed on him with as much delight as before."

"Call him Raoul?" Caedon asked, his voice careful.

"Raoul. Rafe. Whichever." Gilles made a fretful gesture. Then he looked over at Silence. "I see he still has his amulet."

"No one took it from him," said Caedon.

"That's good. You see. Something in him knows who he is. I'm guessing he fought any attempt to take his amulet from him. I'm right, aren't I, Rafe?"

Silence nodded.

"So," he heard Caedon murmur beside him. "Rafe, then."

Gilles stepped to Silence and began running his hands over him. Silence struggled within himself to keep standing quietly. He struggled to keep from hitting Gilles's hand away, as Gilles picked up his amulet and examined it on its thong. "Let me see my mark," he said to Silence.

By now, Silence understood what that was. He lifted his tunic so Gilles could see it.

The sensation of Gilles's fingers tapping it and stroking it filled Silence with a kind of nausea.

"And yours, Caedon," said Gilles. "Let me see yours as well."

Caedon stepped to Gilles and lifted his own tunic.

"My most beloved boys," said Gilles. His voice was tremulous with desire.

Silence looked over at Caedon. Caedon's strange amber eyes shone with unshed tears. His hands were shaking.

As for Silence, he had started to feel a bit hopeful during this long and troubling interview, had started to feel that he was standing tall as the man he knew himself to be and was not the debased thing other people seemed to feel entitled to use for their own debased purposes.

Now, though, he perceived he was actually reeling at the lip of a vast pit many fathoms deep and filled with darkness.

Feed on him? Those were the words this mighty one used. Not just a nobleman. Not just a king, or close to. A powerful mage who could call up the forces of the Spheres themselves. But the forces Gilles intended to call, Silence realized, were the dark ones. *Feed on him?* What could these words possibly mean?

Silence didn't know, not inside his head, but in his gut, something did know. And that something filled him with revulsion.

CHAPTER SIX

Speak, Silence

Silence trembled to think of the broken thing he'd seen dragged away from Gilles's chambers and taken to a healer. Caedon hadn't even looked like a man any longer. He looked like some shell that a man had been sucked out of.

And now Caedon was secluded in his rooms with his healers.

Silence had his orders. He trained every day with an arms master. He read every day from the books in Caedon's many-volumed library. He wrote down his thoughts on pieces of parchment and then burned them at the hearth so his thoughts would not be seen and known.

He searched Caedon's library for anything mentioning The Rising, but he found nothing.

And every day, he went out into the pleached garden of Caedon's manor where he could be alone. There, he walked
underneath the trees and practiced speaking. Sometimes he
even had a little success. A sound he forced from his lips became
a word.

But not often.

One warm morning he woke with a new optimism. He put on
his practice leathers. He belted on his sword and made his way
out to the stable, where the arms master waited.

He smiled at the man and they walked together to a grassy
area at the back of the stables.

The arms master was named Master Estefan. He lived on the
coast, up a peninsula that stuck like a thumb into the Narrows.
Caedon was from there, and Caedon had paid Master Estefan to
come to his manor near Gilles's castle and train Silence for a season.

"Master Estefan is the best I know," said Caedon, on the day
he made ready to go to Gilles. "I'm having him train my. . ." Caedon's voice trailed off and his eyes went blank. After a moment,
he resumed. "Your reading and writing are fine, Rafe. I'm sure
these weapons skills will come back to you easily, once you have
a chance to practice, and once the effects of several difficult years
have completely left you."

Silence bowed.

"Rafe," said Caedon, putting both hands on Silence's shoulders. "I am to blame. I know that. I'm going to Gilles, to make
amends, but I will make amends to you, too. What I'm about to
do—" Caedon faltered. Silence saw with surprise that he could
barely go on. "It will be hard, but it is necessary. I will return.

Believe me, I will. Gilles has promised it, so I don't think he'll take me all the way down. I must trust that." Caedon swallowed hard, and Silence saw the fear in him. "And then." Caedon resumed with difficulty. "Then, when you are up to it, he'll summon you as well, and you too will have the privilege of serving him."

Silence nodded, tamping down a feeling of dread, and watched as Caedon drew on his cloak and made ready to go to Gilles. What could Caedon mean, *take me all the way down*.

Silence believed Caedon when he expressed remorse. But in some other sense, he didn't. He had the deep-seated feeling that what Caedon might think he wanted to do was not the same as what he would do. He had the feeling Caedon was a man as divided from himself as he was. More divided.

"You're a blank slate, Rafe," said Caedon over his shoulder, as he headed to his cart. "I can work with that. Things between us can be made into what they should have been all along." His amber eyes held an unsettling gleam. Silence found he knew that gleam. From somewhere in the hidden past, he knew it.

More authentic than anything else Caedon said, though, was Caedon's palpable fear. Gilles was about to hurt him, hurt him badly. Silence recognized that fear. He had known it when his old master took him to the nightmare room.

Now, when he thought about it, late at night alone in his bed, Silence shivered. Something told him his fear of his old master and what that man had done were as nothing compared to what Gilles had done to Caedon.

He remembered the feeling he had had, in the hands of his old master, that some cycle of pain and healing had once been his lot in his past life. He remembered his confusion, because he had seen no marks on his body to show that anyone had beaten him or mistreated him in any way.

What had Gilles done to Caedon, he wondered. *What will he do to me?*

But today, with the warmth and the sun, the sharp green scent of summer grass, the vigorous exercise, Silence felt these terrors falling away from him. His hair clubbed back in a thong, he stripped off his tunic and laid it over a fence rail. At Estefan's command, he moved fluidly through the exercises designed to test each muscle group, each position one might assume during the use of the sword in actual battle, as well as the mental fortitude to take these poses and movements inside until they became as natural as breathing.

"Very good, sir," said Estefan, calling a break. "Good effort. You are making splendid progress."

Sir, Silence thought blankly. Was he a gentle? He didn't think he was, but this man thought so, and Kipp had speculated that maybe he was. Besides, if Estefan thought so, that meant Caedon thought so. That meant it must be true.

He thought back uneasily to the day Gilles confronted Caedon, and himself as well. *You did not treat Rafe gently*, Gilles had upbraided Caedon. What did he mean? wondered Silence. Did that mean Caedon, if he didn't treat others gently, was not a gentle? He wore his hair long like a gentle. But maybe Gilles meant something completely different by *gentle*.

He remembered the terror he had felt, when Gilles swiveled his eyes to Silence in the moment Silence stood wondering. *Gentle*, Gilles had laughed, a low grating sound. *What do you lot know about it?* Silence realized then his thoughts had been overheard.

I raise high whom I please. I bring low whom I please. I made a woman a knight, and then I made her a saint.

Silence remembered looking aside at Caedon. He saw Caedon was equally baffled.

A saint, thought Silence. *What's that?*

Without further answer, Gilles had turned to snarl at Caedon. *See that Rafe is taught.*

Now he was being taught. Caedon and Gilles were right about his skill with the sword. That skill was rusty, but it was there, waiting for Silence to awaken it and make use of it. Just as if a sword itself were rusty, and he had taken the polishing stones to it.

Now Silence put aside his actual sword, heaved on a protective leather vest, and took up the bated, heavily weighted practice sword. He and Estefan sparred. In the end, Estefan laid him out on the grass.

Silence lay blinking up into the sun and smiling. Nine Spheres, it felt good. Estefan had dealt him a mighty blow, and he'd be aching for days from the effects of it, but it was clean and good. A useful pain. Pain that indicated how much he was learning, how much his body was re-tuning itself to the way it once was and needed to be again.

Estefan reached a hand down to draw Silence to his feet.

"Nicely done. Pretty soon I'll be the one lying in the grass, defeated," said Estefan. "Tomorrow we'll start you practicing with a shield."

Silence grinned and gave Estefan his best bow. He put away the practice sword and vest, pulled his tunic down over his sweaty torso, scratching where the scar still itched a little. He belted his real sword about his waist.

"Well, after all," said Estefan, clapping his hand on Silence's shoulder. "You were taught by one of the best." When Silence glanced at him sidelong, he saw Estefan was looking a bit frightened. "We must not speak of those days," he murmured. "Those matters. All that's in the past."

Silence gave the arms master a wave farewell and limped to his refuge, the garden, nursing his bruises. And thought about what Estefan had said. He laughed a little to himself. The advantages of being silent. People said things to him they'd never say to a man who was speaking back. An odd matter, he thought. Maybe people who speak feel compelled to rush quickly to fill any silence, and then they say things better left unsaid.

Taught by one of the best, Estefan said. Gilles had said so, too, and he had mentioned a name. Conal. Silence wondered who this Conal was.

Conal. He shaped the name with his lips. He tried to say it. Nothing happened.

Another name rose unbidden to his mind. *Avery.*

Conal and Avery. Something about them. He remembered Caedon telling him something about these men.

He searched his memory. It gave him great satisfaction, doing that, although some things he wished he could forget—the experiences in the hold of the ship, the brothel, his old master and the cruel implements he wielded.

From the time Silence had come back to himself in his coffin, his memory had been fine. More than fine. Sometimes excruciatingly fine. He remembered everything that had happened since his death, down to the tiniest detail. Just not anything that had happened before it.

I suppose I am a blank slate, just as Caedon tells me I am, he thought. A new slate, with new writing chalked across it.

Avery. Conal. He thought these names. Then he thought, *John.*

Not quite a blank slate. As he said these names to himself in the silence of his own head, he felt a deep pounding emotion coming at him from nowhere, overwhelming him. Shattering him.

He put a hand to his head.

Avery is dead. Conal is dead. That's what Caedon had said to him, when he first came to Caedon's manor.

John is dead. He remembered how Gilles had accused Caedon. Caedon killed him, this man John. Brutally, Gilles had said.

A thought exploded into Silence's head.

And then Wat and I tried to kill Caedon.

Silence felt as though a tight band of metal around his brows were tightening further, while the whirlwind of thoughts exploded outward, threatening to rip him apart the way beasts driven in four different directions ripped apart the bodies of the malefactors tied to them for execution.

"John," he said. The breath came out of his body in the form of a word, a name. "John. John." He said this name louder, and louder still.

He realized all this while he had been fingering the amulet at his neck. It distracted him. Calmed him. His ragged breathing slowed. He pulled the amulet's thong off from around his neck so he could hold the little iron bird in his hand and look at it. Was it really the sign of some god, as the people in the ship's hold, and in the brothel, had believed? The way Caedon and Gilles spoke of it, he didn't think it was. But it was nevertheless desperately important to him. *Maybe I'll never know why,* he told himself.

Just now, he believed if he could only keep his eyes fixed on the bird, the overwhelming thoughts would recede into the deep place from which they'd swarmed, and he'd be saved from them.

The opposite happened. As he strung the little bird back around his neck by its thong, a memory came full-blown at him, a memory from before. It came hurtling at him the way a physical attacker might spring for him. He cringed back from it. Cried out.

The cry died on his lips. The memory blossomed around him, painful and beautiful at the same time.

He and a woman stood in a garden, another garden somewhere far from this one. He had the little bird in his palm, and her palm pressed down on it. He remembered closing both of her hands in both of his, the little bird in the hollow their hands made.

He remembered how warm and fine her hands were. He remembered kissing them.

He had looked into this woman's eyes. In his memory, he saw them, dark, intense, looking back.

Her lips parted, and she spoke. *Swearing on this, I feel as though I'm swearing on your life.*

And she had said, *We'll never be parted now. They may try, and they may succeed on this side of that river. But underneath the Spheres, we are one.*

"Diera," Silence said hoarsely.

He fell sideways off the bench where he was sitting. The world tilted sideways and went dark.

CHAPTER SEVEN

A Cry

S peech had come back to Silence, although he didn't speak much. Now he knew his name was Rafe. Or Raoul. But he didn't feel that it was. When he thought of himself, he thought *Silence*. He wondered if he would always feel this way. Shreds of memory had come back. Not everything, though. Really, just a few things.

Now he knew what The Rising was, partly from memory and partly by piecing together chance things he overheard. He remembered his brothers. Avery, Conal, Dru, John, Wat, some more clearly than others. John and Wat most of all. They weren't his brothers by birth. They were his brothers by blood. And Conal, his brother but also his teacher.

Caedon called himself Silence's brother, but Caedon was a grotesque parody of a brother. And he could see Caedon was horribly jealous of the others.

Most clearly, Silence remembered Diera. He remembered feelings more than actual events, but some things they had done together stood out like bright jewels. Their vows in the garden. The first time he kissed her. A frightening time when they fled through a forest.

But he didn't remember the time he supposedly died, or nearly, as he drove her carriage, maybe trying to help her escape from men who would harm her. He had learned it from Caedon. Now that he remembered Diera, he wished it were otherwise. He didn't want what he knew of Diera to be profaned as it reached him through Caedon.

There was something else he only dimly remembered. Some other woman who had somehow come between him and Diera. Silence couldn't remember much about this woman, and he was sure he hadn't loved her.

But Diera herself was a touchstone to him. A flame he followed in the darkness. Her eyes. Her hair. The way she felt to him when they made love, her silky skin against his, the heady scent of her. Her bravery.

Was she out there in the world somewhere, or was she dead? Caedon had said both to him, and he wasn't sure which one was true. Silence did know one thing about Diera above all things. He knew he loved her, and he knew she loved him back. *I'll find her, if she's in the world*, he told himself.

As for his brothers, he knew they were all dead, and at the hands of Caedon. All except maybe Wat. The longer he thought about it, the longer he lived with his shreds of memory, the more certain he became. *Wat is out there somewhere*, he told himself. *I'll find him too.*

In the meantime, he was in the hands of Caedon and Gilles.

Very gradually, Caedon had come back to himself after what Gilles had done to him.

What did Gilles do to him, Silence wondered. He was too afraid to ask Caedon, especially after Caedon had implied the same thing might soon happen to him. It was as if he believed, superstitiously, that if he didn't know and didn't ask, it wouldn't happen.

Then Caedon had taken an abrupt turn for the worse. His healer, panicking, called for the enclosed cart. Men carried Caedon's inert form to it and laid him gently inside. The healer bundled Silence in after him. "You must go with him, Master Rafe. Someone must be with him. If he dies on my hands," she had muttered to herself, "I'm as good as dead myself."

The driver had whipped the team of horses hard. A messenger, sent on ahead, had made sure many servants were there to greet them at Gilles's castle. They'd taken Caedon to a room in one of the towers, and they had put Silence in a room next to him. Several healers hovered about Caedon, directed by a man who seemed to be very important.

"He comes from the university," one of the healers whispered to Silence.

For a long time, Caedon stayed in his bed at Gilles's castle. Silence helped his healers tend him. He held Caedon's shoulders while one or another fed him broth.

Caedon's eyes glittered feverishly. "You are here with me, Rafe. That means everything to me," he whispered during a rare lucid moment.

Silence felt unexpectedly moved by these words, but also unnerved. *This man means me ill. Yet somehow, he loves me,* thought Silence. *How can this be?*

Silence took turns with the healers in watching Caedon while he restlessly slept. Sometimes Caedon went into terrifying spasms, while he slept or tossed half-asleep, and then the panicked healers darted around his bed, trying to revive him and help him to breathe.

Silence helped as much as he could. He saw how frightened the healers were. He thought he knew the reason—not that they loved Caedon so much as that they feared Gilles's wrath so completely. If they let Caedon die—and he seemed on the point of it several times—they'd be the ones Gilles blamed.

It was exhausting work, tending the sick man. Whenever he could, Silence took to roaming about Gilles's castle's grounds to settle himself and breathe fresh air away from the sickroom.

One day he happened into a part of the grounds completely new to him. A vast courtyard lined with little doors. Doors into small rooms. Children lived in these rooms.

Silence came back several times to watch them. They were small children, maybe around six years old, most of them boys. They had minders who seemed to take very good care of them. But what were so many children doing here?

Once, he stopped one of the minders, as she ran from the courtyard intent on some errand. "Why are these children here?" he asked her.

She didn't reply, just stared over her shoulder at him with frightened eyes.

Something kept drawing him back to the courtyard. Once, he saw several minders lining up some of the children, six or seven of them, and marching them in a line out of the courtyard. He followed along after them. They all stopped under a tree in the outer bailey of the castle. The minders sat them down and moved among them with bread and cheese. Then they went off together and sat down to their own midday meal, talking quietly among themselves.

Silence strolled up to two of these children, two small boys. He squatted down beside them. "Hello," he said.

"Hello," they chorused back. They seemed like ordinary happy children.

"Are you on an outing?"

"No, sir," said one of them. "We've been given leave to go home to our parents now."

"You've been taken here away from your parents?"

The boy nodded.

The other boy said, his voice tremulous, "I miss me ma."

"What a baby," the other boy said, shoving him.

"I'm not!" this boy cried.

"Here, now." One of the minders stood over them. "None of that. You, sir. What are you doing here?"

"I'm here at the castle to tend Lord Caedon," said Silence carefully. So many words at once were hard for him.

"Oh, I see," said the minder. She shook her head at the two small boys. "For shame, quarrelling. You're about to be taken in to the baron, to say your farewells."

The two little boys hung their heads.

"Safe travels to you," said Silence, getting to his feet and smiling at the boys. The minder was looking at him oddly. He nodded at her, too, and began walking away. When he looked back at the little group, he saw the minders were getting the children together now, and leading them over to one of the castle's mural towers. Leading them into a narrow door.

Something about what he'd seen was disturbing to Silence. He wasn't sure what.

That night, on another of his breaks, he made his way through the shadows of the outer bailey to the foot of the tower, the same one he'd seen the children enter. He looked up. Far above, a lone high-arched window glowed with the yellow of many candles. Silence shook his head and turned to go. He wasn't sure what he expected to see.

Then something stopped him mid-stride. A high childish screaming, terrified. It cut off abruptly.

Silence felt himself turn to ice. A guard was passing. Silence rushed to the man. "Screaming—" he said breathlessly. "Someone in trouble. A child." He gestured to the tower.

"Oh, that," said the guard. "It's one of the owls they keep up there." The man walked on.

Silence stood in the darkened bailey. *That wasn't an owl*, he told himself. *That was a child.*

He tried questioning Caedon about it, but Caedon just stared at him blankly. Silence wasn't sure whether Caedon was in his right wits. He didn't appear to be.

Silence tried questioning the healers, and their evasive answers just frightened him more.

Soon after, the day came when his healers judged Caedon well enough to go back to his own manor. Silence accompanied him in the closed cart. Caedon lay against the cushions, his eyes closed. But his hand stole out to Silence's and held it.

By then, Silence knew not to ask about the children, so he didn't try. And anyway, it was too difficult to get such a complicated question, the question he wanted to ask, out of his mouth.

At the manor, Caedon still had a healer who tended him, and he spent another fortnight in bed. Some days were good, others not so good, sometimes alarming. But at last it seemed Caedon was mending. At last he could sit up in a chair, and he seemed to know where he was and who Silence was.

After Caedon could leave his bed, he took to sitting in the pleached garden of his manor under a pear tree on a little bench in the early harvest-tide sun. He summoned Silence to him there.

Silence loved the little garden and spent a lot of his time there. It lacked only one thing he needed. A pool or pond. Silence felt completely landlocked at Caedon's manor, and that unsettling feeling pricked at him always in the background.

Sometimes, during their time in the garden, he and Caedon played a game Caedon knew, on a game board he had bought as a rarity shipped up the rivers from the Great City by traders from the Ice Realm. The game board was a marvel of beautifully inlaid green and black squares. The game pieces were intricately carved. Small soldiers. An imposing monarch. His queen. His priests. His knights. His castles. These pieces were ranged across the game board in patterns, and the game pieces fought a war on that board, a war such as realms and armies fight.

Caedon always took the black pieces. Silence always took the part of the green army. "Green. The color of The Rising," Caedon said once, with a grim smile.

Caedon always won. Even in his illness, he won.

Silence didn't understand the pleasure Caedon got out of playing the game with him. Caedon had taught him the game, so complex that Silence understood it would be the work of years to master the strategies of it. If Caedon hadn't completely mastered them—maybe no one could—Caedon had become expert. Silence was a novice. The more they played the game together, the more Silence realized how trivial it was for a player of Caedon's skill to play the game with someone at his own poor skill level.

Yet with each inevitable win, Caedon knew immense pleasure.

Sometimes, the two of them just sat together quietly under the trees. At such times, Caedon was used to taking a small leather pouch from his cloak, opening it, pouring four small objects out of it, and tossing them absent-mindedly in his hand. Sometimes he just sat and ran his fingers over them.

When Silence asked him about them once, he said only, "The solids," and didn't explain.

They were odd little objects. One six-sided, a little cube. One spiky and four-sided. One many-sided; the last one nearly round, with a sort of pebbled texture. They glowed like rich jewels. The more he looked at them, the more Silence was convinced that someone had carved each one of them from a gemstone, then polished it until it glittered.

It was clear to him, then, what a wealthy man Caedon must be.

"But there's a fifth solid," Caedon murmured once. "I don't have that one. I want it." And once he had said, of the little objects, "These are all I possess, from my life before." Silence didn't know what to make of that statement.

More often than these other activities, Caedon had Silence read to him from his books.

"My eyes are too weak yet for reading," he told Silence. "And reading aloud will be good practice for your voice."

Sometimes he took Silence's hand in his and stroked it absently.

Remembering the brothel, Silence felt himself inwardly cringing.

"Don't worry," Caedon said once, catching Silence's expression. "You're not to my taste, in that way." He smiled at Silence, amused. "As for you, it's women you love, and they've always loved you in return."

Silence knew there were a number of young boys in Caedon's employ. He knew why. But there was a young girl, too. Silence pitied her. She had long honey-golden curls and a face like a flower. Her name was Jillian. Caedon puzzled Silence. He knew Caedon craved the attentions of his boys, but he also knew Jillian was Caedon's favorite.

"Jillian will be a woman soon," said Caedon. "Then I won't want her any longer. But I'll still treasure her. I lost her for a while. Now I have her back."

Silence stopped mid-sentence in the book he was reading and stared at Caedon, when Caedon said this. Silence knew he didn't know much about the world. But he knew he had landed in a strange corner of it. He knew now that in the past, Caedon had meant him ill, and had damaged him. He knew Caedon had damaged Diera. But he knew these things in an abstract way. He didn't remember any of it as experience, just a hazy understanding. An inkling. He had a hard time knowing how to feel about Caedon.

"I may marry Jillian," Caedon said. "It won't be the politically expedient thing to do, I suppose. Although—" he stopped and looked over at Silence. "She's the daughter of an earl, you know." He waited.

Silence thought he was waiting for some sign of recognition from Silence, and when Silence didn't give it, he resumed.

"And then I'll gain her lands. At one time, that earl was the richest man in the Sceptered Isle, and his father before him. His former holdings are fragmented, but if I go to the lesser men who own them now, and show them persuasively that those lands actually belong to me, I'm sure they'll give up their claims in my favor. They'll be pathetically eager to do it. There were no sons to muddy the succession, and only a bastard older sister. A half-sister, I suppose. She has no inheritance claims. Jillian does." He stared at Silence as if this too might mean something to him.

Silence shrugged and went on reading.

Caedon kept interrupting him. He kept talking about the little girl. "I've taken her lands by force. It will make me look good, to people, when they see I've a legitimate claim through marriage.

I'll get children on her, and that will strengthen my claim. Some of these children I'll send to Gilles as my allotment."

Silence determinedly read on, trying not to think about what Caedon had just said to him.

"And he who becomes master of a state accustomed to freedom and does not destroy it," Silence read, *"may expect to be destroyed by it, for in rebellion it has always the watchword of liberty—"*

"The watchword of liberty rallies the rebels of a subjected state. These rebels must be crushed. Hah. Important advice," said Caedon. Silence was relieved to see he was distracted from the girl back to the book. "I intend to take this advice to heart," Caedon continued. "I intend to stamp out every trace of rebellion. Every trace of The Rising. Divide them. Scatter them. That's what this sage of the Primacy recommends." He nodded to the book in Silence's hands. "What you're reading. It's precious to me. Gilles brought that book back with him from a plane he visited. From the Primacy, but on a different plane."

"You told me," Silence began. Then, haltingly, "Gilles can't bring things from—" he paused, thinking how to say it. "back from these planes."

"Interesting," said Caedon. "When you read, you have no trouble with fluency. Only when you're trying to think of your own words and say them. But yes, you're right. Gilles can't bring anything back, anything material, like a book. He carried these words in his head. All of them. An entire book of them. Something he can easily do. Then he allowed me to transcribe the words. He knew I'd value them. One of the many gifts he has given me."

Silence looked down at the finely written page. *Caedon taught me to read and to write*, he thought. *Caedon knows these skills better than I myself know them. He wrote down all the words in this book I'm reading, and the words were a gift from Gilles.*

Then he thought, *Caedon gives gifts too. This is a gift Caedon gave to me, being able to read these words, and write words down. What kinds of gifts are these, fine gifts tied to suffering and evil.*

"You see how much Gilles loves me," said Caedon.

Silence looked up at Caedon, wanting to know the answer to his unspoken question. "He hurt you."

"I offered myself to him, as is my duty, and he took it, as is his right."

Unconsciously Silence put his right hand to his left armpit, where Gilles's mark lay hidden.

"Yes," said Caedon. "You too, Rafe. Soon you'll go to him."

Caedon's words filled Silence with terror.

"While you await his pleasure," said Caedon, "I have some small errands for you. These will be a test of your devotion to me."

I'm not devoted to you, thought Silence, *in spite of your gifts*. But he kept his eyes down.

"These are matters I should have trained you to attend long before. Now you'll perform these duties, and your faithfulness will determine where we go from here. Put the book aside, and I'll tell you the first of them."

Silence closed the book and laid it carefully down on the stone bench.

"Do you know how it is you came to be Gilles's best beloved, along with me?"

Silence shook his head.

"When you were very young, your parents sent you to Gilles to be fostered. Gilles sends word out around his domains. Bring me a son to foster, he demands of the noble families, and some of the lowly ones as well. The families hasten to send him a son. Sometimes they send him an infant, to be done with it. Gilles likes that. But he likes it better when they send him a boy of around six years. Sometimes a daughter, if they have no sons. Your parents sent you to Gilles at six, Rafe. Do you remember this?"

Silence shook his head, but now, the memory of the children he'd seen at Gilles's castle rushed at him with terrifying force. The scream he'd heard.

"You remember nothing of your parents?"

Silence shook his head again.

"We'll remedy that. I'll send you to meet them. It may jog your memory."

Silence raised his eyes to Caedon's. He had parents. They lived in the world.

"Let's make that your first errand. The other can wait," said Caedon. "Do I really want that, jogging your memory?" he muttered to himself. "Gilles wants it."

Silence looked at him curiously.

"The more whole you are in mind as well as body, the greater the savor," Caedon explained. "Gilles feeds on the body, but he feeds on the mind as well. Memory. Thoughts. Yearnings. All of that." He laughed as Silence shivered. "You'll find out," he promised Silence. "But I." He stared at Silence. "I like you as the blank slate I can write upon." He sighed. "Gilles's wishes are far more important than mine. I'll send you to your parents."

Silence tried, once more, as he'd tried many times unsuccessfully before, to find the words to ask Caedon about the children he'd seen, while Caedon lay ill.

"Yes, as I told you. Gilles brings children into his service," Caedon said, brushing aside Silence's other attempts to question him.

He brought their conversation back to Silence's impending visit to his parents.

Silence tried to distract himself from the deep uneasiness this idea of meeting his parents had roused in him, and the outright fear prompted by thoughts of the children.

It helped that Master Estefan was teaching him mounted skills now. The work was hard and physical. It took his mind off the dread Caedon's words caused him to feel, and the headaches that came with it.

Charging at a quintain with heavier and heavier weights attached. Using a shield while he rode. Holding a lance. He worked hard, and each night he fell into his bed, exhausted. Sleep took him.

He was grateful he did not dream. Because when he did dream, he heard, over and over, that childish, terrified, choked off scream.

CHAPTER EIGHT

Meet the Parents

A few days after their conversation about Silence's parents, Caedon led Silence out to his cart. "My man will take you to your parents. Perhaps you'll retrieve some important memories. Wear these." He handed Silence two beaten gold armlets, wide cuffs of gold that Silence slipped on.

"We don't want your parents seeing that brand," said Caedon. "They'll think Gilles and I didn't take good care of you." He smiled his wolfish smile. "The left armlet will hide the brand." But then Caedon's eyes darkened. "A bondservant in a brothel. Shameful. I've suggested Vigilia should be punished. How could she not realize you were alive? How could she allow you to be taken off and treated so shamefully?"

Silence tried to hide his dubious look. As far as he could tell, Caedon himself had tried to have him killed, for reasons he only dimly understood. His disobedience. His work for The Rising. *I was trying to save Diera*, he thought, *and he didn't want that. Maybe I did save her.*

He was relieved to step into Caedon's cart and have his thoughts to himself. The cart dropped Silence off in the center of a small village not very far from Gilles's castle. "Two leagues that way," said the driver, pointing down a road leading off into the hills. "I'll wait in the inn here. Master says make sure to come back by nightfall. I've engaged a room at the inn for you. I'll bring you back to Master in the morning."

Silence nodded. He began walking down the road the driver indicated.

Although the sun was warm, the harvest-tide air was crisp, the sky a chill blue with small wisps of clouds. After a few furlongs of walking, Silence threw off his cloak and folded it over his arm.

It felt good to be out in the countryside. Birdsong sprang from every hedge. Out in the fields, peasants and bondservants labored to bring in the harvest.

Struck with a sudden thought, Silence stopped to gaze out over the fields. Suppose Kipp were in those fields, he thought. He had never forgotten the man. *He took care of me*, thought Silence. *Where is he now?*

He remembered how Kipp valued freedom. Clearly Kipp must have been a member of this Rising Caedon kept talking about. A rebellion. Kipp's ideas about freedom came from it. *The watchword of liberty.* Gilles's book had said rebels clung to such an idea, and so rulers must stamp rebellion out. That's what the book advised, and that's what Caedon thought. That's what he had set out to do, with the approval of Gilles.

What had life as a bondservant done to Kipp, Silence wondered. A man dedicated to that liberty the book warned against, as it was connected so strongly to rebellion. Silence knew too well that his masters must have branded Kipp, as his had branded him. What would that have done to the spirit of such a man as Kipp?

What did it do to my own spirit? thought Silence. *But Kipp told me freedom was inside a man. He told me tyranny did not last forever.* Silence could only hope Kipp really meant the words he had spoken and had not just been mouthing them to keep Silence from despair.

After a long time of gazing out into the field at the laborers, Silence resumed walking. The idea of his parents had left him unmoved by any longing. He had only some unsettled feelings he couldn't name. Now that he was actually about to meet these parents of his, he felt suddenly unnerved. When he thought of them, *my parents*, he felt only a blank. How would it be to come face to face with them?

Another thing bothered him. His parents had given him to Gilles. What kind of parents would do that? Didn't they realize what they were sending him to?

Because finally, probably to shut him up, Caedon had told him more about the children in Gilles's service. Silence had doggedly kept asking. He was driven to keep asking.

As Caedon talked, Silence had listened carefully to Caedon's descriptions of their boyhoods, his and Caedon's, under Gilles's care. Yes, Gilles had cared for them. In his own way, he had loved them and still did.

But he loved them and carefully tended them so he could devour them. Not devour them entirely. Feed on them little by little. Harvest them. Tend and manage them so he could harvest them again, as if they were a kind of crop.

That was terrible enough. Other boys whom Gilles had taken, mostly boys but sometimes girls, too, did not fare so well. Gilles did things to them. Silence was not sure what things, but as he listened to Caedon's roundabout cautious descriptions, he became more and more certain that these children died as a result of the things Gilles did.

And now he knew, with horror, the meaning of what he had seen and heard when he stood beneath Gilles's tower.

He does things with the dead as well, Silence reminded himself. *That's what he planned to do with me, when he thought I was dead. He was glad to find me alive, but he had looked forward to the pleasure he'd have had with me dead.*

Tormented by these thoughts, Silence did not realize he had come to the end of the road until he saw he had walked into a circular space rimmed by a crescent of stone buildings. The central building was fairly imposing, or once might have been. Now it looked to be in disrepair. The other buildings were little more than tumble-down hovels.

Silence drew a breath and closed his eyes. If Caedon was correct, Silence had spent his early days of life in these surroundings. But they meant nothing to him. He felt nothing, standing there.

He opened his eyes. A man had come to the door and was looking out cautiously.

"Who's there?" he called out. Then, in a quavering frightened voice, "Raoul?"

"Yes," Silence said, mastering his own sudden tremor of fear and striding to the door. "Are you my father?"

"But you are dead!" the man burst out, his eyes widening in shock. And some other emotion. Silence wondered what he saw there. Guilt, perhaps.

Silence shook his head. He made his voice calm and even. "Not dead. They thought I was dead. I'm not."

"Catelot, come quick!" cried the man into the interior of the house. Silence's father, it seemed, old, white-haired, and bent.

An equally old, equally white-haired woman appeared in the doorway beside him, although her posture was erect. She looked at the man in confusion, then at Silence. "Raoul," she whispered. She turned pale, put her hand to her head, and fell over in a faint.

Silence rushed to help this man, his father, carry the woman who must be his mother into the stone house where a hearthfire smoldered in the one large room. He helped his father lay his mother down on a bed of furs in a shelf set into one of the walls.

"She thinks you're dead, Raoul," said his father. "I thought so too."

"It must be a shock," Silence murmured sympathetically. He tried to imagine how he would feel under similar circumstances. As it was, he felt nothing at all beyond normal human compassion.

"There now, Catelot. It's Raoul. He isn't dead," said Silence's father. "They were wrong when they sent us word."

Silence's mother was sitting up, rubbing her eyes in confusion. Then she realized and flung herself on Silence, sobbing and laughing.

Soon all three of them were gathered at the hearth.

"Onfroi will be overjoyed," said his mother.

"He's at the market town buying a pig," said his father.

"Vauquelin will know joy as well," his mother said. "If he ever got word you were dead." She looked a bit dubious. "We haven't heard from him in a while."

As they talked together further, Silence began to gather that Onfroi was his oldest brother, his father's heir. Vauquelin was the second brother, off at the wars.

"Losing you. It was too hard. First Bernardus, then you. But you are not dead!" His mother marveled at this, saying it over and over, stroking Silence's hand as Silence smiled at her.

Bernardus, he gradually realized, was another brother who had somehow died.

"Look at this, Catelot," said his father, reaching out for Silence's amulet.

Silence kept himself from drawing back.

"You've kept it always," his mother said.

Now both of these people, his parents, after the first shock, were looking shifty-eyed and guilty. Well, they would be, thought Silence. They should be. Look what they'd sent him off to.

For Silence, the little bird had come to signify the love of a woman. To his parents, he saw now, it signified something else.

He drew a deep breath. Time to let them know what had happened to him.

"My mother and father. I must tell you something."

They looked at him warily.

"I was hit on the head," he said, pointing. "A man with a club, during war. I lost my memory. I didn't know who I was for a long time." Silence stopped and took another deep breath. Saying this much this fast was difficult. "The baron Gilles found me."

"Thank the Lady!" cried his mother.

"I have put some things together, and now I have a few memories. I know my own name now," said Silence.

His father was staring at him. "But you don't know us, Raoul. You don't remember."

"I'm sorry," Silence whispered.

"My poor boy," said his mother.

His father looked uneasy. "Perhaps it's just as well," he muttered.

Silence's mother exclaimed at this, and he turned a warning look on her.

"The baron sent me to you," said Silence. He wasn't sure if they knew who Caedon was, but he knew they knew the baron. After all, they had given him to the baron. He suppressed a flash of anger.

"Our kind lord," said his father.

Silence overlooked that. "This," he said, raising the amulet on its thong. "This has meant everything. I kept it always."

"You see," said his mother to his father. "He did remember."

"I knew it meant something. Something important. But I wasn't sure what it meant."

Again his father reached out for it and took the little bird into his own hand. Again Silence had to stop himself from jerking it back.

"The eldest son inherits. That's Onfroi. The second son goes for a soldier in the service of the overlord. That's Vauquelin. The third and fourth sons, any others, now they have a different road to travel, a different life to live in this world. They must make their own way in the world. Wander far. But in these lands, for a generation, the youngest has always been our good baron's portion," said his father. "It's only right," he said, taking his hand away.

Silence nodded. He was beginning to see what his father was driving at. His father threw another warning look at his mother, who looked on the point of speaking. His father put his hand out again and tapped the little bird hanging about Silence's neck. "This is the martlet, boy," he said. "The martlet is the sign of the fourth son."

"Ah," said Silence. "Now I understand."

"The fourth son goes to the baron," said his mother. "Most who send their sons to his lordship, or sometimes their daughters, never see their children again. I suppose the baron sends them off around his vast domains. We were lucky he kept you close. You've been able to visit from time to time."

"Ah," said Silence again. Now he really did see, although he had to suppress an incredulous exclamation. All those families, believing their children were safe somewhere in the world. Surely someone must have questioned this lie over the years. It was as if they all willfully blinded themselves. But his mother was right. He was one of the lucky ones.

Or, he thought to himself with a chill, *maybe I'm not all that lucky.*

Later, after Onfroi, his eldest brother, had come home and they'd exchanged some uneasy pleasantries, Silence left his family. They all told themselves comfortable lies about the frequent visits home Silence would now be able to make.

Silence felt a vast relief once he was away from them all and back at the inn. His brother Onfroi's barely concealed hostile looks were particularly troubling.

In the morning, cart and driver would take him back to Caedon's manor. Strange to think of that place as a comforting refuge.

When he came down from his inn room to break his fast, he was astonished to see Onfroi standing before the hearth fire, twisting his cap in his hands.

"Onfroi," said Silence. "Brother," he made himself say.

"Walk with me, Rafe, I have something to tell you," said Onfroi, a stocky solid man maybe ten years older than Silence.

Silence left the inn with him and they walked down the lane past where Caedon's cart stood waiting for Silence.

Silence forced himself to say nothing.

"Listen," said Onfroi at last, turning to face him. "You must never come back. It hurts our mother too much. When she thought you were dead, it was better."

"Better?" Silence echoed faintly.

"Yes. Surely you see it. Father is displeased."

"No, I didn't see that. Onfroi, you must realize, I hardly know any of you. In fact, I don't know any of you at all."

"Better that way," Onfroi repeated.

"Yes, I see that it might be," Silence said carefully. He wondered whether Onfroi was worried about his inheritance, but how could he be? The first son inherits. It was established law.

"You open old wounds, for my parents," Onfroi said bluntly. "When you went away to the baron, I tell you truly, Father was relieved. But then you kept coming back."

"Most of them don't," said Silence softly.

"Most of them don't."

"And you know what that means," Silence said.

"Of course. Everyone knows what it means."

"But they pretend they don't. They pretend their children are just—elsewhere."

"Easier on everyone, that way, since there's no help for it."

"I see," said Silence. "I had wondered about that."

"Then," Onfroi went on, "after all those years of returning, and returning, and everlastingly returning, you stopped coming, and everyone could feel relief."

"Huh," said Silence, half-amused, half-horrified.

"You're not my brother," said Onfroi. "Or not really."

"No?"

"No. But you're our mother's son."

"Oh," said Silence, realizing now. "Sending me to the baron was a good solution to her problem."

"She never saw it that way. The rest of us did. Father did. Many families with such problems are glad of the baron's quota."

"I understand," said Silence.

"Think about it," said Onfroi. "Think about us, and then yourself. You'll see I'm right. You don't belong amongst us. Don't come back." He started walking away.

"I won't," Silence called after him. *Think about it,* this part-brother of his had said. He did. He saw. All of them were stocky with light brown hair and fair, ruddy skin. The Earth Child's. They all had brown eyes.

He was dark and slender. He was of the Sea Child, with the Sea Child's own eyes. They were not.

So I still have a father out there somewhere, thought Silence, *and I suppose I'll never meet him.*

As he got into Caedon's cart, he felt unsettled. But in many ways, he felt relieved. He had no obligation to these people, and he didn't need to see them again. When he thought of his mother's farewell kiss, though, and the anguish he realized he had seen in her eyes, he knew pity for her.

Overall, though, relief was what he felt as Caedon's cart jolted away from the little village.

But then, as the ramparts of Caedon's manor appeared at the end of the last turning of the road, an equally profound dread.

How can I live like this? Silence thought. *I don't belong to myself. I don't have a family of my own, not really. And I've fallen in with people who do terrible things.* With a bitter laugh at his own expense, he realized he thought nothing could be more horrifying than the master with the nightmare room.

I didn't know the half of it, he told himself.

Once again, he found himself fingering the little amulet at his throat. Now he understood better what it was supposed to mean, but for him, it meant something different, something much deeper. Holding it was a comfort to him, a kind of light in the darkness.

The little bird was a wandering creature, betwixt and between. It had no feet, symbolizing the wanderings of the fourth son, or maybe the bastard son, no land to call his own, no place to alight.

Silence felt himself unmoored from ordinary life, condemned to wander from one place or situation to the next, and to the next, and to the next, each new situation more terrible than the one before.

Would there ever be rest, for him? He thought maybe, like the martlet, there would not.

CHAPTER NINE

The Temple-Haunting Martlet

Y ou're restless and troubled. I can see it, brother," said Caedon to Silence. "I had hoped a visit to your parents would
settle you down, remind you of important matters in your
past. I see that's not the way of it. You remembered nothing?"

"No, nothing," said Silence.

"Your parents always treated you very affectionately. So I
came to understand, over the years. Not everyone can say as
much."

"They welcomed me," said Silence, deciding he didn't need to tell Caedon about Onfroi's words. "But I shocked them."

"They thought you were dead."

"Yes."

"They must have been overjoyed to find it was not so."

"It seems they were," said Silence.

"And that didn't move you?"

"It did. The way a moving story about strangers is moving."

"I see. No feelings at all, in their presence?"

"None."

"Well, then," said Caedon. He was sitting on his bench underneath the pear trees in his garden. "This may be a good thing that you've learned about yourself. You're not sentimental. You may be uniquely well cut out for the work you're about to do on Gilles's behalf." After a moment, he said, "Yet you are very troubled. I sense this."

"Why would they send me to Gilles, the way they did?" Silence burst out. "Even if that man thought it would help him get past his anger at his wife. Who would do that to a child?"

"So you do see," Caedon murmured. "I didn't think you would."

"And you. Why did your parents send you? How could they bear to do it?"

Caedon shrugged. "I had no family. None to speak of. I had no one to think twice about it. The baron sent for me, and I went to him."

"But you weren't a small child."

"No."

"So why—"

"He saw something in me," said Caedon. "I'll always be grateful to him for it." Caedon leaned toward Silence. "Somehow, you need to find that sense of gratitude in yourself. You're not considering this the right way, considering truly what you are. Look," he said, as if struck by a sudden idea. "There's something you know how to do, and it has always soothed you. You learned it as a half-grown lad."

"What is it."

"Look there. Look to the horizon."

Silence stood and gazed over the garden wall, squinting into the sun. "Mountains."

"One mountain in particular. A cliff face, a giant among crags. You know how to climb it, Rafe. When you were a boy, and troubled, you went there and climbed it." Caedon regarded him narrowly. "That does mean something to you."

"Yes," said Silence. He felt a gathering excitement.

"Take a few days. Hike there. Climb the mountain. Then come back to do your duty."

"Suppose I don't know how to climb any longer. It must be a difficult skill."

"There's an old goatherd in a hut at the base of the cliff face. He is the one who taught us. Gilles would send us off to him, to challenge ourselves."

"We climbed together?"

"Yes, for a while. I didn't care for it, so I stopped. But you. Every chance you got, you were over there, until Gilles sent us across the Narrows to the Sceptered Isle. That's when it stopped, for you. But I'm guessing that this skill of yours, like the skill of the sword, like riding, is still inside you as strong as ever. You see, don't you, Rafe. This is what Gilles values in you. This is what I value. You have something important inside." Cadeon reached out his hand and caressed Silence. Silence kept himself from hitting Caedon's hand away from him.

At dawn, with only a walking stick, a lump of bread, and a skin of water, Silence found himself trekking toward the mountains.

At the end of the day, he had found the hut. The old goatherd welcomed him with tears in his eyes. "Master Raoul!" he exclaimed. "You've come back! You're a man grown, but I remember you. How could I not?"

Very quickly, with the goatherd's help, Silence remembered everything, all the preparations. They were simple. Loose clothing, his hair tied back, supple leather shoes on his feet, thin strips of leather wrapping his hands.

His body remembered how to balance, how to lean against the cliff in order to feel its contours and know it. His feet remembered how to search out cracks in the limestone, his hands how to reach for holds in the rockface.

He thought about nothing at all, just about the cliff and his body learning the cliff.

The quiet was profound.

Caedon is right, he thought. *I need this.*

After an indeterminate time of climbing and concentration, his body gleaming with sweat, he realized he was nearing a ridge of rock that looked to be the very top of the cliff.

He pulled himself up and lay at full length there.

For a long time, he let the sun beat down on him, soothing body and mind. Finally he scrambled to his feet, and then he gasped. He was not at the top. Not even close to the top.

He was in a bowl-shaped niche. Sheer walls set back from this niche rose all around it. More to climb, he supposed, if he wanted to.

But he did not.

He wanted to stand quietly and look.

Someone had carved out columns from the rock.

In the bowl at the top of the cliff face, someone had constructed a small perfect temple, open to the open sky.

He went to the temple, edging past two imposing rock monoliths, mammoth and weathered, ending in bird-like structures far above him. He stepped into the center of the columns, maybe eight of them. There he saw a deep pool. He put out his hand to touch the columns. Who had carved them, erected them, placed them? Whose temple was this, he wondered.

There was no designation. No incised inscriptions or designs to let him know. No statue of any god, unless the bird monoliths represented gods. It wasn't a temple to the Lady. It didn't appear to be a temple to any of the Children, either. He wondered if the Old Ones had erected it here. Whoever did it, the difficulty must have been almost overwhelming. But not completely overwhelming, for here the temple stood. The ones doing the carving would have had to be accomplished climbers as well as accomplished stonemasons.

And the pool. Of course he would have loved this place, in boyhood. He was a child of the Child of Sea, far away from the sea, cut off from it. But here was this pool. He stood and looked into its depths. He could not see the bottom. A memory came surging at him. A memory of diving deep into this pool, and knowing solace.

On impulse he kicked off his shoes and shrugged out of his light trousers. It was all he had been wearing. He unwound the leather strips from his hands. He bent down to touch the surface of the pool with his hand. It shimmered slightly beneath his touch, as if it had a life of its own, a skin of its own that he alone could penetrate. He stood up on his toes, threw his arms overhead and made his hands into an arrow. He sprang up, flipped over, and dove straight down, arrowing down strongly toward the bottom. There was no bottom, or if there was, it was deeper than his deepest breath allowed him to go. Reluctantly, he swerved and made for the surface. For a while, even after he had surfaced, he couldn't make himself get out. He wanted to stay in the pool forever. This was his own element, and he had been away from it too long.

At last he heaved himself out of the water and onto the lip of the pool.

He sat down cross-legged in the midst of the columns and looked around at the surrounding cliff walls. A flicker of movement caught his attention. He drew in his breath.

Now he saw that birds, many of them, maybe hundreds, were nesting in the surrounding cliffs. Darting swift-winged curved-winged birds that circled and cried and wriggled into crevices where they had their nests.

Silence reached up to finger the amulet at his neck. These birds of the cliffs were his birds. The wanderer without a home, his amulet signified. But they did have a home, these birds. Here it was.

After a long time of gazing and simply breathing, Silence got back into his shoes and trousers, and wound the strips of leather around his hands again. He got himself back down the cliff.

He thanked the goatherd.

"Did you see? Did you pray at the shrine?" whispered the old man.

Silence nodded. He supposed that was what he was doing, as he sat there in that still high place. As he dove into its waters. What he did was a kind of prayer.

He slept in the goatherd's hut, ate from his kettle in the morning, thanked the old man again, embraced him, and headed back.

Caedon was there to greet him, leaning against the lintel. "I can see it in your face, Rafe. You found peace during your climb."

"Yes," said Silence. "And look at you. You're standing."

"We've both healed, at least a little," said Caedon. "And now you'll be ready to do your errand."

Even those words could not undo the peace Silence had found on the mountain. "Did you ever climb all the way to the top?" he asked Caedon.

"No, not I," said Caedon, with a laugh. "I got maybe halfway up a few times, before I lost interest. But you kept on."

Silence saw now. Caedon didn't know what waited at the top. He guessed that as a boy, he'd never told Caedon. He guessed that he had kept the sacred place entirely to himself. Who would ever know of it, if they hadn't climbed up to see for themselves. The top was set back where no eye could ever spot it, unless that eye belonged to a bird.

The goatherd knew. Silence saw that now.

Caedon seemed to have thought the climbing would be a soothing thing for Silence to practice, make him more tractable. He had no idea what had really happened to Silence on the mountain. What had probably happened throughout Silence's boyhood. Silence did not tell him now, either.

Maybe this is what sustained me, all those years in the custody of Gilles, he thought. But if so, Gilles must surely have seen it in him. So how had Gilles allowed it? That was a mystery to Silence.

Shortly after Silence returned from this expedition, Caedon gave him his instructions. "It's time to see if you will truly obey. Always in the past you were willful and disobedient. We'll see if anything has changed. I know your former life is banished from your mind, or much of it. Those snatches of memory hardly concern me. They shouldn't be enough to make you head off mulishly in some unfortunate direction counter to my wishes. But what about your essential character?"

"What errand?" said Silence, trying to push aside all the insulting things Caedon was implying about him.

"As you know, our mighty lord brings children into his service when they are around six years. There's a family on the coast with two sons near that age. The older is six, I believe, and the younger close to it. You're to go to them and bring back the older. Or, seeing as they are almost the same age, whichever one the family decides to give in homage to our baron. The younger son usually goes. But do you understand? It's their choice."

Silence nodded. He felt sickened by the whole enterprise, knowing what he now knew. Sickened that he'd be a part of it. But there was something else. Something unsettled him about the way Caedon emphasized the choice these parents would be offered. And the look in Caedon's eye. The way it was directed to him. Was it malice he saw there? A gleeful kind of knowing malice that unnerved Silence.

"Tomorrow, head off to meet the parents of these boys and find out which they will give. Then you're to bring that boy back to me. I'll see that he goes to Gilles."

Caedon's words filled Silence with deep misgivings. *Can I do such a thing, knowing what I know?* he thought.

"This is a test, Rafe," Caedon said, turning him and looking deep into his eyes. "A test to see whether our mighty lord can trust you. Whether I can."

Silence stood thinking. He was horror-struck by the idea of what he was to do. But as he stood, a deep calm descended on him. Somehow, he knew, it came from the temple on the top of the cliffs. It came from the pool. He put his hand to his amulet and touched it. He was not directionless, rudderless. There was a place for him, and he had been there.

Swearing on this, I feel as though I'm swearing on your life. Diera's words came ringing into his memory.

"Do you feel ready for your test, Rafe?" Caedon prompted.

"Suppose I fail it, this test of yours," said Silence.

"That would be. . . ." Caedon paused, watching Silence closely. "Most unfortunate."

CHAPTER TEN

A Little Boy

The wagon let Silence off along the coast, where surf pounded rocks rosy in the setting sun. He found an inn and engaged a room. "I'd like one overlooking the sea," he told the innkeeper.

"Certainly, good sir," said the innkeeper, his eye fixed on Silence's gold piece.

"No stinting," Caedon had said before Silence left. "At the inn, take a room to yourself. You're traveling on the baron's business. You're representing Gilles."

So Silence had paid for not just a whole bed but an entire room, and in the best inn with the fewest fleas and other vermin.

He threw down his belongings and lay quietly on the bed, soothed by the steady roar and retreat of the waves.

As twilight drew on, he went down the twisted stairs to the hearth, where he ate a hearty meal of stew and ale. Then back for sleeping. Even though in Caedon's manor he slept alone, he felt guarded there, on alert. *It must be*, he thought, *the result of living in a brothel for over a year*. And at the manor, he was always uneasily aware of Caedon's scrutiny. To sleep by himself in this inn was a kind of luxury, no one waking him for some unpleasant purpose, no one spying on him, and examining him, and sizing him up for their own desires and purposes. He slept deep, lulled into it by the sound of the sea and the tang of salt air.

But he woke in the morning with a sour feeling in the pit of his stomach. Now he had to proceed up the coast to a little village, and go to a house there, and take a boy.

He'd long since decided he couldn't do it. He wouldn't.

But then, once he had disobeyed, Gilles would hunt him down. Gilles would find him. He had no doubt Gilles would, and if he had had any doubts, Caedon had assured him of it before he left.

What Gilles would do to him then didn't bear thinking about.

Silence decided he'd go to the house and talk to the parents of these two boys. He'd make them understand what they were doing by giving one of their sons into Gilles's hands. Then they'd refuse. Surely they would. Afterward he'd return to Caedon. Let Gilles's wrath fall on the parents, not on him. He shied away from that little bit of cruelty. Maybe the parents would be able to look out for themselves. Maybe Gilles wouldn't be hard on them, because he'd maybe think they didn't understand the high honor they were refusing. *The honor they thought they were refusing,* Silence amended. What they were really refusing was a fate out of nightmare for their son.

Once he had made that decision, however evasive and cowardly, he could break fast at the inn and hire a driver to take him to the village. *I've suffered,* he thought resentfully. *Why should I have to suffer more?*

The driver's ox plodded up the coast. Silence leaned back into the cushions of the cart and tried not to think.

"Shall I wait, sir?" said the driver, when they arrived in a small nondescript village. He pulled his forelock and pointed with his wagon whip toward the house Silence was to visit.

Silence made a quick decision. "No," he said. "I've other errands here. I may be long."

Because, he thought, *if things go wrong, I'll have to—*

He wasn't sure what he'd have to do if things went wrong.

Before he could think about it and lose his nerve entirely, he walked through the one dusty street of the village and knocked at the plank door of the small timbered house he was expected to visit.

A large man opened the door.

"You're the one from Gilles?" this man said after a long moment of scrutinizing Silence.

"Yes," said Silence.

"You look familiar. Caedon sent you. Didn't he."

Silence was taken aback by the man's hostile stare. No "Lord Caedon" in this man's mouth.

"Yes, he did," said Silence.

The man held the door open and motioned for Silence to come in. "I suppose I'll have to show you the boys. I suppose Caedon will come down on me hard if I don't."

Silence nodded in surprise. He sat where the man indicated.

"I'll get them, and my wife." The man disappeared into the interior of the house. He came back with a woman. She was attractive in a blowzy way. Blonde. Buxom.

She would have done well in the brothel, Silence thought, looking at her appraisingly.

The woman rose from the curtsey she was making to Silence, and then her mouth gaped open. She stared at him. Then she began to shriek.

Silence took a few steps quickly backward and looked to the man in confusion. He seemed just as shaken as Silence was. He put his hands on his wife and hustled her from the room.

Through the hide swinging between the front room and the interior of the house, Silence could hear her screaming and babbling incoherently. He could hear the man's voice, angry, remonstrating. Then a solid thwack.

The man came back out, red-faced. "She's in a state," he mumbled.

"Listen," Silence said urgently. "Maybe she has heard things. Things about what Gilles will do to your son."

The man looked at Silence in amazement. "Are you daft?"

Silence shook his head, hard. He wasn't sure what was going on.

"Wait here. I'll get the boys. My wife knows what will happen. We talked it over. But now the silly cow is overwrought. If you tell Caedon about this, make sure he knows it's she who caused trouble, not I."

The man came back with two young boys. As Caedon had said, they were both around six years old, and they looked nothing alike. One was dark and slender and quick. The other was a big blond lad who resembled his father.

Two different fathers, thought Silence. *It's pretty clear.* He thought of his own situation.

"This one's Gwyl," said the man, shoving the dark slender lad toward Silence. "Make your bow to the gentle," he hissed at the boy.

The boy made a quick little bow and looked up at Silence warily, then over at his father.

Not his father, Silence realized. *And this man hates him, the child of some other man.*

"This boy is Pierrick," said the man, indicating the other boy.

That one is his son, thought Silence, seeing the man's pride, and also his fear, when he gently urged the boy forward. *He'll be glad to get rid of the younger one, the dark one. This bigger one must be the elder.*

"What do I have to do for Caedon, to get him to take the elder?" said the man.

"The baron usually takes a younger son into his service," said Silence carefully.

"But the elder will go," said the man, grabbing the dark slender smaller boy by the neck of his tunic and practically pushing him on Silence. "Take him. Tell Caedon I'll do whatever he requires. Take him and go."

Now Silence saw. The big boy was actually the younger. He sprang for his brother, but his father grabbed him, too, by the tunic and thrust him toward the hide hanging between the two sections of the house.

"Go to your mother. See she's not hurt," he told the blond younger boy, who looked frightened and obeyed.

"And you," said the man to Silence. "Take the elder and get out of my house."

"Good sir," Silence began.

"Out," the man yelled. Spittle from the force of his yelling sprayed on Silence's cheek.

The elder boy stole his hand into Silence's. Silence looked down at him. "We'll go, shall we?"

"Yes," the boy said softly.

"Do you want to send any belongings—" Silence tried.

"Get out. Are you deaf? Get out!" screamed the man.

Silence took the boy and left the house. He didn't know what else to do. "Is there a place in the village we can stay the night?" he asked the boy.

"I'll show you," the boy said.

Gwyl. That's his name, thought Silence. He engaged a room for the two of them from a neighbor, who looked at them both with frank curiosity.

"This is my uncle," Gwyl lied to her. "I'm staying the night with him, while he is visiting. There's not enough room to home."

The goodwife regarded the two of them suspiciously. Silence was about to lead Gwyl outside and head even further down the road.

Before he could, a young woman appeared in the goodwife's doorway. "Goodwife Marcelle, my sister has sent me to make sure you have room for these two," she said breathlessly.

Silence turned to her in surprise. She was a young woman just past girlhood. Her glossy brown hair was drawn off her face and braided down her back, tied off with a piece of yarn. Her expressive brown eyes flicked in his direction, then back to the goodwife.

"If you vouch for them, Mistress Elene," the woman began.

"Indeed I do," she said, fumbling in a small pouch dangling from her belt and producing a few coins. Gwyl had rushed to her and had attached himself to her by holding tight to her skirts. She put down a hand and smoothed the boy's hair.

Silence stepped forward. "Nay, Mistress Elene, I have the funds for myself and the boy, but thank your sister for me, and her husband, for their . . ." he paused, trying to control his tone. "—courtesy," he finished, pulling out Caedon's pouch of gold and producing a coin that dazzled Goodwife Marcelle into a broad smile.

She took it.

Silence bowed.

"I'll come help you get the lad settled, shall I?" said the girl.

"I thank you, young mistress," said Silence.

The goodwife showed the three of them to a tiny room with one bed over the stable.

Silence sat on the bed and drew the boy to him. "Now," he said. "If you can, tell me about yourself. What just happened was—" Silence groped for words. "Confusing." Deep down, though, he knew. Something was telling him. A father who wanted another man's son gone, with Gilles's quota the convenient means. Wasn't that his own story?

"My name is Gwyl," said the boy.

"I know. What else?"

"This is my auntie." He nodded to the girl Elene, who was hovering in the doorway to the room.

"Thank you for taking the lad," she said. "He's not had it easy."

"Father gets angry with me," said Gwyl, "because I am a bad boy. Bad to the core."

"I see," said Silence carefully, looking from the boy to Elene. *Bad to the core*, thought Silence. *Child preserve him, he's quoting his father.*

"He likes Pierrick," said Gwyl. "Pierrick is good. Not like me."

Silence glanced over at Elene.

"Master Maro is not the lad's father," she said.

Just as I thought, Silence said to himself.

"Will you take him to the baron?" she said. "He deserves a better life. My sister doesn't know I'm here. I lied to the goodwife. I saw you taking Gwyl off and I knew I should help you get him away from those two back there."

"No," said Silence. "No one understands, it seems. The baron damages boys like this. I'll not take him there." He hadn't known he'd say that until he did it. But he didn't have to think about it. He wouldn't do it. He knew it without having to think at all. "The baron expects me to, but I won't," he told Elene, as her expression turned from hopeful to confused.

"But the baron has a big castle, and a horse, and a sword," Gwyl burst out.

"The baron is a bad man," said Silence. "I won't take you to him."

He saw one expression after another chasing itself across Gwyl's face.

Gwyl looked as if he were considering, with dismay, the loss of castle, horse, and sword. But then he broke into a huge smile. "I won't go! I'll be with my brother!" Gwyl crowed.

Silence smiled at the boy, and he smiled at Elene over the boy's head. He started to say something, but then he turned at a scrabbling sound on the narrow stairs.

Before he could stand up to see what it was, the younger boy Pierrick had leapt into the room, and he and Gwyl were pounding each other delightedly on the shoulders. They stood arm in arm and grinned at Silence and Elene.

"Why, Pierrick!" she exclaimed. "You were supposed to stay safe behind."

"If Gwyl goes, I go," the little blond lad announced. "Father doesn't like Gwyl, but he can't stop me liking him. I like Gwyl. Gwyl is my brother," he said, all in a rush.

"Well, now," Silence said to Pierrick. "What shall the four of us do about this? Your father wants me to take Gwyl, but I don't want to take him, and I think now he's thought about it, Gwyl doesn't want to go."

"He wants to be with me," said Pierrick with a sunny smile.

Child keep you both, thought Silence. "What does your auntie think?" he said instead.

"This happened before," said Elene to Silence. "A man came to take Gwyl. I heard about it and hid him in the woods. I was afraid Master Maro was selling him into bondage. When the boy came home, Master Maro beat him. I thought this time was different. That the boy would be happier this way. What you're telling me now..." She faltered to a stop.

"I brought apples to Gwyl in the woods," said Pierrick proudly. "So he wouldn't be hungry."

"Who was this other person who tried to take him?" Silence asked Elene.

"I don't know." She looked uneasily away. "Someone who meant him ill."

Silence saw it. She did know who. She just wasn't going to say.

"Someone else," Gwyl burst out. "Some other man came to take me, but auntie didn't let him. It was that man from down the way."

"Gwyl hid. Auntie and I helped," piped Pierrick.

"This is confusing," Silence said to Elene. "Help me understand this boy's situation." He doubted he'd get the full story from her, and he didn't know why. But he didn't doubt her good intentions.

She leaned against the doorframe, considering him. Probably trying to decide how far she could trust him. "I'm the sister of the boys' mother," she said at last. "My sister sent for me when she and her husband had to flee from the troubles over there on the Sceptered Isle. Our parents are dead of plague, and our older sister was killed by The Rising. So I crossed the Narrows to be with my sister and help out with the children." She stood quiet. After a moment, "I've been here a while, and now I see some things I don't like," she said softly. "Especially with Gwyl. His father fought for The Rising, I think." She nodded toward little Gwyl, who looked up at her uncomprehending. "The boy's father was an enemy. Master Maro can't get past that, and neither can my sister. But it's not the boy's fault."

Silence wondered at her words. He knew many women became caught up in wartime chaos and raped by soldiers. An unfortunate effect of wars everywhere. Perhaps this young boy was the result. Whatever the way of it, Elene was right. His mother's misfortune wasn't the boy's fault.

Not for the first time, Silence wondered if he himself had been part of The Rising. He supposed he had. Perhaps they were a violent lot, a dirty bunch of thugs and rebels, as Caedon implied. He hoped he hadn't participated in any vile episodes such as the rape of young women.

But none of that mattered. The little boy was in danger, and Silence saw he couldn't stand by and let that happen. He certainly couldn't bring the child into danger, no matter who the lad was, no matter what kind of criminal his father had been.

"Here's what we will do," said Silence after a moment. "You go home, Pierrick. Your auntie will take you."

Pierrick's snub-nosed, freckled face clouded over.

"I know," said Silence, putting out a comforting hand to the little boy. "But Pierrick. I want you to think about something for me. If you don't go home, what will happen?"

"Come looking for me," Pierrick whispered.

"And then what will happen?"

"Father will find Gwyl and whip him."

"Right. And that would be a bad thing."

Pierrick nodded, his little face miserable. He stole his hand into his brother's.

Silence looked up at Elene. "Gwyl will come with me." At Elene's expression, he hastened to add, "Not to the baron."

"Where, then?" said Elene, putting out a hand to Pierrick and gathering him to her side.

"Somewhere the baron can't find him," said Silence.

"No," said Gwyl.

"No?" Silence felt a sinking feeling. How could he make this boy understand the danger he was in.

"No," said Pierrick, leaning against Elene.

"We stick together," said Gwyl, hopping off the bed and going to Pierrick. "We're brothers."

"I see," said Silence. He did, too. He felt a pang of envy and, chasing right after it, a pang of love. Two brothers who loved each other. Part of Gwyl's story was his own story. This part of it was not. If only he'd had brothers who loved him. He thought of Onfroi and his hostile gaze. He thought of Caedon and shuddered.

Then he realized. He'd claimed brothers of his own, his brothers in The Rising. He knew that now. They couldn't be thugs and rapists.

Suppose he took the two boys off with him.

But where would he go? He had a feeling Pierrick's father might be glad to see the last of Gwyl, no matter who took him, or where, or why. The man wouldn't stand idle, though, if someone took his true-born son.

And the mother. That harrowing scream. What had she known? It must be she knew what Gilles did to boys. How else explain her reaction? And the father had confirmed she knew.

She wouldn't stand for either son being taken away from her, Silence decided, even if Gwyl was the child of a rapist.

Much later he found he was wrong.

But that was much later, when his realization about why she had screamed could no longer make any difference.

"Suppose I take Gwyl to the next village with me?" he said to Elene. "I'll arrange for his care there, and when you judge it is safe, you can go there and get him and bring him home."

He looked down at the dark slender lad with the wide gray eyes, dark-lashed in his small pale ivory face. The Sea-child's, if he didn't miss his guess. For that reason, and for the other reason, that he wasn't wanted by his family, a family ready to hand him over to Gilles, Silence felt a kinship with the boy. "Your auntie will come to get you when the time is right, and then you'll go home," Silence told Gwyl. "You trust your auntie, don't you?"

The boy nodded reluctantly.

Silence looked over at Pierrick, who nodded too but looked to be on the point of tears.

He smiled at the two boys.

Two lovely boys who loved each other and took care of each other as much as they could, and under difficult circumstances. Gwyl, clearly the Sea Child's own. The boy's brother, a fine sturdy lad, completely different, who looked to be one of those dedicated to the Child of Earth. Very different boys who were each other's best support and—Silence intuited this—always would be.

This younger boy, Pierrick, clearly took after both parents. Gwyl must take after his real father, the absent one.

What heartless kind of man is he, to abandon his son? thought Silence. Then he realized this man probably didn't even know his son existed. *Besides,* Silence told himself, glad the man didn't have control over such a fine boy, *this man who fathered him must be a villain.*

"What do you think? Is this a good solution to the boy's problem?" he said to Elene.

"Boys." He turned to Gwyl and Pierrick. "Play for a little while. I need to talk something over with your auntie."

He stepped outside the little room with Elene. "Is this a solution at all? Will the boy even be safe, when he returns home?" he asked her.

"Master Maro beats Gwyl," she said. "Not just that one time. He does it often."

"I'm leaving the baron's service," he told Elene. "I see what he does with the boys he sends me to take. I can't be a part of it. But I can't take Gwyl with me, even if I want to. He won't be safe with me. I'll have to flee. It's best, I think, to find a hiding place for him, maybe a sen'night, maybe a fortnight."

Elene nodded. "This is the only way. The best way. I see that, sir. And I thank you."

"I feel much better knowing he has you to look out for him, as much as you can," said Silence to her. "That may be hard for you. You may be put into a bad position. Look," he said, struck with a sudden thought. "Just say you heard through neighbors that some villainous churl had abandoned Gwyl in a village down the road. That should work, and you won't be suspected. Here is gold for the boy's keep."

"Oh, sir!" she said, demurring.

"You must take it. How else arrange for him to stay in the next village? And afterward, maybe you can use it some way to help him. Pierrick too. I can see it, what fine lads they both are. Take it," he insisted, urging the gold on her.

Finally she did.

Together, they went back into the little room, where the boys sat on the floor intent on a game of knucklebones.

"Boys," said Silence, getting their attention. "Your auntie and I have decided. She'll take Pierrick home, and she'll arrange for Gwyl to stay nearby until she thinks it's safe for him to come home too. What do you think of this plan? Will you keep it a secret, what we've decided to do?"

"Yes," said Gwyl.

"Yes," said Pierrick.

And that's what they did.

CHAPTER ELEVEN

A Needle in a Field

Silence hoped to his god, whether Sea Child or whoever She might be, that he had a little time before Caedon realized Silence had gone missing. Then there'd be the Dark Ones to pay.

He needed the time because there was something he realized he had to do, even if it put him in danger. He knew it with just as much conviction as he had known, in the end, that he could not bring Gwyl to Gilles.

It was Kipp. Silence thought of the laborers he had seen in the fields as he had made his way to see his parents, and his fantasy that one of them might be Kipp. He needed to turn fantasy into reality. He needed to find Kipp and free him.

How in the Nine will I do that? he wondered in despair.

He knew he had to try.

After he had seen Gwyl securely tucked away with Elene, he hired a horse. By now, he knew he could ride a horse, and ride well. He and Esteban had practiced combat from horseback. As they practiced, the skill of it came back to Silence with a rush, just as the skills of climbing and diving had come back to him. He had practiced the skill of the horse before, and he knew now in muscle and sinew and bone that he'd been on horseback since early childhood.

He turned this hired horse's head toward the south. He rode along the coastal trails in the glorious weather of harvest-tide, golden fields to the left of him, the sea with its mighty roar to the right. In spite of the danger he knew he was in, the sea gave him solace and courage.

Late on the first day, he came to the road that turned away from the coast eastward toward Caedon's manor, and far beyond, Gilles's castle. The road he was supposed to be taking.

It gave him a chill, standing there looking down that road. Gilles knew things. Did Gilles know Silence was standing at the crossroads deciding to flee from him?

Silence did not head down that road. He turned away, turned away south again, and he kept going. He wasn't quite sure how to find the port city where he and his fellow prisoners had made landfall, but by asking along the way, he discovered directions to the most likely of the three possibilities. He traveled carefully. He didn't want to ruin his horse, even though he felt a terrible prickling at the back of his neck, all the way, as if Gilles were watching what he did and deciding when to come after him. He stayed in modest inns as he traveled.

By the third day, he had reached the town. The right town.

He made his way down to the shore and stood gazing across the Narrows. *This is the place,* he told himself, feeling a shiver of recognition. Then he walked his horse back into the heart of the town. People on the crabbed, crooked streets stepped aside from him and pulled their forelocks respectfully.

He seemed a prosperous gentle to these people. Silence smiled at those he passed, but his smile was mirthless. As he paced his horse past the blue door of the house that served as the town's brothel, he felt a momentary surge of rage. He wanted to step into the place and throttle the master with his own hands. He wanted to take Alphonsine and most of the others off with him to a place of safety.

But he knew he couldn't save them. There were too many of them, and too many soldiers about. If he stopped to do it, Caedon would hear of it. Gilles would. He'd be taken. With a sick heart, he turned away.

He found an inn and stabled his horse. In the morning, he put aside his guilt about the brothel and began his search.

At the port, he passed himself off as a landowner's son come looking for an easy source of labor. Where might he acquire slaves to work his father's lands? he asked.

Those he talked to pointed his way to a portside tavern.

"That's where you'll find the slave factors," one of the townsfolk told him.

Silence entered the tavern and found a table. An oily fellow made his way over to where Silence sat with a tankard of ale.

"I hear you may be in need of field labor," he said.

"Yes, you heard rightly, my good man." Silence summoned up all the haughty manners he'd observed in Caedon. He drew his pouch of gold from his belt and laid it on the table. He made sure the man got a good look at the dagger in its scabbard and the sword at his belt, too. The man was no doubt indifferent honest. "I understand ships bring prisoners from the Sceptered Isle to this place, and then they are sold as bondsmen to landowners."

"Aye indeed, young sir," said the man. "Plenty of the enemy taken in the wars. A long war's bad for some. Good for others. For me, very good. For me, a steady supply. Good for those who buy from me, too."

"And you arrange such transactions?"

"I do, yes, and some of these others you see around you work in the same trade. But I am known to be the best. Ask anyone. Deal only with me, young sir, and you'll not get cheated."

"Cheated how?"

"Oh, you know," said the factor, giving Silence a shifty look from underneath his beetling brows. "These are war prisoners. They've suffered wounds. Some of my colleagues are not as scrupulous and honest as I. They fix the prisoners up to look hale, and then, too late, their new masters find they are sickly and soon die."

"My father gets most of his labor from the east. He has never bought any of these war prisoners," said Silence, inventing quickly. "Can you recommend a few masters roundabouts who'd talk to me about their bondsmen? How satisfactory they've found men of this sort?"

"Surely," said the slave factor, but with reluctance. After a moment of hesitation, after a few black looks, he mentioned several names.

The factor probably thought Silence was trying to take advantage of him by getting free information out of him. He gave the fellow a gold piece. "A small advance, should I return to buy from you," he said. "If I do not, pray keep it for your trouble, and your good advice."

Now Silence was this man's best friend and patron. The fellow bowed, he pulled his forelock, he made all manner of obsequious remarks. He gave Silence directions to the farms and manors where Silence would find such masters, such bondslaves.

I've done my job maybe too well, thought Silence as finally, with difficulty, he rid himself of the fellow. He felt dirty, just talking to the man.

In the entire experience, only one thing made Silence glad. He was glad he had not come face to face with the slave factor who had sent him to the brothel. He didn't trust what he might have done to the man if he had. He vividly remembered the man's sneering face, the way he'd grabbed at Silence's amulet, the judgment he passed on Silence to send him to a bad fate when Silence was too helpless and bewildered to prevent him. *I'm not helpless now*, he thought. With an effort, he set these memories aside.

Maybe a little bewildered still, he told himself. He clucked to his horse. *Pretty bewildered*, he said to himself.

The very next morning, he headed off to visit the farms and lands he'd been told about. He rode slowly past the fields where the bondslaves were threshing or tying straw into yelms. When it was necessary, he talked to the overseers, telling them the same lie, that he was looking over the bondservants who had been war prisoners, to see if they made good workers. If he could, he avoided the overseers and tried to tally and scrutinize the bondservants on his own.

After three days, he hadn't found Kipp.

I may have gone to find a needle in a field, he told himself. By now, Kipp could have been sold far away from the area. By now, Kipp could be lying dead in some unknown common grave.

But on the fourth day, he was glad he hadn't avoided the overseers completely. One of them was showing him around his overlord's fields. This man happened to mention the fine specimens he had recently seen at work erecting a new outbuilding for a neighboring lord.

Silence realized then. *I heard the slave factor sending Kipp off to the fields, but he might not have stayed there. He might have been put to a different kind of work.*

As he rode toward the neighboring lord's lands, he swatted away a swarm of anxious thoughts. He was staying in Gilles's realm too long. If he didn't get away, he'd be taken. By now Caedon, and probably Gilles too, had had time to realize Silence had double-crossed them both. Not done their bidding. Not brought children to Gilles so that he could hurt them or kill them or anyway ruin them. Made off with their gold.

As he neared the lord's manor, a line of laborers tramped past him, their mauls on their shoulders.

Silence looked down the line of men. Then he began to grin. He controlled his expression, forcing himself to look haughty and overbearing. At the end of the line, the laborers' overseer marched with his whip.

"Get along with you, all you yaldson vermin," this man was crying out. "It's close on noon. I'll whip you all if we don't get the lord's business done by nightfall."

"Fellow," Silence called down from his horse.

The man paused in surprise. He called out a few more obscenities to his charges and told them to keep walking while he talked to the gentle.

"Sir," said the man, pulling his forelock.

"My father has sent me out to find a particularly strong bondservant to move some rocks. Who is your strongest man? I'd like to buy him."

"Halt!" bawled the overseer to his charges. They all stopped and stood drooping in the roadway. The overseer looked up at Silence. "They are his lordship's bondservants," he said.

"But if I gave you this," said Silence, plucking a gold piece from his pouch, knowing it was more coin than the fellow would see in twelve turnings of the moon or more, "perhaps you'd sell me a likely fellow anyhow. I'm sure your lord would find this a fair price, and I'm long overdue back at my father's manor. He'll be angry with me for lollygagging around the country visiting taverns instead of finding a man to do his work." He winked at the overseer, and the man guffawed. "Do us both a favor and sell me someone strong."

Silence knew, and the overseer knew, that the overseer would keep the coin for himself and tell the overlord one of his bondservants had keeled over dead.

"Well, now," said the overseer, looking over the line of men. "That one there, third from the end, he might do nicely. Or how about this one?" he pointed his whip at a hulking bondslave standing with his head down.

"What about that tall fellow?"

"That there's my best worker, good sir," said the overseer with a canny glance at Silence.

Silence produced a few silver pieces to sweeten the deal.

"Done," said the overseer. He walked over to the bondservant Silence had pointed out, unhooked him from the rope that bound the men together in the line, and led him by a chain to Silence.

"You belong to this man now," he said, handing the end of the chain to Silence with one hand and taking the coins with the other.

"Stand here by me," Silence murmured. The bondslave he had just bought stood in the road beside Silence on his horse.

"The Lady knows what you really want with him," Silence heard the overseer mutter underneath his breath, "but do I care?"

Silence and his new bondslave watched as the overseer marched the other men away. As the last of them disappeared over a little rise, Silence slid off his horse.

He grasped this man he had just bought by the shoulders. "Kipp," he said, and his voice broke.

Kipp, who had been looking at his feet through the whole exchange, now raised his eyes. "Silence?" he said, his eyes opening wide.

The two men stood in the road embracing and weeping.

"You talk, Silence!" said Kipp at last, dashing the tears from his eyes.

"A little," said Silence.

"I'm yours now, Silence. I see your fortunes have changed," said Kipp with a smile.

"You say you're mine." Silence's voice was flat. "You must be joking. You are your own, Kipp, and always have been. I've been looking everywhere for you. Let's walk my poor horse to an inn and find you some better clothes."

"I'm a bondslave, Silence," said Kipp, holding up his wrist with the brand for Silence to see.

Silence drew off the armlet of beaten gold from his left wrist. "And here's my own. A wise man once told me, freedom is in here," he said, and hit his chest with his other fist. "He told me, Endure it, Silence. Tyranny can't last forever."

Kipp laughed out loud, and Silence laughed too. They laughed until fresh tears came to their eyes and poured down their cheeks.

Something healed inside Silence then, and he saw maybe the same was happening to Kipp.

CHAPTER TWELVE

Complicated

Silence looked sidelong at Kipp. He saw his friend was frightened. "No fear," he said. "They don't know us here."

He saw Kipp swallow hard. "It's the memory, man."

"I know," said Silence. "And you were hauled away from the place, while I—" They were walking together up the main street of the little port town. From there, they'd book passage across the Narrows and be gone from this realm where so much harm had been done them. "See that door?" Silence pointed to the other side of the crooked little street. To the blue door leading into the tall narrow house that was the town's brothel.

"I called that place home for too long," said Silence. "And now, when I walk past, what I feel—" he stopped. "I want to go in there and kill someone. Several someones, but one man in particular, the master. And I know I can't, because if I do, it will draw un-wanted attention."

He saw the concern in Kipp's eyes.

"They won't know me now. I look prosperous. I look like no-body who would have ever lived there. No one who would have been made to do—" he broke off. "I'm safe from them, as long as I don't do what I want to do to that man." He guided Kipp down another lane. "We'll go back to the inn where I stayed, when I started looking for you."

But the instant they walked in, Silence was recognized.

"Young master! Young master!" The slave factor rushed up to Silence.

Silence looked a warning at Kipp, who nodded slightly back.

"Did you find the laborers for your father?" said the factor, putting his hand on Silence's arm. "Is this one of them?" He nod-ded toward Kipp.

Silence kept himself from jerking away. He thought fast. "Nay," he said. "This man—" and here he nodded at Kipp— "has just come from my father, to summon me home." Silence made himself grin. "I'm in for it now, good man. My father won't be pleased." A plan was forming. It might be risky. Silence realized he had to try it.

"I'm sorry to hear it, young master," said the factor.

"He'll call me a ne'er do well, wasting my time in brothels ra-ther than doing the business he sent me on. But ale will help fortify me to face the worthy old man." Silence snapped his fin-gers at the passing tavern wench and led Kipp to a seat. "Join us, good master factor," he said.

The factor eagerly slid onto the bench across the table from Silence and Kipp. When the tavern wench arrived, Silence ordered ale for the three of them.

"I'm thinking there's one more office you can do me, good man," he said, leaning over the table to the factor and dropping his voice confidentially.

"I'm at your service entirely, good master," said the factor.

"I need you to buy me someone."

"Of course. Is there a laborer you have your eye on?"

"If only I did." Silence made himself sigh again. "No, this is a purchase that will displease my father even more than he's already displeased." He forced another grin. "But if you and I are discreet, he'll never know it." He looked aside to Kipp. "My father's servant knows me well. He won't tell, will you, man?"

Kipp, Silence saw with relief, played right along. "I won't tell, master, but your father will be angry."

"It's a woman," Silence whispered to the factor. "One of the women in the brothel here. I've taken a fancy to her. I'm minded to buy her."

"Your father will be so angry," cried Kipp. He rolled his eyes dramatically.

Silence hoped to his Child Kipp didn't overplay it. But the factor, clearly eager for more of Silence's gold, was not noticing.

"Her name is Alphonsine. Would you buy her for me and bring her here to the inn for me? I won't want anyone seeing me in talk with a brothel master."

"I'll be happy to do you this office," said the factor with a wink and a gap-toothed grin. "Wait here, and I'll see what the brothel master will sell her for."

Soon after, he returned, naming a price that, Silence was sure, included a generous markup for himself. Silence thought of dickering over the price. If he didn't, would he set off any alarm bells?

"I confess, I'm besotted with the girl," he said instead, taking out his purse and counting the coins into the factor's palm. "Bring her straight here to the inn. I'm going above to my room. Hand her over to my servant, if you please. He'll bring her to me."

After the factor had gone, Silence looked over at Kipp. "You must think I've gone mad," he said.

"Love," Kipp said, a bemused expression on his face. "It makes men do strange things."

"I don't love this girl. I just need to get her out."

Realization dawned on Kipp. "Oh. I see it now."

"I'll engage a room for us. As a kindness to me, Kipp, keep pretending you're my servant and get Alphonsine above stairs as soon as that awful man brings her here."

"I'll do it, Silence."

Silence waited in the room he'd taken for himself and Kipp. *Every time I do something like this*, he thought, *I increase the risk that Caedon will find me.* But he knew he couldn't leave the port with this last thing undone.

After a long anxious wait, he heard them on the stairs. He stepped to the door of the room. Kipp came up the narrow stairs leading Alphonsine, cloaked and apprehensive.

"In here. Quick," said Silence, holding the door for them. He closed it behind them and barred it.

He turned as Alphonsine was taking down the hood of her cloak. She stared at him in astonishment.

"Alphonsine, I—"

"Silence!" she cried, and threw herself into his arms.

The three of them all perched on the side of the inn room's one narrow bed. Alphonsine couldn't speak, just utter little cries and pat Silence's cheek and weep.

"There, now," said Silence, smiling at her and stroking her hand.

"You can talk again," she said, when she finally collected herself.

"You were right all along. I can talk. I just had to give it time," he said.

"But that awful man took you away. I was so afraid for you, Silence."

"Then some friends found me." *Not exactly friends*, he thought, *but it's too complicated to explain*. "Now I'm free."

"Lady be praised," she said.

"And now you're free."

"You bought me to free me?" Her voice trembled.

"Of course I did. I couldn't let you stay in that place."

"I've been a bondslave since childhood, when my parents sold me," she said after a moment. At their horrified looks, she said, defiantly, "I don't blame them. It was that or starve. My baby brother would have died. But I'm not sure I know how to do it, live freely in the world."

Now Silence started to worry. He'd freed her, but he couldn't stay around to help her. He and Kipp needed to get out of there before he was taken. "Listen, Alphonsine. I'm on the run."

"I thought you said—"

"It's complicated. But Kipp and I have to leave the realm on the morning tide. I'm going to give you a lot of gold. I want you to get a place on a wagon heading up the coast. Can you do that, do you think?"

"I don't know," she said dubiously. "You're going to give me a lot of gold?"

"It's not my gold. It belongs to a very bad man. I took it from him."

"You're no criminal, Silence."

"I know. It's complicated." Silence cursed himself. Is that all he could say? But he'd used so many words, so fast. And his situation really was complicated. Even if the words flowed freely from him, he doubted he'd get Alphonsine to understand.

"You bought me with stolen gold," said Alphonsine."

"Yes," said Silence simply. "And now I'm going to give you more of it so you can get away from here."

She began to laugh.

"Suppose they find out and take her—" Kipp began.

She whirled on him. "They'll never take me."

"Good," said Silence. "Don't let them. Go up the coast to a little village. Find a young woman there. She lives in the household of a man named Maro. The woman's name is Elene. Tell her—" Now Silence was flummoxed. Tell her what? He was putting Elene in jeopardy, he'd probably put Alphonsine in jeopardy. But now he saw it. Alphonsine had made her choice. Freedom over safety. "Alphonsine," he said. "I don't think the risk to you is very great. The master saw only that factor. He didn't see me. Even if someone were to come here looking for me and their stolen gold, I don't think they'd connect me with you. You'll be far away from here by then. And so will I."

Alphonsine nodded, her expression fierce and determined.

"Go to Elene. Tell her the man who helped her with that little boy asks, as a favor to him, if she'll please think of a place you can live. You'll be able to live on this gold for a while, before you have to think of a way to keep yourself."

Alphonsine gave him a strange look.

Please not that way, he thought. But it would be up to Alphonsine, what she did. Silence knew he'd never see her again.

"Here," said Silence. He pulled a piece of parchment from his cloak and drew a little map on it with a piece of charcoal he'd found during his travels. "Don't smudge it. Keep it safe. Tell the wagoneer that's where you want to go. Well, really, Alphonsine," he said, after the three of them had sat together quietly for a moment, "you can go anywhere you like. This is just one place you might go, if you have no other ideas."

"It looks like a good plan, Silence."

"Go now. I think I saw a wagon in the innyard, when my friend and I came in earlier. See if it's there. If it's not, go to the marketplace and find another."

"I will."

He guided her gently to the door. "Child go with you," he whispered, pressing a leather bag of gold into her hands.

She stared at him for a long moment. She pulled him down to her and kissed him. "Thank you for this," she said.

"Thank you, Alphonsine. I don't know what I would have done, back in that place, without your kindness."

And then she was gone.

Silence and Kipp sat on the bed, listening to her diminishing step on the stair.

"She could denounce you, man. Make a lot more gold," said Kipp finally.

"Alphonsine would never do that," said Silence.

"I've seen worse things happen," said Kipp with a dark look.

"Never," said Silence firmly. "Now I have to sleep, my friend. All this talking. I'm too tired to think. And Kipp—I know this is odd, but you can have the bed to yourself. Ever since that place, that terrible place, I can't sleep beside anyone else, not if I can help it, no matter how friendly I feel toward the person."

Silence took his cloak and looked about the floor for a place to roll up in it and sleep.

Kipp leaped from the bed and seized Silence by the elbow. "No, friend," he murmured. He guided Silence to the bed, made him lie down there. He pulled up the cloak around Silence. "You sleep, Silence. Sleep well, my friend."

Then Kipp rolled himself on the floor in his own cloak, and soon the two of them had fallen into an exhausted sleep so long and so deep they almost missed the tide.

It must be true. I'm the Sea Child's, Silence thought. Being on the open ocean invigorated him. He saw most of the mariners had eyes like his, while most of the passengers had eyes like almost everyone else. Eyes of the Child of Earth. Those passengers were cowering on the deck, even Kipp.

Not Silence. He stood at the top strake of the cog and reveled in the stiff breeze carrying them across the Narrows.

Maybe this is how I'll get away from Gilles, he thought. *On the sea. Maybe he can't reach out for me, over the waters.*

Otherwise, he had no idea how he'd accomplish such a feat. Caedon assured Silence that Gilles would find out where Silence was, if he ever crossed the mage, and then he'd hunt Silence down.

Silence saw his hope of safety was a hollow one. The sea might stop Caedon. But he doubted it would stop Gilles.

Now, though, he faced a much smaller but more immediately pressing problem. Kipp was terrified.

"How are you doing, Kipp?" Silence went over to the big man and crouched down beside him.

Kipp could only manage a frightened nod, his broad, usually ruddy face a sickly green.

Silence pressed Kipp's hand sympathetically. He wanted to smile, but that would be unkind. Kipp, so brave when they were lying in the hold of the last ship, retching and miserable creatures bound for slavery. Down there, Kipp didn't have to see the ominous green swells that sometimes rose higher than their deck, or the way the horizon tilted, and righted, then tilted the other way.

As if echoing his thoughts, Kipp whispered, "Never thought I'd say it, lad, but our former voyage together was more comfortable."

Now Silence did smile.

"What will we do, over there in the Sceptered Isle?" Kipp asked with an effort.

"You'll look for your family?" Silence said.

"I have none. What about you, Silence? Will you try to find your own?"

Silence shook his head no. "They're in the Baronies. My parents, two brothers. But I don't know them. Strangers."

Kipp looked at him in confusion. Silence thought about explaining, but it was too difficult and besides, it would take too many words out of Silence's meager stock.

He knew two things only. He was going to try to find Diera, and he was going to try to find Wat.

Beyond that, he had no plan at all. He had fled too precipitously. He hadn't thought through what he'd do, when he thwarted Gilles and Caedon over the boy Gwyl, and now he was suffering the consequences of his poor planning. He just had to hope Gwyl wasn't facing any terrible consequences, or Pierrick. Or the young woman, Elene. Or, Child keep her, Alphonsine.

He looked over at Kipp and felt better. At least Kipp had his freedom. At least Silence had repaid a debt and recovered a friend.

Not too much later, Silence stopped mulling these thoughts and recriminations endlessly over. The ship was pulling into a small harbor on the southwestern coast of the Sceptered Isle, so now he had to make some decisions and take action.

To make things more complicated, he'd be in unknown country. Out in the countryside.

If he had gone to Lunds-fort, a city, he might have fared better. There might have been muckspouts and tavern gossips and other denizens of a city's underbelly to pay for information or otherwise pry it out of. Where that confidence came from, that he could have obtained information in this way, he couldn't have said, but he knew he could easily have gone to the big port outside Lunds-fort, in Baronies territory, and then he could have moved into the Sceptered Isle from there overland across the border.

But that's what Gilles and Caedon would expect him to do. *Stay on the water*, he told himself. As long as possible, he did.

"This is my country, Silence," Kipp whispered now, partly rousing to peer at the oncoming land. "My farm was near this coast. I know this land."

Silence felt a kind of hope leap up inside. Suppose Kipp helped him. But then he thought, *I must not ask this of him. Kipp is home. Let Kipp go back to his life, after such a harrowing time.*

Besides, if Kipp stayed with him, he'd be put in danger.

Gilles, directing his attention at a person, knew whatever that person was thinking. Caedon told him that. Gilles would be able to track Silence that way, and when Gilles came after Silence, Kipp might seem a puny obstacle to be destroyed without a thought.

But a few times Silence had noticed Gilles didn't seem to know what he was thinking. Was it because Gilles's attention wasn't directed toward him? Or was it something else?

Because of what happened to the inside of my head, Silence thought, *Gilles might not be able to track me so easily.*

Or not as easily as if he were some ordinary person. Or even an extraordinary person, like Caedon. Silence had begun to notice that Caedon was not ordinary. He wasn't a mage, like Gilles, but he seemed to have some of Gilles's powers.

Caedon confirmed this. When he was telling Silence of all the many gifts he'd gained through Gilles's generosity and love, he mentioned certain powers Gilles had granted him. He had said this when he threatened Silence with the consequences of not doing his duty. "Gilles is gentle with us, when he feeds. But if we need punishing, he's not so gentle. And he has granted me some of that power."

Silence had murmured something, he wasn't sure what. He was too frightened at what he was hearing.

"Rafe," said Caedon, giving him a hard look. "If you ever betray me again, remember this. I'm not gentle."

Silence wondered whether Caedon meant it in both senses. He had no idea what Caedon's origins were. But he remembered how Gilles had berated Caedon for treating Silence ungently. How had he put it? *You near-totally depleted Rafe, and much too fast. You brought him far too close to the edge.*

Silence knew Gilles had not been gentle with Caedon this time, and it was because of his displeasure over the way Caedon had treated Silence. Silence saw how much Caedon resented it.

If I fall into Caedon's hands, after betraying his trust, he'll try to hurt me, Silence realized. *Especially after I made him look bad in front of Gilles. Gave Gilles reason to bring him almost to his death.*

The little vessel was coming into port, chasing these thoughts away. Silence and some of the mariners helped Kipp over the side of the cog and they were rowed to shore from where the cog stood out in the harbor. Silence remembered his baptism in the sea as a slave. How good it felt to be thrown off the ship into the cleansing waters, after such a vile experience in the ship's noi-some hold.

It might be just as refreshing now to swim for shore, but he decided he'd be better off keeping his clothing dry. He needed to look the part of prosperous young lord until he figured out what might be going on in the Sceptered Isle.

He wouldn't abandon Kipp, either, not even for the short trip from the cog to the shore. He recalled the look of terror on Kipp's face as the hard men of their previous voyage had thrown him into the sea to struggle as best he could for land.

Silence kept a comforting hand on Kipp's arm. When they reached land, Kipp knelt on the beach and praised his Child.

"So, my good friend. Here you are. What will you do now?" said Silence.

"I've dreamed of this moment, Silence. Now that it's here, I really can't say. By now my farm is probably in the hands of my neighbors who denounced me to the beadle so they could take it."

"Your own neighbors?"

"Yes, they'd an inkling I'd joined The Rising, and that was enough to get me taken and my land confiscated." Kipp looked around him at the green of the surrounding hillsides, the blue of the sky. "But here I am, a free man," he said. He rubbed his wrists. "I'll earn my way easily enough. I can work."

"Make yourself an armlet of leather to cover your brand," said Silence. "People might wonder. People like those neighbors might see a chance to make some coin. That's what mine are for." Silence touched his own armlets.

He reached into his pack and handed Kipp an axe, one of the other weapons he had learned from Master Estefan. "Here. You should go armed. But truly, keep your brand hidden. You know a man can make quite a bit of coin, turning in a bondslave carrying a weapon. That's the way of it everywhere, not just in this realm, where neighbor turns on neighbor."

"Good advice," said Kipp. "And you, Silence. What will you do?"

"I need to find someone. No idea how." Silence aimed a rueful look at his shoes.

"Let me help you, then."

"Kipp, I'll put you in danger."

"Let's talk about it over stew and ale," Kipp suggested. "On that ship, I wanted only never to see food again. Now I'm hungry enough for four men."

Silence laughed and pointed to a tavern sign up the hill from the port.

Then Kipp stopped. "No. That's not right. I haven't a coin to my name, and I'll just keep burdening you, Silence. You've already paid to free me, paid for that inn room, paid for us to break our fast—"

"How can you think it?" Silence burst out. "If not for you, I'd be dead. And look." He showed Silence his pouch, still plump with Caedon's and Gilles's gold.

"It's not right," said Kipp.

"This isn't my gold. I stole it."

"Oh, Silence. You said so last night, to that young woman. I confess, I didn't figure you for a thief," said Kipp, but he started to grin.

"It's complicated," said Silence. *I keep saying that*, he thought. He summoned up the will to try to explain. "Powerful men took me. They gave me this gold. Gold enough to perform a terrible deed. I refused their deed. I took their gold. I fled."

Too many words, thought Silence. *Especially after yesterday*. He dragged Kipp off with him toward the tavern.

After stew, ale, two beds for the night this time, Silence felt better in the morning. More optimistic. He had no idea how or where to look for Diera or for Wat, but he'd spend time getting to know this unfamiliar land, and he'd start his search.

He still had a great deal of Caedon's gold left over, even after paying for Gwyl's keep, buying Kipp's freedom, and booking passage on the cog. Buying a whore out of a brothel and giving her a lot of Caedon's gold! That would surely rankle the man, when he realized. One more reason for Caedon to hunt him down.

So some of his optimism had dwindled by the time he and Kipp sat down at one of the tavern's rough tables to break their fast.

"The sleep these last two nights. Best sleep I've had in three years, man," said Kipp.

Silence nodded, remembering his own feelings when he'd first been freed.

"Now what, lad?" Kipp tore into a piece of brown bread and chased it with ale. He put his tankard down on the table and stared into Silence's eyes. "You need to tell me about yourself. I haven't wanted to press you. But if you can, tell me more. I see you know some things now. Who you are. You know you're from the Baronies now. I wondered about that, but then you understood all of us from the Sceptered Isle perfectly well. I can hear it now, though. You have the Baronies accent."

"I'll tell you—" Silence began. He stopped. "It's hard." He pointed to his head. "Words are still hard."

"We have all day," said Kipp.

So, haltingly, Silence told him as much as he could.

Gilles and Caedon, though. They were impossible to explain. If he tried, he thought Kipp would think him mad, so he didn't.

"Who I am. I don't really know that," Silence concluded. "I know some things now, about what happened to me. Before. And I know well what happened to me, after. I have feelings. Strong. About people I need to find. I know my own name. But who I am, really? I don't know that."

"What is your name?" said Kipp eagerly. "Then I can call you something else besides—"

Silence shook his head no. "I do have a name. It was my name before. Silence is my name now. You named me."

"I can't go around calling you that, Silence. People will stare."

Silence thought about it. He nodded. "My name is Raoul. But I spent a long time here. People here called me Rafe."

"Rafe. Should I call you that, then?"

"Yes, it's best."

"Rafe, then."

"But just between us, I'm more comfortable being Silence."

"You should get used to being called Rafe," Kipp argued.

"Those men who keep me now, or think they do. They call me that," Silence said with a shudder.

"They keep you," said Kipp slowly. "But you're not a bondslave. And you've fled them, taking a lot of their gold. I don't understand."

Silence bit his tongue. He knew he was about to say, *It's complicated.*

"Look. You'll tell me about all that in your own time, and only if you want to," said Kipp after a moment. "I'll not press you. So tell me this. You're searching for some people. People here in the Sceptered Isle?"

"I think so. Maybe."

"I'll help you, Silence." Kipp shook his head at himself. "Rafe," he corrected himself, and stared hard at Silence. "Let me help you, Rafe. Start with the names of these people you want to find, and where you think they might be. Then we'll head out to search for them."

"Two names," said Silence.

Kipp waited.

"Wat. Diera."

"Nine Spheres," said Kipp softly. After a moment, with an effort, he said, "Wat is the last of them. The last of The Rising, after the others were killed."

"Tell me about The Rising," said Silence. "You were right when you said so, in the hold of that ship. I was part of it. I know a little about it now. Not much. The men who took me hate The Rising." He gulped down ale, to ease the passing of so many words from his throat and lips.

"Ranulf was our king," said Kipp. "His son Artur was to inherit after him, but when Ranulf died, Artur's younger brother Audemar assassinated him and took the throne for himself. Then the youngest brother, Avery, started a rebellion to restore the throne to the rightful king, Artur's young son. When we say Rising, we mean Prince Avery and his friends."

"But they did not succeed," said Silence, nodding. "This much I've learned. So the young king is disinherited."

"He's dead, killed by Audemar before the boy ever came to his throne. Then Audemar's underling killed all the leaders of the Rising. Everyone but Wat."

"So who is king? This Audemar?"

"No, here's the strangest part. This underling of his, a man named Caedon, grabbed the power away from him. He and his former master, Audemar, fought a war, a civil war against each other. Many think of Caedon as king now. What?" said Kipp, stopping at Silence's expression.

"Nothing," said Silence. "I know Caedon," he made an effort to say at last.

"You know him? That's hardly nothing, Silence," said Kipp.

"He's the man who took me."

"And you took his gold?" Kipp started to laugh and slapped his thigh. "You're in a world of trouble, lad."

"I know it," said Silence with a small smile.

"Wonder why he took you, of all people? That explains your fine clothes. And the gold. So much gold."

"He found me in that brothel."

Kipp's face turned sober now. "I swear to you on my Child, Silence, if I could have stopped them—"

"I know," said Silence, covering Kipp's hand with his own. "It was hard. I survived it. You told me I would. That's the only thing that gave me any comfort or hope. I thank you."

He took another big swallow of ale, hoping it would help ease the words out of him.

"That still doesn't explain Caedon."

"I think, before, I may have been his prisoner, or his servant. Something like that. I spied for The Rising. He found out."

Kipp nodded dubiously. "That certainly explains why you were half-dead in the hold of a slave ship. Although not why you weren't completely dead."

"I think I might have been kind of dead. Kind of completely dead. Then they saw I wasn't. Or thought so. That's when they put me in the hold of that ship."

Kipp was shaking his head. "I don't know what you're telling me, lad. I don't know what to think about you. About what they did to you, and why, and why you're here now."

He sat looking for a long time at his hands. "Back to Wat. You want to find Wat. That will be hard, lad. Wat is in hiding. And as for Diera." He began laughing again.

Silence looked at Kipp with a question in his eyes.

"You know I said Caedon maybe thinks he's our king? Maybe is, in the eyes of many?"

Silence nodded.

"But our real monarch is a woman."

"A woman can't be monarch." Silence wasn't sure how he knew that.

"Avery changed the law. She is. Diera is our rightful queen. I was at her coronation."

Diera's name on Kipp's lips burned Silence all the way through to his very marrow.

"Maybe it's not the same Diera. The one I want to find," he whispered.

"Maybe not. But you say Wat's name, and then you say hers. I have to think you mean our queen. She is Wat's near relation, you know."

"I didn't know that. Suppose I'm looking for a different Wat."

"It's possible. Common enough name, at least around the area near Lunds-fort. Diera's not that usual a name. Saying those two names together, man. Knowing that you were part of The Rising. Knowing you're on the run from Caedon. It's Wat, man. It's Diera."

"Children keep me," Silence whispered.

"You're right about that, Silence. Rafe." Kipp regarded Silence carefully. "You've taken on quite a task, man, and you don't even really know why."

Silence nodded assent. "I just feel it. Here." He whacked his hand against his chest, hard.

"Look, man. I was part of The Rising myself. Can't say as I ever even met Wat, but of course I know about him. I saw him at Diera's coronation. She gave him a fancy sword in thanks for his part in The Rising. I can help you find some people who maybe know some things. We can go from there."

"We," said Silence. "This will be dangerous. I see it now. Much more dangerous than I supposed. You must keep yourself safe, Kipp. Don't go running after trouble."

"Look, lad," said Kipp. "I'll help you. I was in it. The Rising. What do you think I'll do with myself now? I know it well, I'll try to find any of my former companions at arms and see if I can join them. All hope may not be lost. As for family, there's nothing for me there. I didn't have any family, when I joined Avery's cause. Wife and son both dead of plague, and now my farm's gone too. I'll help you look. Let me help you, Silence. Rafe."

Silence nodded finally. "I thank you," he said.

They clasped hands.

"No," Kipp said, resting his chin on his hand. "Don't remember seeing Wat, except from a distance at the coronation, and maybe in a battle we fought. Conal, now. I remember that man well. He trained me. Turned me from a ploughman to a soldier."

"He trained me too."

Kipp looked at Silence in amazement.

"So I've been told. I don't remember Conal. But I know what he taught me."

"You can fight?"

Silence nodded.

"And Conal taught you how to do it?"

Silence nodded. He could see Kipp only half-believed him.

"Conal was the best there is."

Silence remembered Estefan's words. *You were trained by the best*, he had said. He wished he remembered this man Conal.

But his arm remembered. When Estefan awoke the skills of the sword inside him, those were Conal's skills.

"Conal, man." Kipp sighed reminiscently. "He was full of words about how to defeat an enemy, how to keep myself safe, how to keep the man beside me safe. They weren't just words. They were my life. In war, they saved me time and time again, and they stood by me when I encountered my enemy. I remember the most valuable piece of advice he gave me. Cut to the body—"

"Not to the sword," Silence finished. Then he sat astonished at himself. The words had risen from some deep place inside.

Kipp was whispering across the table from him, and Silence found himself whispering along.

Cut to the body, not to the sword.

They stared at each other.

"Brothers," said Kipp. "Through thicket and thin wood, brothers."

"Brothers," said Silence, and they clasped arms.

Silence had felt himself alone. He didn't any longer.

CHAPTER THIRTEEN

Getting to be a Habit

We'll pay a visit to some men I know in a village up the coast," Kipp told Silence. They decided they'd better try to find Wat before they looked for Diera.

"Diera has been in exile somewhere across the Narrows. She has an uncle over there. But some say she and her army may have landed to the north and east, here on the Sceptered Isle. You talk to one fellow, you get one story. Another fellow will tell you something completely different," said Kipp. "Wat's whereabouts may be easier, if you know the right one to ask."

"Won't Wat be fighting with Diera?"

Kipp shrugged. "The Rising fragmented when the leaders were all killed. Then I was taken, and after that, I don't know."

"The leaders were killed," said Silence quietly. "I know this from Caedon. Conal was killed, and—"

"And Avery. The prince. He was king for about a day before he was killed. The leaders of The Rising learned Artur's two sons were dead, they decided Audemar should be passed over due to his treachery, and Avery assumed the crown."

"Could that have been his plan all along?"

"No!" Kipp exclaimed. "His enemies spread that rumor, but it was a false calumny."

"I'm just asking," said Silence. "I don't know. I think I was there, maybe in the thick of it, but I don't remember any of it. I just have some strong feelings that won't let me get any rest."

"Talking to you, lad, I'm guessing you were in the thick of it indeed. I'm guessing you got your head wound when Avery and Conal and that other man got killed."

"The other man?"

"The earl was already dead, and John was. Then, that terrible day, Caedon's men killed the rest. Only Wat escaped with his life. Avery dead. Conal dead. And there was another man."

"One of the leaders too?" But Silence was thinking, *The earl.* He remembered Caedon's half-taunting words about the young girl Jillian, whose father was an earl, whose lands Caedon hoped to possess. Maybe that dead earl, one of The Rising's leaders, was the earl he meant. Silence remembered how Caedon had stared hard at him, when he told Silence about the death of this earl, as if the news of it might mean something to Silence. He glanced over at Kipp.

Kipp was looking Silence over with a very strange expression on his face.

"What?"

"Nothing. It's nothing, lad. You say you don't remember any of this? The fight that ended The Rising? It was the fight to get Diera out of the hands of Caedon. Very dangerous, but very necessary. Avery must have known The Rising was doomed. But he saw something he could do, and he did it. Bring a brave young queen to her throne. He gave his life for that."

Silence nodded slowly. "I wish I did remember. It seems important that I do. I have a feeling it is. Beyond that feeling, though—"

"Four of the leaders. Wat, who survived. Three who died. Avery and Conal. And another. Another with them, who maybe died too. Another one." Kipp put out his hand. "Child keep you, my lord," he said.

"Don't call me that," Silence said, trying to laugh. "I'm not a lord. My father. . ." He groped for words. "He's a kind of minor gentle. Not a yeoman. Not a lord. Betwixt and between." To himself, he said, *And I'm a wanderer betwixt and between.*

Something he saw in Kipp's face unsettled him badly. He rushed to explain something he saw he needed to do. *Keep focused on the practical,* he thought. Let these frightening big matters take care of themselves. "Not a lord. I need to get out of these clothes. I must find clothes more like yours, Kipp. I stick out too much." Silence unsheathed his dagger and began hacking at his hair. "And this. I have a lord's hair. I shouldn't. My hair should be short."

Kipp put his hands on Silence's shoulders. "Silence. Rafe. Stop. Listen to me, now. I want you to think hard about something. I want you to try to remember something. Someone. A man driving Diera's carriage."

"Let's wait until we get to Wat, Kipp. There will be time for explanations then." Silence felt a bit dizzy. Maybe one of his headaches coming on. Hadn't Caedon said something about his role, how he drove Diera in her carriage, how Caedon shouldn't have allowed it? But he couldn't think about that and what it must mean. Not now. "Let's wait," he whispered.

"All right," said Kipp. He dropped his hands and sat looking intently at them.

"You see something. I can tell. I want to remember too. But right now, I don't. I want things just as they are. This way I can act. If I learn something bad about myself, what if—"

"It's not bad."

"It may be bad for me to know," said Silence. Kipp left it then, and Silence was glad. He was afraid to know what Kipp seemed suddenly to understand. If the knowledge of it shattered him, how would he accomplish the two things he felt, deep inside, he desperately needed to get done? Find Wat. Find Diera.

What if I'm a traitor, thought Silence.

Then how explain Caedon's anger? he thought. He knew he had betrayed Caedon. Caedon had told him so.

I could have betrayed both sides, he thought. *Or suppose I was a coward, and that's why I'm alive.*

Suppose, when I get to Wat, he hates me, he thought. *Suppose Diera hates me. Suppose there were things I could have done to help but didn't. Couldn't or wouldn't. Suppose what I did, or didn't do, somehow led to Avery's death. Conal's, and that earl's. Suppose I was sworn to these men but I let them down. Suppose, instead of dying with them, I lived on, damaged and useless, to become a tool in the hands of their enemies, mute clay to be molded by them into their weapon.*

"Silence," said Kipp gently.

"You see? I can't think about these matters."

"I do see. You're right. Let's talk instead about what we have in front of us right here, right now."

Three days later they were high up in the hills, up a river Kipp identified as the Dourdin. Three men were with them, three whom Kipp had fought beside. They were overjoyed to see their comrade.

"Wat has taken a small group and is making his way up north to join Diera's forces," said one of these men. "He's been over on the Western Isle. Now he's back here with us."

The five of them were lying along a ridge looking across a valley where a castle stood silent in the gathering twilight. "That's one of the castles Caedon controls," said this man. "And not too far away, there's a manor belonging to him."

At these words, Silence felt an uncomfortable prickling of the neck. The surroundings felt all too familiar to him, and an ominous feeling accompanied the familiarity.

"Is that Earl Treddian's castle?" whispered Kipp.

"It was," said the man.

"That's where the fight took place," Kipp murmured to Silence. "Down below on that very road. The fight to get Diera out of Caedon's hands."

Silence felt the nausea beginning to rise, the iron band begin to tighten about his head. He dug his hands hard into the dirt of the bank where they lay.

"Now Caedon has put the queen there," said Tyn, the soldier from Wat's contingent of men.

"The queen?" said Kipp blankly. "He has Diera again?"

"Not our queen. Audemar's."

"Oh, the Lady Ailys," said Kipp. To Silence, he said, "This lady was married to Artur. Then suddenly, after his assassination, she was Audemar's queen. We all think she was one of those around Audemar who planned the assassination. When Caedon defeated Audemar in the civil war, and Audemar fled, the Lady Ailys came under Caedon's protection."

Silence nodded.

"Wat told Tyn here that he was going to reconnoiter the castle. See what the defenses are like now. He remembers them, from before. Tyn says Wat wants to revenge himself on the Lady Ailys."

"So Wat is down there?" said Silence.

"Aye," said Tyn.

Silence felt the familiar pounding in his head, a kind of keening roar in his ears. He shook his head, to clear it. "I know this castle too," he said softly.

The others looked at him doubtfully. Not Kipp. Kipp clapped him on the arm. "It's coming back to you," he said under his breath.

Silence nodded curtly.

"Wat went in there yesterday," said Tyn. "Now he has missed our rendezvous. He hasn't come out."

"I know a way in," said Silence. *Where had those words come from?* he asked himself. *Where had the knowledge come from?* He did know a way in. As if a picture in his head were slowly unfolding, he saw the very place.

"We should wait til daylight before we do anything," Tyn was saying. "Let Wat do his work. We could upend all his plans if we rush in."

Reluctantly, Silence agreed to wait. Tyn left then for the place where Wat's people were hiding outside the castle. The pounding in Silence's head was a warning. Wat was in danger. Somehow he knew it. This man Wat. A man he was connected with, as close to him as a brother. Waiting was an agony.

"When it's near day, I'll get down the hill to Tyn," said one of Kipp's comrades-in-arms. "Then I'll bring word back. It may be we'll need your way in, if you really do know one," he said to Silence. "I pray to the Child we don't need it. I pray to the Child Wat is back with Tyn and the others by now."

They could all tell by moonset and by the wheeling of the stars across the Spheres that daybreak was near. They'd heard nothing. Their man slipped away into the dark.

Within a candle's measure, he was back. "No word from Wat. But they've seen a bad thing, down there. Yester eve, Caedon himself came to the castle."

Caedon is here, thought Silence. The dizziness and nausea were so overpowering now that he had to sink down on the ground with his hands wrapped around his head. Ever since he had come back to himself, in the ship, in his coffin, he had had the same terrible headaches. The blow on the head, Gilles had said. He was having one now.

He made himself sit up.

"I'll show you the way in," he heard himself say.

He could tell in the dimness that the others were doubtful of him. Was he weak, a coward? Silence could see the others coming to this conclusion, and he realized with a sick feeling that they wouldn't follow him.

Kipp saw it too. He spoke. "Rafe knows the castle well. We'll follow you, sir," he said.

Silence saw how the others jolted upright as Kipp spoke his name. It meant something to them. They all looked at Silence, their eyes amazed.

And now something beyond him took Silence over. Something in him told him, *Stand.* He stood. Something inside him said, *Get Wat out. You failed with John. You must not fail now.*

Silence did not know what these words meant, but he had no fear at all, and no hesitation. The headache was gone. "Follow me," he said, and began making his way down the ridge. He didn't look back to see if the men were following. He knew they would.

They needed to get to the castle before first light.

Silence did not think about what he was doing and where he was going. He just did it and went there. "Here," he breathed, as they crouched against the curtain wall of the castle. By then, Tyn and the others had joined the four of them. Silence pushed aside a tangle of vegetation. "This is a passageway out of the castle, a secret way in case of siege. It leads directly to the stable and mews. Follow me, and make as little noise as you can." Silence slipped into the passageway.

At the end of it he cautiously lifted the trapdoor in the flooring of the stable, making sure no one was about. A horse whickered softly, but the passageway's opening into the castle grounds was at the far end of the stables where the tack and the horses' caparisons were kept, not down by the stalls. Silence pulled himself up and into the stable, holding the trapdoor open so the other four, and then Tyn's men, could follow.

"Listen, if Wat has been taken, I know where they are probably keeping him," he breathed to the others.

"He must have been taken," whispered Tyn.

In his bones, Silence knew the man was right. "We need to cut across the outer bailey. That will be the moment of highest vulnerability. Three guards stationed here, and here, and here." From their vantage under the eaves of the stable, Silence pointed out the places. "If we skirt the inner wall this way, they won't see us. They're mostly looking for those coming up on the castle from without. We hug the wall and make our way up the motte to the inner bailey. See that tower?" He pointed out one of the castle's mural towers, looming in the luminous gray that precedes dawn. "Just at the corner there, a latrine shaft drops inside the walls to a cesspit below. The masonry is broken in several places. I'll show you where. We'll drop down to the cesspit, which lets directly into one of the cells of the dungeon. That's the place they take prisoners when they want to damage them." Silence gulped air.

Don't fail me, he cried to the thronging words that threatened to stick inside him. The things that poured out of him were things he knew. *I know this*, he said to himself. *I need to tell them what I know.*

"That cell is where Caedon has taken Wat." As he spoke the words, it was as if the tumbling of the inner workings of a lock had fallen into place. All of the blocks of knowledge, locked from him, had tumbled out of him, solid and definite. He knew. He knew everything.

The man named Tyn made a skeptical noise.

"That's where they tortured and killed Wat's brother John," said Silence, rounding on the man. "We were too late. We got there too late. My body to the Dark Ones before I let that happen to Wat."

"Nine Spheres, lad," said Kipp. "Your memory—"

"It has come back," Silence whispered to him grimly. "It's all back. All of it. Consequences to the Dark Ones. Let's go."

When the ten or so of them poured out of the noisome slit of the sewer into the cell that opened out in a familiarity horrible to Silence, they saw a huddle of men. One was Caedon. Three others were guards. And a man who lay on the stones of the cell, vainly attempting to shield himself from their blows and the hacking of their swords. With a howl, Silence leaped for them. He drove Caedon and his men away from Wat, where they had been standing over him with their clubs and swords.

For a sick moment, Silence thought he was replaying that terrible time when he and Wat had tried to rescue Wat's brother John from Caedon, and had failed. They'd only brought John's broken body out of the cell with them.

"Not this time," Silence snarled, a savage sound ripped from between his gritted teeth. He let Kipp and the others do the fighting. He darted to Wat.

"Wat," Silence cried. "Dark Ones take you if you die on me."

"Rafe?" Wat whispered back.

We're too late, thought Silence, his eyes raking over the blood, the mangled limbs, the smashed in face.

"Dark Ones take you, Wat. Why is it I have to go all over your turd-cursed country rescuing you and yours. You're coming with me, and a sard to Caedon in the place the sun won't shine. Don't fucking die on me. Don't dare do it. Are you listening to me?" He shook Wat.

"Yes," Wat muttered.

"I'm getting you out of here, Wat," Silence said to him. He stared over at Caedon, who was being backed away toward the doors of the cell by Tyn and his men.

He and Caedon exchanged a long look from across the roomful of struggling bodies.

"Rafe, I'll see you fed to the dogs for this," screamed Caedon.

"Not if I feed you first, you horse-pricker," said Rafe in a low penetrating voice. "And I hope the dogs eat all the juicy bits while I watch."

He circled his arms around Wat and tugged him toward the slit in the broken masonry. "Some of you help me here. The rest of you keep Caedon occupied so he can't summon help and cut us off," he called out over the din.

Kipp leapt to him and together they wrestled Wat up the slit and out into the dim light of early dawn. The rest of their group were out of the slit now, too. They formed a cadre of men around the two of them carrying Wat, and they fought their way into the passageway past the few startled sleepy guards.

Once they were in the open, Kipp and Silence, carrying Wat like a sagging sack of oats between them, made a rush for the woods and their horses. The others were just behind. They galloped away, Wat jouncing across Silence's saddle. They made it to the river, then forded over it, then threaded through a difficult series of defiles in the surrounding hills until they came to an overgrown place, the entrance to a cave the men had known and had been using as a hiding place for the past few seasons.

Silence and Kipp got Wat inside. Once they were safe within, Silence lay Wat gently down on a bed of furs before the hearth fire and put his ear to Wat's chest. Wat was breathing. Wat was alive.

"Wat. Wat." Silence stroked Wat and patted him. Kipp pushed him aside. "I know a lot of doctoring. Let me see to him," he said. Silence got up out of his crouch and let him.

"He's losing a lot of blood. We need a belt, fast," Kipp barked. He tightened it over Wat's upper left arm.

Silence, looking on, could tell Wat would never use that arm again.

Sea Child, let him live. Earth Child, take Your son into Your care, Silence prayed.

Wat, battered and bleeding, lay without movement.

Kipp stood. "The arm will have to come off," he murmured to Silence.

Silence started to protest, but then, as he stared down at the arm, he could see Kipp was right. It was greenish and torn, hanging at a strange angle from Wat's shoulder. Shards of shattered bone poked through the skin.

"He'll die if we don't," said Kipp.

Rafe nodded. "Do it," he said. But he was thinking, *He'll die if we don't, and maybe he'll die if we do.*

The thing that sickened Silence most was Wat's face, swollen almost beyond recognition. One eye was completely gouged out.

He watched while Kipp gently cleansed the bleeding, empty socket and bandaged it.

Wat was unconscious when his arm was taken. *Thank the Children*, Silence thought.

Day after day he sat by Wat as Wat drifted in and out of knowing. Day after day passed as Wat's body fought its battle hard and very gradually began to win. The stump of his arm, which Kipp had cauterized, did not fester. His face, except for the missing eye covered by the bandage, became Wat's familiar face, once the bruising had eased, and now Silence knew it and remembered it. Remembered the boy Wat had been. The young man he'd fought beside.

He almost felt it as a curse, that he remembered everything now.

He held Wat's hand and stroked it.

The other men came and went. News from Diera's army was not good. One day the word came. Diera's army was defeated. They were in retreat north.

One by one, the men in the cave drifted away to resume ordinary lives. After a while, only Kipp and Rafe remained in the cave with Wat, although a few of the men brought them news from time to time, and supplies.

Caedon proclaimed himself king, and no one was left to gainsay him. Caedon, Silence learned, had sentenced Diera in absentia to die.

One morning after Kipp left to find something for them to eat, Silence sat alone beside Wat.

Wat spoke.

"Rafe. Is that you."

The voice was so weak Silence thought he might be imagining it. "Wat. How do you feel."

"I feel strange. If that's you, I must be dead. I must be in the Land of the Dead with you."

"I didn't die, Wat. I'm alive," said Silence. He wasn't sure he was actually telling the truth. Was he alive? Silence had begun to wonder about that. But one thing was clear to him. He was here, here with Wat. So then, that must mean he was telling Wat the truth. He must be alive.

"I'm dreaming, then," said Wat. "I watched you die, Rafe. I saw you draw your last breath."

"Well. A lot of people thought that. Caedon, for example. But here I am, and you're not in the Land of the Dead, and you're not dreaming."

"I can't see a thing," said Wat. "And tell me if I'm wrong about this, but I'm missing an arm."

"You're missing an arm," Silence agreed. "But Caedon only damaged one eye." He passed a hand over Wat's face. "Can't you see out of the other?"

"Not a thing," said Wat. After a while, he said, "I have a dim memory of a lot of screaming and fighting. In the middle of it, I had a beautiful vision. That's why I figured I must be dead. I saw my wife. I saw our child."

Silence smiled at Wat. He hadn't known Wat had a wife and child. "You'll see them again."

"I won't see anything again, Rafe."

"You'll be with them," Silence insisted.

"I'm completely useless."

"No," said Silence sharply. "No, you're not. You think so now, but you won't if you let yourself heal. I mean inside."

Wat lay quiet.

"Doing that needs a long time," Silence said.

"Dark Ones take it, Rafe," Wat murmured. "You going around the countryside rescuing me and mine. It's getting to be a habit." A ghost of a smile formed on his lips. "Do I recall you threatening me with words very much like those? Threatening me with a dire fate if I should presume to die?"

"You do recall it. I did threaten you, and I meant it," said Silence, wanting to cry. Not letting himself.

"You called Caedon a horse-pricker. And did I really hear you telling him you would feed his juicy bits to the dogs?"

"You did," said Silence.

After a while, Wat said, "I suppose I've come back from the edge of that shore, thanks to you and those men. So you, Rafe. How did you manage to come back from the dead?"

Silence shook his head, even though he knew Wat couldn't see it. "Telling you that. I don't know how to begin."

Kipp came in then.

"Here's Kipp. He took care of you. If not for him, you'd be dead for certain," said Silence.

"Welcome back, sir," said Kipp. "You're the last hope now."

"Don't pin any hopes on me, good man," said Wat.

"Oh, I do," said Kipp. "You're the hope, and we are all waiting for you to regain your health so you can resume the fight."

"What about this? and this?" said Wat, pointing to his eyes and his missing arm.

"What about them?" said Kipp.

"Is he always like this?" Wat directed his words to Silence.

"Always. I owe him my life too. And a lot of other debts I owe him," said Silence. "Another thing getting to be a habit."

"I'm thinking he can't save Diera, though," whispered Wat. "I'm thinking you can't, either, Rafe. And I certainly can't. Not like this."

Silence swallowed a sour taste of despair. Wat had heard, even though they'd all tried to keep it from him. *Nothing wrong with his hearing, anyway*, Silence thought, and then he got the eerie feeling words like that had been spoken about him, too.

"Maybe we can't save her," he said finally. "But we can try. As soon as you are well enough, I'm going to find her."

"Better hurry," said Wat. "Leave me here and get to her fast. Caedon is after her, and he's angry. You know what he'll do."

"Yes," Silence whispered. "Yes, I do."

CHAPTER FOURTEEN

Back on the Horse

Once Wat was better, Silence roamed the countryside leading Wat's horse with Wat on it so he could get used to riding even though he couldn't see where he was going. Kipp took on the task as well. Silence wanted to get to Diera, but something equally strong wouldn't let him leave Wat until he was sure Wat was ready to take charge of himself.

After a few days of being led around on the horse, Wat refused to go on any more rides. "It's useless. Just being trotted around by someone else—why would I need that?"

"You will," said Silence.

"I won't."

"Wat," said Silence. "You're the last of us. You're The Rising. If you don't lead it, no one will."

Wat was huddled by the hearth fire of their hiding place. The weather had turned cold. He sat shivering in his cloak, pulling the cloth tight over the place his missing arm should have been.

"Look at me, Rafe," said Wat. "How in the Nine can I lead The Rising like this? And you're wrong. I'm not the last of us. You're here now."

Silence sighed and stared into the fire. How to help Wat understand about his own situation when he only partly understood it himself? He had been doing a lot of thinking about it lately, as he had sat day after day at Wat's side. The rush of memory as he led the men in to get Wat out of Caedon's hands. Then the aftermath, long hours of searching his thoughts and wondering about himself.

"Wat, you know that day." They sat together quietly, remembering. They both knew the day Silence meant. "I was driving the carriage. We heard Mirin's signal, and I whipped the horses. You, Torrin, and Lorel rode out of the woods on one side, Avery and Conal from the other, to intercept us. But there were too many of Caedon's men."

Wat flinched. "Yes," he whispered.

"You fought well. Valiantly, I'd say. While you fought Caedon's men off, Torrin and Lorel closed in. Avery and Conal were doing their best to hold Caedon's men off on the other side of the road. I was trying to control the horses."

"And then Avery went down," said Wat. "The cry I heard from Conal, when that happened, will ring in my ears til my dying breath. He tried to stop them killing Avery, and he couldn't. Then he went down too."

Silence wouldn't let himself say aloud what he thought about that. After Avery went down, Conal wouldn't have wanted to live.

Wat sighed. Clearly he knew what they were both thinking, because then he said, "Conal wouldn't have wanted to go on, but he would have, if he possibly could. He loved us all. Avery most, but all of us. And he gave himself to The Rising. He wouldn't have quit."

The sounds and images of that event, surging back, were too painful, but Silence made himself continue. "What I remember is the carriage overturning. I was trying to protect Diera. You were the only thing between us and Caedon's men, and you fought, Wat. Nine Spheres, how you fought. "

"But then, out of nowhere—" said Wat.

"And that was the end of it, for me. I don't remember that part. I don't remember anything after that part."

"A man wielding a large club rode up behind you and took you out. Diera was standing over your body, sobbing. I leaned down to you, but you were gone. I lifted her out of the wreckage of the carriage, and Torrin and Lorel took her. They got her away, and I fought my way out of there. I left you. How could I have done such a thing. I left you there."

"I was dead, Wat."

"It seems you weren't."

"Here's the strange thing. I'm pretty sure I was."

"How is it you're sitting here talking to me, then? How is it you got me out of Caedon's hands when you and I couldn't do it for Johnny? Explain that."

"You know, I didn't even remember all these things, everything that happened, until a fortnight ago. Until we went in to get you."

"Kipp told me," said Wat.

"Seeing you in Caedon's hands. It triggered something. It brought everything back. Trying to get John out of there, failing. Burying him under those trees. Everything about that terrible day."

"The same cell!" Wat burst out. "I have to tell you, Rafe, when Caedon started in on me in that cell, I felt it was only justice. I couldn't save Johnny, and now in some strange revisitation of fate, the same was happening to me. Let it happen, I said to myself. But then—well, then I had this vision of Mirin, and our daughter, and—"

"Mirin!" exclaimed Silence. "Mirin is the woman you wed."

"Yes, and that is another whole story in itself. I'll have to tell you about it sometime. I wonder, too. Are they dead? How is it they came to me in a vision? They must be dead. Even if they aren't, I don't see how I'll ever look for them." Wat stopped and laughed. "Ha. I don't see how," he mimicked himself. "Nine Spheres, I don't see anything now. Not that, not anything else. But about Mirin—you probably know we worked together. You don't know that Mirin was captured by Caedon during our rescue of Diera. After a long time of searching, I found her. And here's another remarkable thing. Caedon's manor was burned out by Audemar's men, and Jillian, Mirin's young sister, got away from him. He had taken her, too, I'm not sure when or how. She wandered the countryside, and we found her, Rafe! Diera took her across the Narrows, to keep her safe. But tell me," said Wat. "Tell me how you found me."

Jillian, thought Silence. *That's who Jillian is.* But he couldn't bring himself to tell Wat that Caedon had Jillian again.

"Tell me how you found me," Wat said again.

"There's no mystery about that. When I knew Caedon had taken you, I knew where. The mystery is how everything came flooding back to me to let me know." Silence thought about Gilles's strange words, trauma to the brain, memories triggered and retrieved. All his unsettling words of power. "As we went in to get you, I remembered everything about The Rising. Before that moment, I had had flashes of memory, often vague and uncertain. Some of the things Caedon told me were starting to connect with some of the memories, so I had begun to piece together what must have happened, but it was as if these events had happened to a stranger, and I was hearing about them as if I were a character in some story someone was telling me. I had two intense urges, two only, and I didn't know where they came from or what they really meant: to find you, and to find Diera. You have to understand this strange urging came after several years of struggle trying and mostly failing to remember. When I came to myself after I died, I couldn't even speak. I was sold as a slave. I spent over a year in a brothel."

"I'll kill Caedon," said Wat. Then he laughed, a bitter sound. "But of course I can't. Not like this." He was still for a moment. "You say these things happened after you died. But you didn't die. I suppose you nearly did. You had a tremendous blow to the head. I know you did, because I watched a fellow do it to you, and then I killed him."

"Listen to me, Wat. I think I did in fact die. I think Caedon was transporting my body in its shroud, tucked into its coffin, and then there was a mix-up during a storm at sea, and somehow I found myself with prisoners being transported to the Baronies. With Kipp."

"Kipp told me about that. A strange accident of fate."

"Do you remember Labinia?"

"Vaguely."

"You were burning with fever the last time you saw her. John killed her, but you were so out of your head you probably didn't even notice. She was a witch woman. The woman tending me on the ship was her sister, Vigilia. Look at this. No. Wait. I'm an addle-pate. Here. Run your hand over my scar." Rafe guided Wat's hand down the center of his torso. "That's no wound made by an enemy as he slashed out. That's a deliberate cut made by someone with a very sharp knife."

"Yes, I feel it. I understand what you're saying. This witchwoman did it to you?"

"I think she did."

"But why?"

"She was preparing my body. She was preserving it for Gilles de Rais."

"Gilles," said Wat. "He has some strange connection with Caedon that I've never quite understood."

"That's because you've never understood what I was doing at Ranulf's court. Why I was brought there as a half-grown lad."

"Running errands for Audemar."

"Yes, but why? I found out why. Gilles de Rais engineered Caedon's travel to the Sceptered Isle to be Audemar's companion. I was sent along to help with practical matters. Running errands, as you say. Wat." Silence took a deep breath. "Gilles de Rais was the one who masterminded the entire coup. The assassination of Artur. Everything. That's why he sent Caedon."

"You never told us this," said Wat quietly.

"I only gradually realized it. At first, I was just trapped in my own situation. Just trying to get away from the influence of Caedon and Gilles. It was difficult. But once I began to understand a little more about Caedon and Gilles, I knew I'd be in a good position to get information to The Rising. Caedon trusted me, in some ways, because he thought he had a hold on me. Gilles too. And I could find out what they were doing and get that information to Avery. Meanwhile, I could protect Diera. Because by then—"

"You'd fallen in love with her," Wat said softly. "It was a dangerous game you played, Rafe. Avery knew all this?"

"He knew a lot of it. The person who knew all of it—" Silence swallowed hard. "That person was John. He saw up close what Gilles and Caedon were doing to me, because they tried to do it to him. That's why Caedon had him. That's why Caedon killed him. John was resisting them."

"I don't know what you mean," Wat whispered.

"I know. It's hard to explain. You know about witches, right?"
Wat nodded.

"What about mages? What do you know about them? Gilles is a powerful mage, one of the most powerful underneath the Spheres. He uses his skills to gather power over others. And the way he gets his power—" *How can I explain this to Wat?* thought

Silence. "Gilles feeds on people. He sucks their life force out of them. I know this is hard to understand."

Wat said nothing.

"You probably can't understand it. John could. John was a mage too, you know."

"I do know that," said Wat. "We all saw it."

"His powers were nothing compared to the ones Gilles wields, and even if they had been, John would never have gone to the evil lengths that Gilles does to extend them and use them to control others. Never. Gilles wanted John to help him. He wanted John. To study him. To—" Silence hesitated. "—to taste him. John refused. So Caedon killed him."

"Caedon is a mage?"

"Gilles grants Caedon some of his powers, but no, he's not a mage. He's just completely under Gilles's control. His willing tool." Silence felt a moment of doubt. How complete was Gilles's control over Caedon? Maybe it wasn't complete. Pretty nearly complete, he decided.

"And you?" Wat whispered. "What about you, Rafe."

"Gilles took me when I was a small boy. He tried his mightiest to corrupt me, as he fed, but there's something inside me— I don't know what it is. Some kind of cussedness. A will to fight back. I wouldn't let him take me under his control, or not completely. I fought him." Silence paused, miserable. *I'm one of the enemy*, he thought. *I fought, but I was Gilles's creature, and in some ways I still am.* He made himself keep going. Wat needed to understand. "I fought, and Gilles enjoyed that." Silence's voice dropped low. "He enjoyed the challenge of the fight. Otherwise, he would have killed me in boyhood."

Wat put his hand out and felt for Silence's arm. He clasped it. "You are my brother," he said.

"I met you lot, and at last I had found my brothers," said Silence. *That is the truth*, he thought. *Child keep them all, on this side of the river or on that far shore. These are my brothers, my true brothers.*

"Now I understand a little better some things Johnny told me, after he escaped from Gilles. Now I understand how you rescued him over there in the Baronies, the time Gilles had him. It wasn't some ordinary rescue, was it?"

"No," said Silence.

"Now I understand some things he told me about you, Rafe."

"So," said Silence, "Here's the hard part. The part you'll have difficulty accepting." He took a deep breath. "Wat, I died. Between them, the witch-woman and Gilles were keeping my body going, in some elemental, basic way, until she could get me to Gilles and he could end me completely. Something interrupted her. She had made the cut. Child knows what she did to my body. She strapped me back together until Gilles could finish me off, because he wanted to be the one to do that. I think I was dead, Wat."

"That's not possible."

"I think I was."

"Those who go across that river never come back."

"I don't think I made it across that river."

"Then how can you say you died?" Wat's voice was practical and brisk. "You didn't die, and here you are, and now you are the one who will lead The Rising."

"Wat. This is hard. I think I died. I'm stuck wandering betwixt and between, my journey interrupted. I think it will resume. I don't think I was intended to remember any of these things. I was intended to ease across that boundary without ever knowing them. But I'm such a rebellious lad that I've remembered them anyway." An echo of something Caedon said to him rose into Silence's memory. *You never do as you're told, do you, Rafe?*

"Nine Spheres, Rafe," Wat muttered.

Kipp came in then with a load of wood, which he dropped with a clatter by the fire.

"I can't even die properly, not without a lot of fuss and bother," Silence concluded glumly.

"You can't die at all. I won't let you do it, Rafe," said Wat.

"I think I will, though, whether I want to or not. In that regard, I'm like anyone else. And you know?" Silence laughed a little. "That's an oddly comforting thought. None of us wants to, and we all do it anyway. I think that's what will happen. But first I have to find Diera. I can't die until that happens. Don't ask me why. I don't know why."

"Caedon has condemned Diera to death," Wat whispered. "I failed her, Rafe."

"Don't you see, Wat? We go around thinking we can right these wrongs and fix what's broken, and sometimes we can, but most of the time we can't."

"We can try," said Wat.

"That's it exactly. We can try. Since I won't be here to try, you'll be the one to do it. That's the reason—" said Silence, hoisting Wat to his feet, "—that you need to learn how to ride a horse even though you can't see. And you know what? Maybe wield a weapon too. And use your brain, man. Let these others be your eyes and ears, your arms and legs."

Between them, Silence and Kipp tugged Wat stumbling after them to the entrance to the cave.

"There's the horse, Wat." Silence led Wat over to the beast and placed Wat's hand against its withers. "So now. I'm telling you this, Wat. I'm commanding you from the Land of the Dead. Or close to it," Silence muttered to himself. "Near enough to it." He flinched away from Kipp's expression. He raised his voice and got a firm hold on Wat, preparing to hoist him into the saddle. "I'm telling you. Get back on the horse."

CHAPTER FIFTEEN

A Refuge

N ow that I'm better, you need to go, Rafe," said Wat to Silence. "Spring has come. Travel is easier. Everything we hear tells us Diera and her army have fled north."

"What remains of her army," said Silence glumly. "Yes, we should make ready. Head north ourselves."

"I'm not coming with you. I'll just slow you down."

"Wat. Do we really have to go through this again? Yes, you are coming with me. Do you know how many are ready to go with us, because of you? Me, they barely know who I am. Just a name they've heard."

"You're their inspiration, my lord. They've fought beside you. They know the iron in you, man," said Kipp to Wat from his side of the fire.

"If there is any iron in me, it's only because of the ones who've helped me. I'm not a lord," he added. "All the ones who have helped me. You, Rafe. Avery and Conal and Dru. Child bless her, Mirin. Diera." He paused. His voice dropped. "And Johnny." He laughed a little. "Do you know, I even have a father? Avery adopted me before he died."

"You see," said Kipp, his voice stubborn. "A lord."

"You didn't know Ranulf, did you?" said Silence to Wat. "Not really."

"I only saw the king maybe three times in my life, except sometimes at a distance in some procession."

"Ranulf changed toward the end," said Silence. He turned to Kipp. "King Ranulf was Wat's father," he explained. Kipp's eyes grew big. "You would have felt differently about the king, if you'd known him then," Silence said to Wat.

"But I didn't," said Wat. His head swiveled in Kipp's direction. "I was only his bastard son." He made a dismissive gesture with his hand.

"Avery became your father," said Silence.

"In a way, Johnny was the only father I'd ever had. Then he was gone. Avery saw that, and he stepped in. Avery and I didn't grow up together, the way he, Johnny, and Dru had. But during The Rising, I'd become close to Avery. I'm a man rich in brothers. John, Avery, my little brother Aedan. My actual brothers. And then the brothers I chose, you and Dru and Conal."

"I feel the same," said Silence.

"You're the only one of them left, Rafe," said Wat. "And I thought I'd lost you, too. That's why you must head north without me. I'll hinder you. Put you in danger."

"I'm already in danger. Come on, Wat. Get yourself ready. We're going north."

Without further argument, Wat began packing up. Very subtly, Kipp was helping him.

Wat is getting around more and more easily, thought Rafe. *He's learning fast. He'll be fine.*

In only a few candle-measures, the three of them were on the road north. Rafe and Kipp took turns riding close beside Wat, one hand on his own reins, one hand on Wat's. By then, their horses had gotten used to the arrangement, and so had they.

By then, Wat had realized he had some glimmers of vision in his remaining eye. "I can't really see out of it," he said, "but I can see light and dark," he had told Rafe. "I know when it's day and night. I know the direction of the hearth fire. I can feel the warmth, but if I'm at the far end of the cave where I can't really feel it, I can still see a patch of light and walk toward it. I can see a patch of light, when it's day, where the cave mouth is."

Rafe marveled. He hadn't known such a thing was possible.

Kipp was blunter. "I always thought blind was blind."

Wat laughed. "Me too," he said. "Guess I was wrong."

Sometimes Silence found himself staring hard at Wat's remaining eye. It looked fine. What had happened to it? What had happened to the other one, that was perfectly clear. Caedon had plucked it out. Whenever Silence thought about that, a dull red rage began rising inside him. But this remaining eye. Silence scrutinized it.

Out of Wat's hearing, Kipp cornered Silence. "Remember when you couldn't speak? You could, but you couldn't. I'm not putting this very well," he concluded lamely.

"I know what you mean, though. No one saw any reason why I couldn't speak, not even I myself. But I couldn't do it. "

"So do you think Wat's eye can maybe really see, but somehow, he just can't? That eye looks fine."

Silence thought about it. Finally he shook his head. "I don't think it's the same," he told Kipp. "I don't think he'll ever see out of it, except that little bit of light."

As the days went past, Silence marveled at how Wat made the most of the little he could see, and he saw Kipp was marveling as well. Wat could do a lot with his one arm, too, and every day, he could do more.

On the road, though, it became harder. Wat had learned his way around the cave, but now they were in new surroundings every night as they came to an inn or paid a farmer for the use of a bed.

Silence tried to learn how much help Wat needed from him, and give him just that much, but nothing beyond. He saw Kipp was doing the same. They both saw how eager Wat was to do as much as he could for himself. Sometimes it was hard to judge, and he and Kipp overstepped. Wat grew angry and lashed out.

Silence let him. He remembered that feeling, too. He remembered how Kipp had helped him.

Wat was a young vigorous man, and his body had failed him. Even worse, it had failed him because of the actions of an evil opponent. Not in battle. Not in some accident. Through a deliberate act of evil. Someone to blame was walking free out in the world. Silence could see how thoughts of revenge were festering inside Wat, and how deeply they connected with his feelings about his brother John's death at Caedon's hands.

To occupy himself, Wat had fletching materials by him always. He made arrow after arrow. "My hands know how to do this," he said. "Hand," he corrected himself. "I don't need to see to do it. I just needed to figure out a few things so I can do it one-handed." That was the first time that Silence realized how much Wat's identity was bound up with his bow. He remembered the excellent bowman Wat had become, a skill he had developed from boyhood when court politics denied him the weapons training of other boys his age. Now all that was gone. Later, Conal had trained him in the sword. That too was over for Wat.

A fragment of memory flashed into Silence's mind. Wat, young, eager, somehow improbably keeping six cloth balls in the air at once, making them fountain up into an impossible shower.

"There are things I can do to an enemy, one-handed," Wat told Silence grimly.

Silence remembered Dru telling them that Wat was as good with a garotte as anyone he'd ever trained.

They had been on the road north for maybe a sen'night when they came upon a ragged band of wounded men walking dazed down the road in the other direction.

"Good man," Silence addressed the one who seemed to be their leader. "You've met with some disaster."

The man stared through Silence and trudged on without replying. The three of them pulled their horses to the side of the road while the ragged column limped past. Silence caught the eye of another of these refugees, little older than a boy.

"Lad," he called. "Here's a skin of water for you." Silence held it down from his horse.

The boy scurried over and took it. He upended it and drank. "My thanks," he gasped at last, handing it back.

"Lad. What has happened here."

"We're the remnants of Diera's army, good sir," said the boy. Then he looked frightened.

"No fear, lad. You're speaking to friends. My companions and I are riding to join her."

Before he finished saying this, the boy was shaking his head. "Don't go up there. They're all dead, up there. Only a few of us survived. We all fought, but Caedon's forces outnumbered us ten to one."

"Dark Ones take him," said Wat.

The boy looked up curiously at Wat, his bandaged face and missing arm. He nodded.

"Where has our queen gone?" said Silence. "Does anyone know? Has she been taken?"

The lad shrugged. "No telling," he said.

"Here, lad." Silence handed over all their foodstuffs to the boy, and then he and Kipp and Wat turned their horses' heads northward and resumed their journey.

The farther north they went, the deeper Silence's forebodings grew.

A day after that, horsemen emerged from the woods to block their path.

Silence's hand went to his sword. He could see Wat was on alert. *He probably heard the jingling of harness*, thought Silence.

"Too many of them," Kipp murmured beside him.

But before Silence could think how to act, one of the men dismounted and came to them and knelt in the roadway. "My lords," he said. "We're here to join The Rising."

Not too many candle-measures later, the men were ushering them into the manor house of a very prosperous man. "My lords, welcome," said this man. "I am Sir Hugyn Crom, at your service. I am the Prince's man. I am sworn liegeman to our queen."

The prince, thought Silence. *He means Avery.*

"Welcome to my house," said Sir Hugyn, old and bent, supporting himself with a stout stick. "I have some thoughts about how I may help, now that our queen's forces are broken and destroyed."

Silence tried not to let his skepticism show.

"My lords, it's clear to me. I'm old. My fighting days are over, and soon that usurper Caedon will be here to take my lands. But my lords. These lands of mine stretch to the sea." He gestured. In that direction, Silence knew, lay the straits between the north of the Sceptered Isle and the shores of the Western Isle. "My lands stretch to the sea," the old man repeated, "And I own a ship."

Silence looked startled into Sir Hugyn's eyes. Sea Child eyes.

"I own a ship, for in my youth—" Here Sir Hugyn's old Sea Child eyes began to sparkle. "—I bent King Ranulf's rules, ye might say." He laughed. "I went in for a bit of smuggling. And I know of an island. It's a secure refuge. Come inside, my lords. Have a bit of a sup with me while I tell ye everything about the place, how ideal it is for marauding, how hidden away it is."

CHAPTER SIXTEEN

Quarreling

D on't worry, my lord," said Kipp. He kept on calling Silence that, over Silence's objections. "The lad will be fine."

They had decided amongst themselves that Wat would go to the island refuge of Sir Hugyn, far into the Northern Sea, and that Kipp would go with him to make sure he grew used to his new surroundings.

"I'll get settled in, and then you'll leave me and join Rafe," Wat insisted to Kipp as a condition of his cooperation with their plan. "Once I know my way around, I'll be fine. You know I will."

Silence and Kipp gave each other skeptical looks.

Wat laughed. "You think I don't know how you're looking at each other? I do. Don't try to hide it. But think about it, and you'll realize I'm right."

"I suppose you are, lad," said Kipp reluctantly.

"I am. Tomorrow we'll leave for the isle, and Rafe, you'll go to Hakkon, as we've agreed."

They had talked it over and decided Silence's best course of action, if he were to find Diera, was to head as far north as he could go. All reports suggested she and a few faithful retainers were somewhere in the far north of the Sceptered Isle.

"But the longer you stay in the realm, Rafe, the more likely it is Caedon will find you. He knows you're here. He knows he wants to stomp you into oblivion. Feed you to the dogs, is that it?"

"That's what the man said." Silence grinned. Wat couldn't see it, but he knew Wat could hear it in his voice. Then again, Silence thought, with Caedon, that might not have been some idle threat. What did Gilles and Caedon do with the leftovers, once they'd sucked a person dry? Silence shuddered.

Wat had gone somber too. "If we'd only had you with us, Kipp, when Rafe and I went in there to get my brother John. Maybe—"

"Wat." Silence made his voice gentle. "You know John was drawing his last breaths, by the time we got to him."

"I know," said Wat, but Silence could see the blame Wat laid heavily on himself would likely never go away.

As for himself. He desperately wished he hadn't let the others talk him into waiting until daylight to go in for Wat. Since there was nothing to be done about it now, he resolutely shoved these thoughts away.

"We've never talked about Ailys, Wat," Silence said now. "She was in that castle too?"

Wat nodded. "I wanted paid back for that time she had me in Tam Fort," he whispered.

Silence wondered not for the first time what Ailys had done to Wat, when she'd held him prisoner some years ago.

"Going after her. That turned out to be a mistake." Wat's smile was bleak. "I went into that castle to destroy her, and I never even saw her. Caedon and his men were lying in wait for me. A trap baited by my own thirst for revenge. My own injured vanity. I should have picked my battles. Saved my strength. And now look. I'm to blame."

"Nay, lad," said Kipp. "She's a viper. Someone needs to take her out. It was the worst kind of luck Caedon arrived when he did."

It amused Silence that Kipp insisted on calling him "lord" but when it came to Wat, actually by adoption a lord—a prince, even—Kipp sometimes called him lord, too, but mostly called him "lad."

He wondered about Caedon's untimely arrival, though. Was it true, what Wat assumed, that Caedon and Ailys had devised a trap for him? Maybe Gilles had tracked Silence and he was actually the one who had drawn Caedon there. Gilles and Caedon between them were tracking him. He knew this. And then there was Ailys. If he was right about why Caedon was in the castle, he wondered about the role Ailys had played.

"Do you think Ailys practices witchcraft?" he said suddenly.

"Maybe. She's thick as three abed with Caedon, isn't she?" Wat looked thoughtful. "When I was her prisoner, I got an inkling maybe she does practice the arts of the Dark Ones. So you see, Rafe. You have to get away from the realm."

He's not far wrong, thought Silence, but he kept Gilles' tracking abilities to himself. "Hakkon Hardaxe. You think that's really the place?" Silence was a little dubious, himself.

"Hakkon's realm is close enough to the north lands of the Sceptered Isle that you can take a fast ship and be back in a day or two, if you get word about Diera," said Wat. "The Northern Sea and all its rough waters won't even bother the likes of you, being the Sea Child's and all. Me, now. I dread our passage out to Sir Hugyn's island. I don't mind admitting it."

"I dread it too, lad. Just getting across the Narrows was almost too much for me." Never one to mince words, Kipp added, "But having no sight, you won't have to look at the waves heaving back and forth, as they do in that wicked way of theirs. I call that luck, lad."

"I'm happy to know there are some advantages to this," said Wat drily, gesturing at his eyes.

Kipp patted his hand, oblivious and fond.

Silence bit back a laugh.

"When Silence and I lay in that stinking hold, we counted ourselves lucky we didn't have to watch, especially during that storm, didn't we, Silence?" Kipp continued. Then he caught himself. "Ah. Rafe, I mean. Your lordship, that is."

Now Silence and Wat both laughed at Kipp, and he laughed at himself a bit too. By the time they went to their beds, Silence's bleak mood had lightened.

In the morning, Silence and Sir Hugyn went to the shore to bid farewell to Wat, Kipp, and the men who had joined The Rising to serve at Wat's side.

"A good voyage," said Silence to Wat, gripping him hard. And then Kipp.

"Pray to your Child for us, Silence," said Kipp, forgetting again, looking greenish already.

"I promise I will," said Silence with a grin.

He and Sir Hugyn waited until they'd seen the tops of the cog's sails dwindle over the horizon.

The next day, Silence headed out for the nearest port to board a ship bound for the Ice-realm.

Caedon's gold was at last dwindling. Silence decided he'd have to hire himself out as a mercenary when he got to Hakkon Hardaxe's port city.

Thank you, Caedon, for your rich gifts, thought Silence with a cynical smile. *Your gold, that I have appropriated for my own cause, and your arms training.* But then he thought how the arms training was actually due to Gilles, and Gilles was no joking matter. Thinking about Gilles at all might draw his attention. So Silence became properly serious again. He saw he'd frightened himself a little.

When he got across the Northern Sea to the Ice-realm, spring had come even to Hakkon's cold lands, although the wind was still piercing, the air chill.

Silence drew his cloak close about him. He sought out the fort in the port city, Traderstown, where he disembarked, and presented himself as a mercenary. He didn't see any reason to assume a false name. No one would know him here.

"Well, then, Master Rafe," said the fort's commander. "Some of my men will take you out into the courtyard and see how well you fight."

Silence had donned his beaten-up leather armor for the occasion. A close-fitting leather helmet strapped under his chin. Protective strips of leather crisscrossed his leggings. He wore a cuirass of leather scales that came down almost to his knees, and he carried his splintered iron-bound linden-wood shield. The best piece of war equipment he had was his sword. It was a fine short-sword, two-edged, with a fuller, the blade brightly patterned from the strikes of the forger's hammer. Its pommel was richly decorated. The weapon was a present from Caedon, and Silence felt the irony. Caedon had had the pommel fashioned into a martlet. Silence wore it at his belt in a scabbard of sheep's leather, fleece side inward, oiled to prevent rust.

The man who led him out into the practice courtyard of the fort looked askance at his shabby gear. This man was in a mail shirt and a conical steel helmet with a nose guard. He looked away, but Silence caught the sneer.

I'll wipe that off your face, thought Silence. He stood on his guard with his sword drawn.

The man came at him. In only a few moments, Silence had laid him out in the dirt.

"Well-fought," the man gasped, grabbing at Silence's offered hand and pulling himself to his feet. "I'll tell the officer. Wait here."

I probably took him off-guard, Silence thought. *He probably got one look at this battered armor of mine and underestimated me.*

The man was soon back. "The lord says," the man began, then shook his head to clear it. He was having trouble with the language of the Sceptered Isle. "Go to him to make your mark," he said at last. "He'll give you proper armor."

From this officer, Silence got his own mail shirt, an iron helmet, a better shield, and a bed in the fort's barracks. He made a crude mark on the parchment the officer presented to him. No point in letting anyone see he knew his letters.

"Get rid of all that old beat-up stuff, but keep your sword," said the officer. "It's a fine one, better than any we can give you."

Silence found his bed and stowed his gear. He was a soldier of the Ice-realm now.

After a sen'night, Silence had begun to pick up the language of the Ice-realm. He could talk to his fellow soldiers about ordinary things—food, weapons, women. They all had their women at home, or their favorite whores. Often both.

"Come with us to the brothel," said one of them after they'd all dined together one night at board.

Silence shook his head, summoning up a smile. "Not for me. I'm a married man."

"That's not stopping Aalf," said the man, nudging his buddy, who gave a big guffaw and made an obscene gesture.

"My thanks for the invitation, but it does stop me," said Silence.

"Your wife wears the spurs, does she?" said the man.

Silence turned aside with a smile, and the others let him alone. *Dark Ones take me if I ever visit a brothel*, he thought savagely, *unless it's to burn the place to the ground and stick my sword up the master's arse.*

One of the fellows had stayed behind to gather up his gear. "Hit a little too close to home, did he?" said this man with a knowing smile.

Without thinking it through, Silence knocked the man on his back.

The fellow got to his feet, rubbing his jaw. "You're stronger than you look," he mumbled. "I promise I won't say a word more against that wife of yours."

That's not why I hit you, Silence thought, but he didn't correct the man's mistake.

Unfortunately, that moment was the one an officer happened to be strolling past. So Silence was up for punishment, three blows across the bare back with a whip.

He took it stoically. It was nothing to what that terrible master of his had done to him.

As he was pulling his tunic back on, the officer in charge of whipping him looked him in the eye. "I see by your back you've been in trouble before, fellow," he said. "Better control yourself. We don't need your kind of trouble here."

Silence earnestly promised not to lose his temper again. *Nine Spheres,* he thought. *I can't let these bad memories rule me. I have a task to perform, and an opportunity too precious to waste on stupid mistakes.*

But the others were wary of him by then, and they were careful to steer clear of him. No one bothered him. No one befriended him. *So much the better,* thought Silence.

After a fortnight, he had learned the language there pretty well, but he didn't let anyone else know how well. He remembered his former life of silence, how others would say things around him they'd never say if they knew he was listening and understanding.

One of the men even took to calling him "Master Silence," but only when he thought Silence wasn't listening. Silence had to bite back a laugh at that.

In spite of his resolve to make no friends and travel light, a season into his employment as a mercenary in the Ice-realm, he did make a friend.

A very unlikely friend, and he didn't know what to make of it.

CHAPTER SEVENTEEN

Lists

B y then, Silence had been reassigned. One day in high
summer, the men were all called into the fort's outer bailey.

Their commanding officer stood with a scribe at his elbow.
"I'm sending some of you to Old Town," he cried out to them. Silence knew Old Town was the Ice-realm's capital. "King Hakkon
of great name has asked for a guard of picked men to serve his
heir, now the young prince has come into his majority. Only the
best will go. It's a rare honor to be chosen, men. If you are one of
the ones chosen, remember to live up to the standard set you
here, and do us proud."

Silence's attention, after the first few words, wandered. *It won't be me.* Even though, after that one violent incident, his behavior had been impeccable throughout the season he had spent at the fort, he was one of the newcomers and had been styled a troublemaker early.

After making his speech, the officer now turned to the scribe. "I have a little list," he said.

The scribe looked down at his parchment, whispered a name into the officer's ear, and then the officer called it out.

Name after name. Silence recognized these men as the best fighters and the most experienced.

Thank the Child my name won't be called, thought Silence. The port was exactly the place he needed to be. He spent all his free time down at the waterside taverns, where he carefully listened to tavern muckspouts and gossips and far-travelers for any shred of news about Diera he could garner. Every so often, his efforts paid off, and he was cultivating a possible informant, a mariner who made the voyage back and forth from the northernmost reaches of the Sceptered Isle to the Ice-realm once a fortnight or so.

"Master Rafe Quarrel," the officer called out.

It was the last name on his scribe's list.

It is my name, thought Silence, stunned.

"Master Rafe?" the officer called again.

Silence shook himself out of his astonishment. *I mustn't stand here like a stone*, he told himself. *I must move over there with the other chosen men.*

He hurried to do so. He caught the officer's irritated gaze on him.

Now the others were dismissed. The officer moved to the group of chosen ones.

"This is a great honor for you, lads," he told them. "I won't lie to you, I'm displeased, myself. I'm losing my best men, and I don't like it. But that's of no consequence."

"Neither here nor there," murmured the scribe helpfully at his elbow.

He shot the man a glare, and the scribe cowered back.

"Here's the thing. You need to uphold the standards you've learned under my command. Don't let me find out later I shouldn't have chosen you. That goes double for you, Rafe Quarrel," he said, looking at Silence hard.

Silence dropped his eyes.

He stepped over to Silence. "Look at me, fellow."

Silence raised his eyes again.

"The thing about it is, is. . ." he paused, struggling for words. "You're the best we have." His voice dropped low. "The best trained. So I've chosen you. Don't make me regret it." He turned aside, muttering, "Some higher up must love you. Nothing to do with me."

Silence nodded, wondering, with a chill, *What higher up?* and then in the few remaining days before the chosen men were to pack up their gear and head to the royal city, he set out to disobey the officer as exactly as he could. *Don't make me regret it.* He'd force the officer to regret it, and then the officer would remove him from the group of chosen men.

He tried picking fights with the other men, but they stepped aside from him with uneasy smiles and didn't rise to his bait.

He incited a brawl at the roughest tavern down on the docks. Heads were knocked in. Arms were broken. In the end, no one realized he was the instigator, and he wasn't the one blamed, not even after he planted a few rumors that he should have been. *Maybe I could have arranged to have my own arm broken*, he thought glumly. *That would have kept me well out of it.* But by then, it was too late.

Finally, in desperation, he decided to insult the officer himself. He thought over his newly acquired catalogue of obscenities in their language, especially aspersions upon mothers. He rejected as childish the ever-popular "Your mother's a hairy reindeer-sarder," settled on the anatomically improbable "Your mother got you on a man-troll," and headed to his commanding officer's quarters.

"His Excellency is away from the fort," the officer's aide told Silence with a prissy little grimace. "He is off visiting his mother in Njardarheimr."

Silence slunk away, his plan to stay in the port city thwarted. Only a day later, he was marching inland with the others. And by the next, he was part of Prince Ansgar's retinue.

The crown prince was a lad of twenty years or so. He was fine-looking, blue of eye, blond and strapping and handsome, and Silence saw at once he had been well-trained to the sword and in other martial skills, without a doubt since boyhood.

Silence and his fellows lined up for the prince's inspection.

The prince was completely at ease with the members of his new guard. Some of them were his own age but many, like Silence, were much older. Silence was twice the prince's age, he figured, or close to.

The prince went down the line of new men, finding out each man's name.

He's getting us all on his side, thought Silence. *The lad's a politician, and a good one, looks like.*

When Ansgar got to Silence, he tapped Silence on the chest. Silence raised his eyes. The young prince already overtopped him.

"You. You're from the Sceptered Isle, they tell me," he said, shifting easily into that language. "Rafe Quarrel, is it?"

"The Baronies, actually," said Rafe, switching into that one.

The young man beside him startled a little.

Ansgar looked over at that man. "You, you're from the Baronies as well, I hear." He too had switched to the language of the Baronies, just as fluently as he had switched to the Sceptered Isle's tongue. Rafe was impressed.

"Yes, Your Highness," said the young man softly.

"And your name is—" Ansgar consulted a list he held. No scribe murmuring to him at his elbow.

He is lettered, too, thought Silence.

"Yann, is it?" said Ansgar to the young man.

"Yes, Your Highness," said this young man whose name was Yann.

"Well, then," said Ansgar easily. "You and Rafe Quarrel have something in common. Master Rafe." He turned to Silence.

"Yes, Your Highness?"

"Rafe. That's a strange name for a Baronies lad."

"It's actually Raoul, Your Highness, but I lived such a long time in the Sceptered Isle that—" Silence began.

"Ah, yes, I see it," said Ansgar. "What about Quarrel? Are you quarrelsome, Master Rafe?"

Silence's lips twitched. He didn't know how to reply.

"Don't quarrel here," said Ansgar, and swept on.

"Are you?" murmured the young man Yann at Silence's ear.

Silence turned to him with a smile. "I had that reputation, but no. I'm not, actually." He scrutinized the lad. Not one of his own group. "I was sent from the fort. My commanding officer made a point of telling me not to quarrel, after one unfortunate incident there, and the name stuck to me like tar, Child help me. And why are you here, Master Yann, if one may ask? If one may not, pray don't take offense. I'm not here to pick fights, my surname to the contrary."

"No offense taken," said Yann. "My father sent me here. He thought it would be good for me. Advance my training. He's away, mostly, and can't train me himself very easily."

Silence noticed Yann wore his hair long, like a gentle. Silence was still shearing his own short.

"You'd better not invoke your Child here, Master Rafe," Yann added under his breath. "The Lady neither. They're strict about the old gods in this realm."

"Good advice," said Silence, cursing himself for forgetting such a simple thing as that.

Then Silence noticed something else about Yann, and his heart stopped in his mouth.

Before he could think it through, the man commanding them was lining them up and marching them to the practice courtyard of the prince's manor. As they entered, a serving man handed them each a gambeson. Silence shrugged out of his mail hauberk, put the padded garment on, and then the hauberk over it.

"Pair up," this commander called out.

"Shall we?" said Yann.

Silence nodded and drew his sword from its scabbard. Yann was doing the same.

They fought a practice match. *No bated blades here*, thought Silence. The gambeson offered a bit of extra protection, but the practice bouts were dangerous. They felt real.

He was older and, he supposed, more experienced than Yann, but they were evenly matched. The lad had had excellent training.

As their arms master called out the stances, everyone began with their swords raised overhead, aiming at their partners' heads and throats. Except that Yann held his sword up just beside his temple and at a slight downward angle. Silence was amazed. That's where he positioned his own blade. It was as if the two of them were mirroring each other. Master Estefan had always said it was easier from such a position to drop down into the second position with the sword at hip level, angled slightly up, the position called the Plow.

And again, Silence noticed that while all the others stepped forward to lower their swords at the side of the hip, he and Yann, as if synchronized, pulled their sword hilts a bit past their hips, long edge down on the right side of the body, but when they switched their swords to the left side, long edge up.

As they moved from the positions into actual fighting, their efforts intensified into fast, aggressive attacks and counter-attacks, each attempting to get under the other's guard, each attempting to reach the other's body with lethal blows, neither gaining the advantage. Finally the arms master called time. When they lowered their swords, Silence saw to his amazement that the others had formed a ring about them and gave a cheer as they stepped aside from each other, their chests heaving, each on the point of exhaustion. Silence hadn't even noticed these spectators, and he doubted Yann had. They'd concentrated on each other, and they hadn't realized the others had long since given over their own bouts, some the winners, others the losers, and had come to watch.

"Excellent," said the arms master.

Silence bowed to him, and to Yann.

Silence was streaming with sweat. He hauled off his mail and then the bulky gambeson.

Yann stepped to him, his eyes shining. "That was amazing, Master Rafe. It's as if we were taught by the same arms master."

Silence nodded, considering. "Perhaps we were," he said slowly.

"Master Estefan," said Yann.

"Master Estefan," Silence echoed.

They laughed.

"Strange, isn't it?" said Yann.

"Not so strange, considering we come from the same place. You must come from that part of the Baronies along the northern coast," Silence said.

"I do, yes. And you must as well. What village do you—"

Silence was shaking his head. "My home is more in the central eastern part of the Baronies. But I was trained by Master

Estefan, right enough. He was brought to me, to train me, at the place where I lived."

"Baron Gilles's lands," said Yann slowly.

"Yes," said Silence. He turned away. He didn't want to talk any further about it. He was getting an eerie feeling, looking at Yann. It was Yann's eyes. They were a strange shade of amber.

"Brought there specially to train you?" Yann was still trying to make sense of what Silence was telling him.

"Yes, although I also had a different arms trainer for a long period of my life. He was even better. He used a different style. But Master Estefan has had me in hand again in recent years, and it must have stuck."

"But—" Yann began. Then he gave it up.

Silence smiled briefly and walked away. Yann was about to ask him too many questions. Silence didn't appear to be a gentle. Then how was it the best arms master in the Baronies had been brought from a distance to train him? And in that case, what was he doing here as a common soldier in Hakkon Hardaxe's realm?

Yann, too, was a kind of enigma, thought Silence. His father, he said, had sent him to Hakkon's realm for the experience. His father, he said, hadn't the time to train him himself.

And who is this father of his, thought Silence. *And how many men have eyes as strange as that.*

CHAPTER EIGHTEEN

Highly Unlikely

In spite of his misgivings, in spite of his firm resolve to keep away from Yann, Silence found himself paired with Yann over and over. The officer of Ansgar's guard had seen how well they worked together, and he wanted such a convenient arrangement to continue. He saw no reason for it not to.

So their acquaintance grew, and with it, friendship.

Silence found he liked Yann. Liked and respected him.

This is very dangerous, thought Silence. He kept resolving to question Yann about his parentage, in a roundabout way, and he kept hesitating.

Suppose I'm wrong, he told himself. Then he'd shrug. If he was wrong, well then, he was wrong.

Suppose I'm right. That was the thought that haunted Silence.

Sometimes, in the darkest hours of the night, *Suppose this is a trap Caedon has set for me.* He remembered the words of the officer back on the coast. Some higher-up maybe seeing to it Silence was reassigned.

Yann himself appeared to have no misgivings about Silence at all, except for the strange coincidence that they had shared an arms master, and that this pointed to something odd in Silence's background.

So, underneath the Spheres, the season wheeled around into harvest-tide. The air rapidly grew chill and the men were issued their winter cloaks and leggings. The first snows flew.

They nearly always wore their gambesons now, not so much for the protection during drills and practice bouts as for the warmth the padded underclothing gave them.

And always Silence and Yann were thrown together: on watch, during practice bouts because they were so evenly matched, and on extra duties such as the one they were preparing to undertake the day after the first real snowfall.

Yann played a small harp common in his part of the Baronies, and Silence enjoyed listening to it. They sat in the firelight after board, the evening of the snowfall. Outside, the snow was hissing to the ground, a comforting quiet background wall of sound. Inside, it was warm and cheerful by the fire. Silence let his mind run idly. He thought of John and his rebec, watching Yann as he bent over his harp. Listening with great pleasure. The lad was good.

Finally Silence stretched and yawned. He should head for his bunk. They were to rise early the next morning for this special duty.

The king had sent for his new concubine, a young woman he had acquired from the Sceptered Isle, although actually she, like Silence and Yann, had been born in the Baronies.

There was much talk about this young woman. As it circulated around the prince's manor, Silence saw that Yann was becoming more and more uneasy.

"Tomorrow we're to join the party riding to get the king's new concubine when her ship comes to port," said Silence now.

Yann nodded. He fixed his eyes on the fire.

"You don't like this duty," Silence observed.

"No," said Yann.

"Why is that? Sounds like a simple matter. They say pirates have been sighted just off shore, but I don't see how we'll protect her from those. If they attack her at sea, that's the mariners' lookout. As for the road between here and the port, it's generally quiet. Easy duty. We'll probably be there more as a ceremonial gesture than as real protection." Silence had to stop himself from smiling when he brought up the matter of the pirates. He had a pretty good idea who was harrying the shipping between the northern ports of the Sceptered Isle and the Ice-realm's.

Yann looked miserable.

"Yann. Something's the matter, lad."

"No," said Yann. "It's nothing. Or, well. I don't know."

"Does the idea of a concubine bother you?" said Silence.

He knew he was bothered by it himself. To him, a concubine was only a step away from being a whore in a brothel. Maybe an exclusive, high-class whore. A whore nonetheless. Yet almost no one else thought anything of it. Powerful men and their concubines, that was an ordinary thing. Mistress Cicely, Wat's and John's mother, had been King Ranulf's concubine.

"Yes," Yann whispered. "It bothers me."

"I don't wish to pry," said Silence.

But he did. He saw a chance to learn more about Yann and why he was really at the fort. He hoped Yann would talk about his misgivings. Maybe he'd learn more about the mystery that was Yann.

"I never thought this before," said Yann. "I know my mother died when I was very small. I don't remember her. But now I keep wondering—"

"Wondering?"

"Whether she might have been my father's concubine and not his wife," said Yann all in a rush. "Whether I might be my father's bastard and not his true-born son."

"You've never thought so before? Your father has never given you reason to think so?"

Yann shook his head no.

"Why now, then?"

"It's—" Yann stopped. "You'll think me very foolish, Master Rafe. You're so much older than I am, and you've seen so much more of the world."

"You make me sound like a graybeard," Silence said, laughing, trying to lighten Yann's mood.

"Until now, my father kept me close, close in our house, in our village. I never had other boys to play with, just the son of the serving man. I never got the chance to grow that crop one is supposed to regret sowing, as one grows older."

"I never regretted sowing that crop." Silence chuckled. Then he stopped.

He barely remembered what he had been like around women, when he was Yann's age. Only what Wat had told him, how all his friends had teased him about the ladies liking him and making big cow eyes at him.

He didn't remember those days, or just barely.

But he remembered the moment they ended. They ended the moment he met Diera, even though she had barely reached womanhood. He might not remember very well his earlier life as a carefree young man with a different lady on his arm every sen'night, but he remembered that moment when he first locked eyes with Diera, a girl sitting pensive on a bench, her quill held in her hand, her book before her on the table.

This moment was etched inside him forever, a bright faceted jewel. It was one of the first things he had recalled, coming back to himself. He remembered how he waited for Diera to grow older, and how he had watched over her, to try to keep her from harm.

Then how their love had blossomed.

"You look sad, Master Rafe."

"I'm remembering my wife."

"She died?"

"I haven't seen her in many years. She's not dead, but she probably thinks I am."

"That is sad indeed, Master Rafe." After a moment, Yann said, "There's a girl I love. She lives in the next village. Father doesn't approve. I think he sent me here to get me away from her."

"Ah," said Silence. "You are gently born, and she is not?"

"She is gently born!"

Silence saw he had touched a nerve. "I tell you truly, Yann. Whether a man is or is not gently born makes no matter to me. Nor a woman neither. I myself may not be gently born, and if I am, it's only barely. It's a good bet I myself am a bastard."

"If I'm a bastard, I'm not a gentle at all," said Yann. "The girl I love is gently born. But her family fell on hard times, and most of them died, and one sister was killed by The Rising, and the other sister has to work for her bread to support her shiftless husband."

Child keep me, thought Silence, staring at Yann blankly. Could the lad be talking of that little boy Gwyl's parents, and the girl Elene? The village where Yann came from looked to be in the very region where Gwyl's family lived. It was not impossible.

But he said only, "In that case, it's a mystery why your father would keep you from the girl."

"He loves me, but he controls everything I do," said Yann.

"Why do you think you're a bastard? That doesn't seem very likely, lad."

"Why did he send me here, to live as a common soldier?" said Yann. "No offense," he added quickly.

"None taken," said Silence, but *Why, indeed?* he asked himself. "It seems like an extreme measure, if the only reason is to get you away from that girl."

"I can see why you're here. It puzzled me for a while, Master Rafe, I do confess it. But then I realized."

Silence's heart leapt into his mouth. How much did the lad know of him? How much suspect?

"It's your amulet. In the Baronies, the martlet is the sign of a fourth son."

"Indeed," said Silence, breaking into a smile, putting up his hand and fingering the little bird on its thong. "You're very observant. Not everyone knows that, even in the Baronies. As I say, my family is just at the edge of gentility. My father's farm can barely support one son, let alone the four of us. My oldest brother inherits, my second-oldest has gone for a soldier, the third of us died, and in childhood I was sent—"

Silence stopped abruptly. He began quickly talking about his father's farm and its dilapidated state.

By then, they were walking from the manor's great hall, where they had lingered after board, and through the manor's courtyard underneath the first frosty stars, the thin crust of snow crunching underfoot, heading for their bunks.

"I see all that," said Yann, rounding on Rafe. "What you say about your family. But it doesn't explain Master Estefan, does it?"

Silence couldn't help himself. He burst into laughter.

When he could calm himself, he turned to Yann. "You're a smart lad, aren't you. I confess, I have tried to stay away from you, but circumstances keep throwing us together, and now I count you as a friend."

"And I count you as a friend," said Yann.

"All this while, Yann, I've asked myself question after question about you. And you've been asking yourself question after question about me."

"Yes," said Yann simply.

"You're Caedon's son, aren't you?" said Silence. After so many seasons of caution, he was feeling suddenly reckless.

"Yes," said Yann. "You know my father."

"We are enemies, Yann. I'm trying to get away from him. Now, I suppose, I'll have to find other employment."

"No!" said Yann. "I won't tell him!"

"Yann, you love and honor your father, do you not?"

"Yes, I do," said Yann, and Silence was moved by him.

"Then I'll have to leave this place. You can't be false to your own father."

"Rafe!" said Yann, stricken.

"It's fine, lad. Don't feel bad. What was that you said, about your girl's sister? How the men of The Rising killed her?"

"Yes. They are villains," said Yann.

"I fought for The Rising, Yann, and your father fought against us. Anyway," he said, as he watched that thought sink in under the dim light of the stars hanging from their golden chains, "I doubt you're a bastard, Yann. Your father is just a very private and secretive man. Even if somehow you are a bastard, I'm sure he loves you dearly."

"You know my father well."

"Too well. He'd never let anyone know he had a son. Not if he could help it. He has a powerful enemy who would—" Silence stopped and slowly shook his head. "Not me. I'm not a powerful enemy. No one in The Rising is powerful enough to do him any hurt. The Rising is shattered and broken. If your father catches up with me, he'll kill me easily. No. The powerful one is someone else. Actually, he's an ally of your father's, but if he knew this secret of your father's, he'd turn on him."

"Why?" Yann stood still, shocked.

"It's complicated why."

"But anyway," said Yann. "Just in these past days, I've learned something about my father that I didn't know. I suppose you've known it. He's a very powerful man."

"Yes," said Silence. "I just hadn't known Caedon was your father, not for certain."

"How did you know at all?"

"Your eyes, Yann. You have your father's eyes."

"Many have eyes like their parents'." Yann stood confused.

"Not like yours. Not like those eyes, Yann."

Yann passed his hand over his face. He looked troubled. "This concubine being sent to King Hakkon, the Lady Jehanne," he said finally. "My father owned her. Everyone's talking about it. That's how I learned who he is. The king of the Sceptered Isle. My own father, and I didn't know something so important about him. So I must be a bastard. Why else keep something like that from me? Why else bring me up in an obscure village across the Narrows?"

Yann stopped for a moment, thinking it through. "This powerful enemy you mention. Maybe he's a threat, as you say. But my father is very powerful, too. Almost as powerful as Baron Gilles de Rais."

"Ah," said Silence. He looked at Yann with pity.

As for the girl they were to escort in the morning. *Concubinage is the least of what your father did to that girl, I'm guessing.* Clearly she'd be better off with Hakkon. She was a lucky girl.

But the thought of Caedon being almost as powerful as Gilles. Silence suppressed a bitter laugh.

Beyond everything, he saw how odd it was that so fine a son should come from the loins of such a despicable man. Truth to tell, he was just as floored as Yann was about these revelations. When had Caedon had a child? He didn't even like women.

Silence stopped stock still and leaned against the stones of the barrack's walls, passing a hand over his forehead.

No, he thought. *Not possible.* But then he counted up the years, Yann's age, the birth of Diera's child. The child Caedon had forced on her. The child he had told her had died.

I'm right, he whispered to himself. As Yann turned to look up at the stars and Silence caught the fine planes of Yann's face in profile, and the curve of his lips, Silence knew he was.

We are the playthings of mighty forces, Silence thought. No wonder Gilles hadn't caught up with him.

Silence cursed himself for stupidity and arrogance. He'd thought of himself as some wily opponent getting away from Gilles.

No.

Gilles was letting him run. Unbeknownst to himself, Silence was Gilles's own stealth outrider, surveying the land ahead of Gilles's reconnaissance to smoke out a possible betrayer. *Caedon, you foolish man, thinking you could keep something like this from Gilles.*

He looked over at Yann, marveling. *On the day you were born, I stood just outside, listening to your cries as you drew your first breath.*

Caedon was supposed to send this son he'd gotten on Diera across to Gilles. But he didn't. He said the child died of plague.

Caedon could easily condemn the sons of others to suffer a terrible fate at Gilles's hands. Gilles prized infants. If they escaped his notice at that point, he took them at age six. That poor little Gwyl, hundreds of others. Caedon was willing to sacrifice them all to Gilles's appetites, but he couldn't bring himself to visit such a fate on his own son.

As for Silence, and as for Yann, Gilles would crush them as easily as flies, if they stood between him and the object of his vengeance. Collateral damage, he'd heard Gilles call it once.

Silence put his hand on Yann's arm, summoning up the will to speak. "Don't let these things trouble you too much," he got out.

You could be my own son. Mine and Diera's, if there had been any justice underneath the Spheres, he thought with a pang.

"In the morning, we'll go to escort this Lady Jehanne to King Hakkon Hardaxe. I won't say goodbye then. I'll say it now. Sometime during our journey up the road, I'll slip away, and you won't see me again."

"You don't have to go. I won't betray you," said Yann.

"I know," said Silence, and believed it. "But I'll put you in a terrible position. And I need to keep moving. I've overstayed my time here as it is."

"Let me come with you!" Yann exclaimed.

"I wish I could, lad. No. Serve this prince honorably. I'm guessing your father will see that it's time for you to move on to some better post. Everyone sees your talents are wasted here. Sooner or later, someone is going to tell your father that, if he doesn't realize it for himself first. And Yann. This life of ours under the Spheres is chancy and short. Get back to your Elene."

"How do you know her name?" Yann stood dumbstruck.

Now that Silence had looked past the Caedon in Yann, all he could see was the Diera in him.

Diera, he said inside himself, and his heart twisted.

He didn't answer Yann. "Tomorrow I must go," he whispered. "There's someone I have to find."

CHAPTER NINETEEN

Pirate Hospitality

Before Wat had left for Sir Hugyn's island refuge, he and Silence had worked out a signal for his men to pick Silence up on a remote shore of the Ice-realm. The headland of this shore was visible in good weather from the island.

"Just in case, brother," said Wat to Silence. "Suppose something goes wrong over there in the Ice-realm? Suppose Caedon tracks you down? Get to the headland and set a fire each night for a sen'night. We're sure to see it, unless the weather is unrelentingly bad. Then I'll send my mariners to get you."

I suppose it's time for that plan, thought Silence. He trusted Yann, but he didn't trust what he sensed from Gilles. It would be as well to get himself away from Prince Ansgar's manor and the royal city. It only took three days before Wat's men saw the signal and arrived to take Silence off the headland. In less than a day, he was on the isle. It was a massive rock outcropping, a natural fortress hollowed away over the eons by wind and weather.

One of the mariners took Silence to the outcropping. They entered by a tunnel into the base and then up a narrow stone stairway spiraling along the inner hollow to the very top, a vast room open partway to the sky.

Wat stood at the hearth fire talking something over with a few of his men, Kipp among them.

"There he is, my lord," said Kipp, spotting Silence.

Silence was amused. Kipp had stopped calling Wat "lad." Now it was "my lord." Wat was clearly in charge here. He had moved past his injuries, as much as anyone could, and he was in command.

Wat turned in his direction and hurried over to embrace Silence. He seemed to know his way unerringly around the space.

"Wat, it's water to a thirsty man, seeing you again," said Silence, returning his embrace. Kipp rushed over for his own embrace, and then he backed tactfully away to let Wat and Silence talk in private.

"Tell me everything you've been doing," said Wat. "But first, tell me why you needed to come. Did Caedon find you?"

"Not really, no. But things went awry. I thought it just as well to come to you here and decide on my next moves here with you, where I can find out what you've been doing yourself. Not that everyone in the Ice-realm doesn't know." Silence laughed. "Hakkon's ships can scarcely nose out of his harbors without running the risk your men will send them and their cargo to the bottom of the sea."

Wat smiled. "As long as Hakkon is Caedon's ally, that will be the way of it. Caedon has consolidated his power in the Sceptered Isle. Most there acknowledge him as king."

"No sign of Diera?"

"We get reports from time to time," said Wat. "She's in hiding in the north still. I'm guessing you haven't had any success finding her."

"None. I was making good progress, and then, almost a full year ago, something strange happened. I had signed on as a mercenary with Hakkon's forces, and I was stationed at the port city, where I had good hope I'd find where she was and get to her. But then I was transferred to the royal city, to serve with the crown prince's elite guard."

Wat's single eye twinkled. *It's heartbreakingly blue*, thought Silence. *It looks fine. But I know he can't see out of it. Or not much.*

"You're a victim of your own success, Rafe. Johnny always complained that you made him look bad in Conal's training sessions. You were smaller and younger, but you outfought him and just about everyone else in the courtyard."

"I suppose it was the early training I received from Caedon, Dark Ones take him. I barely remember it. But when I came back to myself, Caedon gave me the best arms master in the Baronies, to refresh my skills. Arms Master Estefan is not as good as Conal. No one is. But Estefan is very good."

"They say Caedon himself is the best there is," said Wat.

"They do say that. Here's an interesting thing. While I was in his household, before I got my memory back, he said something strange. He said he wished he hadn't killed Conal. He wished he and Conal could have fought man to man, to see which of them would have prevailed."

"He told that to you?"

"Unlikely, isn't it. But he did. If you can't speak, and you can't remember, people underestimate you. They start forgetting you're there. They start speaking their minds."

"I think I understand," said Wat drily.

Of course you do, thought Silence. *People do the same around you.*

"So then, you needed to get away from Prince Ansgar's service in order to make any progress," said Wat after a moment.

"Yes. That. But something else. Maybe I'm imagining it."

"Tell me," said Wat. He led Silence over to the hearth stones and they sat down together. Kipp urged some ale and bread on Silence and went quietly away again.

"I don't know how I'd manage without Kipp," said Wat.

"He's one of the kindest and most loyal friends I've ever made. Well, then. Let me tell you about this strange happenstance." Silence told Wat all about Yann. "It seemed like the unlikeliest of coincidences, at first, and at first I counted it up to sheer bad luck. Or good luck, depending how you look at it."

"How was that good luck?" Wat's voice was grim.

"You'd have to meet the lad. He's a fine person. I have no idea why Caedon would father a son with honesty and kindness and courtesy, but he did." Silence hesitated. He hadn't told Wat yet about his other suspicions. "Wat," he said. "There's something else. I hardly know how to tell you. You know some things about Gilles de Rais now. I've told you that he's a powerful mage, and

I've told you how he tried to damage John. I've told you how he has damaged me."

"Yes," said Wat.

"I've told you my parents sent me to Gilles when I was only a boy."

"Yes," said Wat.

"There are people Gilles takes in adulthood, people who intrigue him. People like John. Caedon came to him as a half-grown boy, almost a man. That's unusual. Gilles likes to take his victims when they are young. He likes infants, Wat. If he can't have a baby, he'll take a child of around six years old. I was sent to him at six. Most of the children I met in Gilles's manor, when I first arrived, were dead within the year. But he kept me."

"That's horrifying, Rafe. Weren't you afraid?"

"I had no idea what was happening. A playmate of mine would disappear, the rest of us would speculate he'd been sent back to his parents for some infraction, and soon—there was only me. But by then an entire new crop of children had moved into the fort. When you're that young, you don't even think to question things that would terrify an older person."

"What do you think Gilles saw in Caedon?" said Wat.

"I've thought about it. I don't know. I have some ideas."

"And?" said Wat.

"I think maybe Caedon reminds Gilles of himself. Just a speculation."

"And you?"

Silence shook his head, even though Wat couldn't see him do it. "I don't know," he whispered. "He says I taste good."

"You haven't let him—"

"He did some things to me. Bad things. Never the worst. Never the things that go so deep he ends up owning you. I got away before he could, thank the Child. But if he had wanted to, he would have done it. I wouldn't have been able to stop him. Caedon would have, too."

"Caedon?"

"He can do it too."

Wat looked a little sick.

"So I can't let them catch me," said Silence. "If that happens, I'll be useless. They'll have me in their power. And I still have my other task to accomplish."

"Me being the first of them." Wat sounded amused now.

"You being the first. I've checked you off my list."

"You've—wait, what?"

"Just an expression of Gilles's," Silence muttered.

"You've been telling me all this, Rafe, and as you've been explaining this very disgusting life you've had to lead, I've been thinking about this boy Yann."

"Yes," said Silence.

"Caedon had a son. Caedon is Gilles's minion. Why didn't Caedon turn this son over to Gilles?"

"Exactly," said Silence. "Why indeed."

"Are we to understand Caedon has some human feelings tucked away inside him somewhere? Are we to understand he has fatherly feelings?"

"Apparently so," said Silence.

"Are we to understand some woman could stand Caedon's presence long enough to allow him to father a child on her?" Wat stopped, thunderstruck. He put out a hand and gripped Silence's arm, hard. "That horse pricker."

"You can't use that. I thought that one up," said Silence.

"Too late. I'm using it. Dark Ones take him. Are you suggesting what I think you're suggesting?"

"Yes," murmured Silence miserably.

"What are you going to do, Rafe?"

"What can I do? I grew very fond of the lad."

"He's almost more your son than Caedon's."

"Not quite," said Silence. "And Diera doesn't even know he exists. Caedon told her the baby died. He told me the same."

"Gilles doesn't know he exists, either."

"Now that," said Silence. "That I wonder about. All these coincidental meetings. Suppose Gilles is setting them up? Suppose Gilles's real target is Caedon. Suppose Gilles is furious that Caedon has betrayed him by withholding this son, and now he is setting out to destroy Caedon."

"Couldn't happen to a nicer horse pricker," said Wat.

"But in the destruction, he'll take us all down with Caedon. Me. You. Yann. Diera."

"He's not getting his hands on me."

"I don't think any of this will happen right away," said Silence. "Caedon is still too useful to him, and now Caedon is in a position to help Gilles consolidate his power. Once Caedon's usefulness fades, that's when I think Gilles will make his move on Caedon."

Wat clenched and unclenched his hand at the neck of his tunic. When he spoke, he sounded shaky, panicky. "Caedon had Mirin and Jillie. They got away from him, but he had them. As he was trying to kill me, he told me he'd found Mirin, where we were hiding from him. Suppose he has already killed Mirin? He told me he did kill her. Right before he set to work on me. And if I do have a child—" He stopped, a look of anguish twisting his features. "And if Caedon got his hands on her—"

Silence put a hand on Wat's arm. "Wat. You know how Caedon operates. Suppose he was only saying it to send you across that river in a state of despair. One more way to torture you. Mirin and the child may be alive. They may be well."

"They may be," said Wat slowly. "But maybe not. I didn't even know I had a daughter. The vision showed her to me. A child of flame. The Fire Child's own. I think it was a vision of the dead."

Kipp interrupted then. "Apologies, my lords. Your captain has had news of another of Hakkon's ships taken. There were survivors."

"Ah," said Wat. He shook himself, hard, as if he were shaking the terrible thoughts away from him. "Let's go down to the pier," he told Silence after a moment. "We sink Hakkon's ships, and most of his men drown, but we rescue a few clinging to the wreckage." Silence could tell Wat was forcing himself to speak calmly.

"What do you do with these men you rescue?"

"If they are gentles, we ransom them back to their families. We make a good bit of coin that way. If they're not, we try to convince them to join us."

"And if they won't?"

"The next ship out drops them off on some remote shore to fend for themselves," said Wat. "We're pirates, but we're not bloodthirsty."

"If Hakkon or Caedon catches you, they won't think of that while they pass judgment."

"They're not going to catch me," said Wat with a grin so like the Wat's of old that Silence's heart twisted inside him.

They were making their way down the long treacherous spiral of the staircase. Silence was amazed at how nimbly Wat negotiated it, shaking off Kipp's offer of help.

Once they were outside the pile of the rock outcropping, into the stinging cold of winter, Silence could see some of Wat's mariners with one man held prisoner amongst them at the end of the pier. As they neared, Silence's heart leaped into his throat. He rushed to the men.

"Yann!" he exclaimed. "You're half-frozen, lad. What were you thinking, making a winter voyage, knowing pirates were patrolling the waters?"

"I had to find my father, Master Rafe. I had to. He has kept me in the dark too long."

"And now these dread pirates have taken you."

"They seem to have taken you, too, Master Rafe Quarrel."

"Not exactly," said Silence. Wat stood aside, listening. "Yann," said Silence, taking the dumbfounded lad by the arm. "This is the leader of The Rising, Sir Walter the Steadfast, Queen's Companion, Defender of our good Queen Diera the First, legitimate monarch of the Sceptered Isle."

"I am the son of your enemy," said Yann to Wat.

"So I understand," said Wat to Yann. "And if you don't get inside to the fire, you'll be his frozen solid son, and we'll only have little gelid pieces of you to chip off and send back to him. As for

Master Rafe, as you call him, he's my second-in-command in The Rising."

"I'm glad to see you, Yann. Then again," said Silence, "I'm not so glad."

"Likewise," said Yann.

"Master Rafe Quarrel?" Wat tested it out under his breath. "What in the Nine? Quarreling, Rafe? Really?

CHAPTER TWENTY

A Dilemma

Having Yann around presented Silence and Wat with a dilemma. He couldn't be ransomed the way a regular prisoner could, because he was Caedon's son and now he knew the location of Wat's hideout. For the same reason, he couldn't just be dropped off on some shore. And Silence didn't want to try to persuade Yann to turn on his own father. It seemed unsavory, no matter how much they all hated Caedon. No matter how much damage he had done to them all. Then again, others in the hideout wouldn't have trusted Yann even if he had turned on Caedon.

Yet Silence loved him.

Yann was an uneasy guest in the fortress.

Some wanted him stuck in a cell. Silence suspected a few of Wat's men wanted to kill him.

He wondered if Wat did.

Yann was at loose ends and clearly miserable. He had found an old harp somewhere about the fortress, had tuned it, and went off often to some remote niche to play it. Or he took to prowling restlessly up and down the pier and around the perimeter of the island during milder weather.

About a sen'night after he was settled into the life of the fort, the weather turned unseasonably mild. Yann furled his cloak about him. Silence watched from a window embrasure as the lad went down to the stony beach. Silence saw he had taken the harp with him.

"What do you think of Yann?" said Silence to Wat, seizing the moment to probe Wat's feelings about the lad. Wat had gone unusually quiet during Yann's time at the fort. Silence worried what this could mean.

"He seems like a fine young man, as far as I can tell," said Wat. Silence saw he was choosing his words carefully. "I'm trusting to your impressions and your judgment, Rafe. You've known Yann for the better part of a year, or close to it, and you've worked with him. You've seen how he is around others when he had no reason to try to impress you."

"Caedon kept him completely in the dark," said Silence. "He's had nothing to do with Caedon's evil. The trouble is, Caedon apparently really loves Yann and has treated him lovingly, for the most part."

"What do you think of his name?" said Wat quietly.

"His name?" Silence looked at Wat blankly. Then he realized. "Nine Spheres," he breathed.

"Do you think it was meant as some kind of taunt?"

"That would fit everything we know of the man," said Silence. "But Yann was born a few years before that terrible time, so maybe it's just a coincidence." Silence broke off. *Like so many other coincidences lately*, he said to himself. "Whatever the reason Caedon named him that, hearing the name every day and knowing it is attached to Caedon's son must make it hard for you, Wat."

"Yes, I have to admit, it does."

Silence decided the next occasion he had to talk with Yann alone, he'd sound him out carefully on the subject.

That time came a few days later.

Silence had gone down to the pier to relay an order of Wat's to one of the mariners. He found Yann there too, looking out to sea in the direction of the Ice-realm.

"You're in a difficult spot, Yann," said Silence.

Yann nodded briefly. "I keep wondering when Sir Walter will decide to kill me," he said. "Makes me tense, you know?" Silence saw he was managing a half-smile.

"I don't think he will do that," said Silence.

"Because of you?" said Yann.

"Partly."

"I owe you my life, then," said Yann.

"That's maybe a bit too dramatic. Wat doesn't usually kill his prisoners."

"But I'm in an unusual situation, aren't I?"

"Yes. Listen, Yann." *To the Dark Ones with subtlety*. "I must ask you something."

"What's that? I'll tell you anything I honorably can."

"I would never ask you to do anything dishonorable. I have just been wondering about your name."

"Yann. What about it? It's a common name in the Baronies, especially on our peninsula."

"Yes, I know, of course," said Silence. "But do you recall anything about why your father named you that?"

"Well," said Yann. "He has always told me it was the name of one of the most valiant and honorable men he had ever met, so I have always felt privileged to carry it."

Silence had to look out to sea to compose himself. He saw what Wat had seen. Yann. John. They were the same name. Finally he said, "Did he ever tell you who this man was?"

"No, nothing beyond that. Oh, one other thing."

"What's that?

"For a few years I didn't have a name. My father said it was because he was off campaigning and had only seen me once or twice after my birth. Finally my minder asked him for something to call me, and that's when he named me Yann."

"I see." *So the timing is right after all,* thought Silence. Caedon named him Yann very shortly after he killed John in the most brutal way possible. The same way he tried to kill Wat. The rage in Silence rose unbearably. He wanted to strike out at something, at someone. At Yann. He knew it wasn't right to feel so. Yann had no idea. It was not his fault.

I need to tell him, thought Silence. *It needs to come out in the open. Otherwise, the matter will fester with Wat. If I feel this way about it, what must he be feeling?*

"Listen, Yann. This is a hard thing to talk about. Very hard for me. Much harder for Wat."

Yann turned his eyes, completely trusting, on Silence.

Silence fought down nausea. "Walk with me, Yann." They began walking together down the shingle. Not looking at Yann made it easier for Silence to go on. "My very best friend in this world, when I was a younger man, was another member of The Rising, a man who was killed. He was Wat's older brother. Wat and his brothers were the bastard sons of Ranulf the Fourth, which meant Wat essentially had no father, as the king ignored them. This friend of mine, this older brother of Wat's, served in the stead of a father to Wat. But then a man captured Wat's older brother and set out to kill him. Wat and I tried to save his brother from his killer, but we arrived too late. Wat's brother was brutally butchered. Wat and I got the body out of the killer's hands, and then we buried it. So Wat and I have ties as deep as anyone can have, just about."

"I see that," said Yann. "That's a terrible story."

"Yes." Silence composed himself to go on. "You see how Wat is. Missing an eye and an arm."

"Yes," said Yann.

"He was a fine bowman. A fine soldier. Now, of course, he can't do those kinds of things any longer."

"Yet his men clearly love and respect him."

"He has a sharp tactical mind. He learned those skills from others in The Rising, especially from the leader, Prince Avery, who fought against his older brother Audemar's usurpation of the throne."

"Ironic, then. My father has defeated this Audemar and has taken his place. Will the prince now attack my father?"

"The prince is dead. Your father killed him years ago."

"I see." Then Yann shook his head. "Actually, I really don't see. I was pretty ignorant of all those matters, when I was a boy."

"This prince was also Wat's brother. His half-brother."

"So Wat must hate my father."

"Yes, and your father was the one who brutally killed Wat's older brother, his full brother. Now, just last year, he attacked Wat."

"My father is the person who took his arm and his eye?" Yann cried out in horror. "My father did that to Wat?"

"Yes."

"In battle, many terrible things—" Yann began.

"Not in battle. He captured Wat's brother and did that to him in a cell underneath a castle now owned by the Lady Ailys. And that's where he took Wat, to do the same."

"How did he escape his brother's fate?" said Yann, his voice subdued.

"Kipp and I and some of the others got him out. And then I fled to King Hakkon's realm, and Wat and the others came here."

"Now I see it all," said Yann. "Why is it you think Wat won't do the same to me?" said Yann. "No matter what you say, he must want to kill me. Why hasn't he? And what does my name have to do with it."

"Wat's brother's name was John. Sounds like your father killed him around the same time he named you."

"What are you saying? That my father named me after a man he killed like that?"

"Looks like it," said Silence.

"But why?"

"Sounds like he admired John very much."

"But then—"

"Wait. I suppose I need to tell you some things. I don't want to, Child knows," Silence muttered.

"Tell me everything," said Yann. "I'm in the dark. My own father has kept me in the dark, and now I see you have."

"Sorry, lad. I was in hiding."

Yann, whose eyes had started to spark with anger, looked down now. "I see that. I'd appreciate it very much if you'd tell me everything now."

"It's not pretty," said Silence. "And it's not easy to understand. I doubt I can tell you everything. It's too hard. Too complicated. I'll tell you as much as I can. First of all, your father and I were raised together as sort of brothers."

Yann's eyes got very round.

"We were both wards of the Baron Gilles de Rais."

"That's why you saw right away whose son I was. And that's why Estefan taught you."

"Yes, but I had two other excellent teachers. The first was your father."

"He's very good," Yann murmured.

"He's the best. I only know one other man who could have matched him."

"They should meet."

"Your father had him killed by his soldiers. They rode him down and destroyed him as he tried to defend his prince." As that sank in, Silence continued. "Gilles disciplined us to perform certain duties for him. Your father was obedient. I was disobedient. Gilles sent your father to assist Audemar the Usurper. I threw in my lot with The Rising. I suppose that's the short version. And so," he concluded, "Your father wants to take me to Gilles to be killed for my disobedience, and he wants to kill Wat because he sees Wat as a challenge to him for the throne he took from Audemar."

Yann buried his head in his hands.

Silence clapped him on the shoulder. "This should not have become your burden, Yann. But now that you're here, it has. It's not fair. I'm sorry, lad."

"What should I do?" he whispered.

"I don't know how to advise you."

"I know you can't advise me to escape."

"No, I can't, and if you tried it, Wat would send someone out to kill you."

"You? Would he send you?"

"I'd refuse, lad. You're my friend."

"But if it came right down to it, me or Wat, you'd choose Wat."

"Yes," said Silence honestly. "In any way that means anything except blood, Wat is my brother. We went in together to get John. We buried him together. You know," he said, "John was my best friend. The finest friend a man could have. One of the finest men I have ever known. I'm glad you bear his name."

"Thank you," said Yann.

And there's another thing, he thought, but he didn't know how he could tell Yann. *Your mother is my wife. She's Wat's best childhood friend. Your father raped her, and that's why you're alive in this* world. "What of your mother, Yann?" *At least let me find out how much the lad knows,* Silence said to himself.

"I never knew her. She died when I was young."

Or so Caedon has told you, thought Silence.

"He was right, wasn't he?" Yann looked at Silence sharply.

"Who would know that, if not your father," said Silence.

"Whatever you say about any of this, I see it well. All of you must hate me. My father has done so much damage to you and yours."

"Yann, I tell you truly, you're the best part of Caedon, a side of him I've never seen. If Caedon can have a son like you, then I have misjudged him, at least in part."

"Very gracefully said." Yann gave a bitter laugh and went off walking down the rocky shore by himself, his found, beaten-up harp tucked under his arm.

The next morning, they discovered Yann had stolen a small boat and had made his way off the island in the night.

"Shall we go after him, my lord?" said Kipp.

Wat shook his head no. "He's not of the Sea Child, is he?" He addressed this to Silence.

"No, I don't think so. Caedon is not." *Who knows what god that man worships?* he thought.

"A man unused to the ways of the sea, in a small boat, at night, in winter. In these frigid waters. It's unlikely he'll survive," said Wat.

With sorrow, Silence had to acknowledge this must be true. He reproached himself bitterly. If not for his interference, Yann might not have given in to despair.

But then, he thought, with a kind of hope, *The breezes have turned mild. Maybe he'll make it. The lad has courage. Maybe he will.*

CHAPTER TWENTY-ONE

A Misapprehension

It was decided the time had come for Silence to leave the island and try again to find Diera. This time, he meant to go directly to the north country of the Sceptered Isle.

"No point in trying to hide my presence from Gilles or Caedon. They know I'm here. I'm a danger to you, here, because Gilles can maybe track me here," he said to Wat, arguing for his departure.

"They'll be able to track you there," said Wat.

"They're able to track me anywhere. Just not as well as they once would have been able to." Silence knew this last statement must puzzle Wat, but he wasn't about to remind Wat about his notion that he was actually sort of dead. Betwixt and between. Not dead yet. Not quite.

He suspected the blanks inside him made it harder for Gilles to find him, when he went looking with those powers of his.

"Kipp will go with you," said Wat.

"I will, Silence. I mean Rafe," said Kipp.

"Silence?" said Wat.

"An old nickname. No, Kipp, I pray you stay here with Wat. I'll be traveling fast and light."

Over Wat's head, Rafe nodded meaningly at Kipp.

Wat laughed. "Don't think I don't know what the two of you are doing."

"Wat, suppose there's an attack. Suppose you need to move fast in unfamiliar spaces. Kipp needs to stay here with you."

Wat made a small, reluctant nod of assent.

"So stubborn." Silence punched Wat in the arm. They all laughed, but it was an uneasy laughter.

So it was decided, and the next day one of Wat's smallest snake ships, clinker-built Ice-realm style, took Silence on the three-day voyage to the northwest-most windswept tip of the Sceptered Isle.

Silence stood underneath the steep coastal cliffs and watched as the little vessel dwindled away.

He began the arduous trek inland.

As always, he stopped in taverns in villages and along the roads to listen to travelers' gossip.

Three hard-faced men dressed in hunting leathers huddled in the corner of one such tavern. From his own place in the opposite corner, Silence noted the gleam of steel hidden under cloaks.

They're not Caedon's, he told himself. Caedon's men had a swaggering presence all too easy to identify. When Silence came upon such men, he quickly slipped away.

Without seeming to now, Silence began to listen.

"We should move camp," one was murmuring. "They may be onto us."

"She's weary," another objected.

"She's strong," the first man said. "She'll understand."

Suddenly Silence felt a hard hand on his elbow. Underneath the table, where the tavern keeper and the other tavern-goers couldn't see, Silence felt the point of a knife jabbing into his rib cage, not enough to draw blood, but a warning.

"Easy, fellow," said a voice at his ear. "Stand up slowly. You and I are going to walk outside arm in arm, boon companions. And don't look at me, neither. What's your name."

"Rafe," said Silence, and stood up carefully. He moved from behind the table. The man stepped up close to him and slung an arm about his shoulder. "Me and my man Rafe, we're going out-side," he called to the others in the opposite corner.

They looked up. One of them made a negligent wave in their direction.

"Walk with me over here. That's right. Nice and easy," said the man with the knife. He walked Silence over to a little stand of trees. He searched Silence swiftly, taking all his weapons. "Now we wait," he said.

In a few moments, first one of the men Silence had overheard came strolling out of the tavern. Then the other two. They stood talking. Then, seemingly casually, they walked over toward the copse where the man with the knife was holding Silence.

They surrounded him. "Listening to us, fellow?" said one, who might, Silence thought, be their leader.

Silence nodded.

"We don't like people listening to us."

"Says his name's Rafe," the man with the knife put in.

"Well, now, Master Rafe. Tell us why you were listening."

Silence decided to be completely honest. "I've been looking for someone. Going all over the north country looking."

"Who is this someone?"

"Queen Diera and her army."

"Army," snorted one of the men. "This is it."

"Will you shut your sarding trap, Elstan?" said the leader. He turned to Silence. "Caedon sent you."

Silence shook his head no.

"Caedon sent you, that arse-licker."

"Call him a horse pricker, myself," said Silence.

The man named Elstan guffawed.

"Funny, are you?" said the leader, apparently not amused. "We know what to do around here with spies." He looked up significantly at a sturdy tree branch.

"Easier just to give him one in the gut," said the man with the knife, prodding it into Rafe's ribs again.

"I believe you're right, man. Much easier, and Child take me, I forgot my rope."

"I need to find Diera. I come from Wat," said Silence.

"Good one," said the leader, looking around at the others. "Man says his name is Rafe, says he comes from Wat." He thrust his face into Silence's. "Wat is dead. Rafe is dead."

"No, we're not," said Silence calmly.

"Wat might not be dead, Nev," said Elstan.

"They took him when he went into that castle after that bitch Ailys, and he didn't come out," said the leader, the man named Nev, never taking his eyes off Silence.

"Ask Tyn," said Silence easily. "He'll tell you. He'll tell you I'm alive, too."

"Tyn's dead," said Nev shortly.

"That is a problem, then," said Silence with a low whistle. "Any of you know Kipp?"

"I know Kipp," said the man who hadn't spoken yet. "Good fellow. One of the best."

"One of the best," Silence agreed. "Kipp and I were enslaved in the Baronies, and then we got out. Then Kipp, Tyn, and I, and some others, got Wat out of that castle."

"You stand here and tell me you know the way into that castle?" said Nev. He spat on the ground.

"Yes. I lived there myself for years, guarding Diera. And Wat and I tried to get Johnny out. But we didn't succeed."

"He knows a lot, anyway," said the man holding the knife on Silence.

"Anyone can know a thing. Proves nothing," said Nev.

"Take me to Diera. Then you'll see."

"Or maybe we kill you right here."

Silence shrugged. "Don't tell Diera you did it. That's my advice." *Diera, of course, thinks I'm dead*, he thought.

"Keep a watch on him," Nev said to the man with the knife. Then he and the other two withdrew and began conferring in whispers.

Silence waited. Finally he had a thought. He began whistling between his teeth. Whistling and humming a little.

I'll sing you one, oh, he whistled.

> *What is your one, oh?*
> *Blackbirds rising, blackbird's eye. . .*

It was the sign of The Rising, the secret sign John had devised to separate those in the know from anyone who might be a spy or a poser. Silence wondered if any of the remnants of The Rising still understood what it meant. *Worth a shot.*

Nev turned around to stare at Silence. He and the others came back.

"All right," said Nev softly after a long moment. "We'll take you to Diera. Then we'll see." To the man with the knife, he said, "Don't relax your guard, not for a minute."

They all went down the hill to the rail where the horses were tethered.

"One of these yours?" said Nev.

Silence indicated with a tilt of the head which one was his.

"Bind him," said Nev to the man with the knife. This man sheathed his knife and brought out a length of rope from underneath his cloak. Silence held up his hands to be bound.

Well, he thought. *That part was a bluff at least. They do have enough rope to hang me.*

The man helped Rafe mount his horse, and then the rest of them mounted up. His minder kept Silence's reins in one hand, and rode close beside him. On the other side rode Elstan. Nev took the lead, and the other man brought up the rear.

They rode at a steady pace for most of the day. They broke for a quick bite of cheese and bread, a swallow of water. They offered none to Silence, although they did let him slide awkwardly off his horse to relieve himself and walk around a little to ease the stiffness.

"We'll be there before nightfall," Nev told Silence. "We're going into our camp, and you'll stand with one of the lads. I'll bring Her Highness out. You won't get near her, fellow. Then she'll tell us if you're a liar or not."

Silence nodded. *Child help her, Diera will die of fright*, he thought. He wished there were some way to prepare her. But mostly his heart leaped in his chest for joy. He would see her! *Maybe I'm the one who'll die*, he thought. *Die of joy.* He'd thought it might take months of searching. And now, after less than a fortnight, he'd be with her.

Just to see her again. Just to touch her hand. By now, she could love another. She might even have married another. It would be enough for Silence to know she was alive and safe.

"You're trembling, man. Afraid of what we'll do to you once we've proven you a liar?" His minder leaned toward him with a sneer.

Silence turned a look on him of such inutterable exultation that the man's eyes opened wide. "She thinks I'm dead, man. I'll see her again!"

"Stars above," the man muttered. "I think you may be telling the truth."

"We're getting close," Nev called back.

After a few furlongs, he drew on the reins, easing his horse to a walk. He stood in the stirrups, peering.

Silence felt a flat cold terror, for he had seen what Nev had seen. A pillar of black oily smoke billowing up from the tree line. And a smell of burning.

"Hurry," said Nev, spurring his horse. They took off at a gallop. Then they all pulled up in the dooryard of a cabin, its ruined shell smoldering and black with the soot of a fire.

Nev swung from the saddle and crashed inside, calling out. He stumbled back out.

Elstan had gotten from his own horse and had bent down, studying the packed earth before the cabin's door. They all dismounted.

"Gone," said Nev hoarsely.

"Taken, looks like. Many men." Elstan pointed to the overlapping prints of hooves.

"And here," said Silence's minder. He stepped to a broken off piece of brush by the path leading away. On it rippled a long torn piece of cloth.

"Hers," said Nev.

Now all of the men swiveled their heads to Silence, who sat his horse, his head down.

"Gone," said Nev. "Taken. Think maybe someone kept us occupied while someone else led a party in and snatched her?"

"I think someone might have," said Elstan. The four of them began striding toward Silence.

Silence had his reins back in his bound hands; he turned his horse's head, gave her the spur, and they careened out of there down the path the snatchers had taken Diera.

With a howl, the others were on their mounts and after him.

Silence leaned low over his horse's mane, muttering prayers to his Child. The horse was worn out after hours of riding. She wouldn't last long at this pace.

The path zigzagged along a steep ridge that had come out of the trees onto a magnificent vista. Below, a lake glistened.

Silence threw himself sideways off his horse into some brush and lay there, his breath driven from his body. His horse kept going, and in only moments the others came thundering after it.

He knew he didn't have much time. Without the heaviness of his body in the saddle, and his urging reins and voice, the horse would come gratefully to a stop, and his captors would then search back up the road and find him.

He got himself awkwardly to his feet, bracing himself against his bound hands, and staggered to the edge of the road.

A steep cliff overhung the lake.

Sea Child stand my friend, he thought. Then he thought, *I can do this*. He got himself to the point of land furthest out over the lake. He raised his arms high, made his arms and bound hands into as narrow a shape as he could, gave a spring, pointed his toes straight down, and speared himself off the cliff toward the water.

CHAPTER TWENTY-TWO

A Weary Way

S ilence sat before his farwydd at her hearth fire. The trek had been a long weary way, but now here he was. Getting to her was the only thing he knew to do. Diera was taken. Her supporters thought he was a betrayer and a traitor. Yet he had his undone task, and until he did it, he felt he'd be stuck betwixt and between forever.

Burdened down with these desperate thoughts, he had realized something important. His farwydd was very close. Silence remembered talking it over with John, how he'd never be able to ask his farwydd for help.

Silence had gotten John away from Gilles, and then he and John fled the mage together. As they parted, John headed off to see his farwydd, the farwydd of the Child of Earth, to plead for her help in understanding the terrible powers the Children had visited on him.

You, Rafe. Why not seek the help of your own farwydd? The farwydd of the Child of Sea is not that far from the Sceptered Isles. Maybe even in a remote part of it, John had whispered to him.

Silence remembered his terrible feeling of abandonment. *I can't,* he remembered telling John. *I'm lost to my Child forever.*

Because of Gilles, and the way he had preyed on Silence, Silence had been sure, back then, that he was too impure and debased to call on his Child. With a chilling sort of pleasure, Gilles had let him know it was so.

Silence remembered how horrified John had been. *That means when you cross to the Land of the Dead—* John hadn't been able to go on. He was too appalled.

It means I'll dwell in the Dark Place forever, Silence remembered telling John.

Go to the farwydd, Rafe, John had urged him. *Go to her anyway.*

And then, when he and Wat had set off to rescue John from Caedon's prison, Wat had given him John's message. *Tell Rafe my Child assures him that his Child stands with him. Tell Rafe his Child will never abandon him.*

It pierced Silence to the heart to recall these words. They meant everything to him. John had gone to his own farwydd for help with his own problems. Instead he had spent part of his precious time with her to plead with her to intercede for Silence.

John, thought Silence, his heart near to breaking.

He had never done what John urged on him. He'd never tried to find his farwydd and solicit her help. In some part of himself, he had felt too unworthy still.

And her lair was indeed remote. He'd never been this close to her abode in his life. This time, the extremities of his despair drove him to set out to find her, and now here he was, a petitioner.

The farwydd wasn't speaking, so he settled down to wait. The light coming in through the mouth of her cave began to fade with the coming of twilight. Maybe she'd refuse to speak to him, in spite of all John's assurances. Silence looked down at the dirt-packed floor of her cave. He fixed his gaze there. He waited, still as any stone.

Many candle-measures later, she sighed. "And so you are here at last, my son," she said. "You have taken huge risks to come to me."

"I need your help."

"Yet when you believed your Child had abandoned you, you did not come to me. Why?"

"I didn't believe myself worthy, lady," said Silence.

"I suppose that man told you that. Lied to you, filled you with despair."

Silence said nothing.

"That mage and his minion. But your friend John spoke on your behalf."

"Yes, and when I received your message, I was overcome with gratitude," said Silence, thinking again of the day Wat brought John's message of comfort to him. Thinking of that terrible day, and what had happened to John, in spite of everything Wat and

Silence tried to do to get him out of Caedon's hands. Thinking of John's grave in the quiet glade, and how he and Wat had knelt there, filled with grief.

"Your Child will never abandon you, Silence." The farwydd's wise voice cut through his painful memories. "His Child never abandoned John."

"I pray you thank Them for me, lady."

"The Sea Child has already felt your gratitude. And now, son, ask your question."

"Why have I not gone across that river?"

"You know that already. Your tasks are still undone. Ask me another."

"This makes me think," Silence said carefully, "that the tasks come from my Child."

"Indeed."

"But why. Why should She care about the puny goings-on between me and my friend? Between me and the woman I love?"

"For balance, Silence."

"I don't understand."

"It displeases The Three, to have someone disturb Their balance, even someone very powerful who strides the planes."

"Gilles."

"Yes, even he. Your Child dislikes it, when one of Her sons is damaged in the way the Baron damages and tries to own those underneath the Spheres. You belong to Her, not to him. When She learned of his attempts to take you over, She complained to the Three."

"And who are these Three you speak of?"

"The Three who uphold the balance. The Three who uphold the Spheres." The farwydd was silent. Then she burst out, her voice filled with rage, "And he has enlisted one of the deep ones of the earth to help him. This is not allowed. The Three are most displeased."

"I don't understand," said Silence. "I don't understand any of this."

"Don't worry about that." Her rage seemed to have dissipated. Her voice, her eyes, were again serene. "You don't have to understand, my dear son. Just go off and accomplish your second task."

"It's hard, lady. I've tried, and I've been thwarted."

"By the minion of Gilles."

Silence nodded. "By him. By circumstances. I really have tried," he burst out.

Now the farwydd, a tiny woman, as powerful a person as he'd ever encountered, smiled at him, and her teeth glinted white and terrible. "I particularly liked the part where you dove into the lake and got out of your bonds."

Silence shrugged. "I'm a floater, not a sinker."

"Of course you are. Aren't you the Sea Child's own? But your hands were bound."

"Only in front of me. Not behind. And my feet were free."

The farwydd looked at Silence thoughtfully. "I suppose the leap from the cliff was the most dangerous part."

"I thought so," Silence agreed. "I realized again how lucky I was that those men had bound my hands in front of me and not behind. If I couldn't have gone into the water as straight as a spear, it would not have gone well with me. But anyway, what was the worst that could happen? I could have died. And I've already—"

"Right," said the farwydd, smoothly evading the question of whether he was dead, or how far dead he was. "Those men would have tried to kill you if the leap hadn't. If they had found you, that is."

They sat quietly together.

"I suppose I'll just have to try harder," said Silence at last.

"Yes, you will," said the farwydd.

"I'm tired," he said.

She sat looking at him, saying nothing.

"Caedon has Diera."

Still the farwydd said nothing.

"If I keep trying, will I be able to get her out of his hands?"

"Suppose the answer is no. Will you give up?"

"If there's a chance I can see Diera again, and help her however I can, then I tell you this. I will never give up."

"There's your answer, son. You didn't need me to tell you this."

"I was hoping for some help."

"The Children help them who help themselves," she said.

A flame of anger rose inside Silence.

The farwydd laughed. "This I can promise you. Your Child loves you always, Silence. Rafe. Raoul." She regarded him through shrewd little eyes. "You and I both know something important about you, Silence. This."

She reached out to his amulet about his neck, and Silence let her. "At the temple on the cliffs, you found what it really means. You have a home. It's lodged here in your amulet. It's there on the cliff top, in the temple. It's in the pool there. You don't need to know who your father is."

Silence looked at her, open-mouthed. He hadn't asked, but that question, too, nagged at the edges of his mind. Who was this unknown man, this father, whom he knew nothing about, nothing about at all, except that he must have encountered his mother in an act of love or aggression, and he must have been the Sea Child's.

All this while, the farwydd had kept her hand on his amulet. And her touch, to him, had seemed right and good. "You have your deep connections with your Child," she assured him. "You've forged them yourself. It's in your deep connection with Diera. Your connection with your brothers, your true brothers. It's in your body, that knows how to climb and dive. It's in here." She moved her hand from his amulet to his head. "And it's in here." She gently pressed her hand against his heart.

She stood and raised her hands in blessing. "No one can take this connection from you. Not Caedon. Not Gilles. They tried to make you think so. They were wrong. They did not prevail. Now go off to do what you need to do, my dear son."

Silence left her cave the next morning, led by her guide Gurr up that arduous pathway. As Gurr departed with a friendly wave, Silence looked around him. He felt as though he stood on the top of the world underneath the Spheres. He felt as though, if he waited til dark there, he'd be able to reach out and touch the stars hanging down on their golden chains.

Instead, he told himself, *I need to keep going, no matter how weary I feel. The world is wide, and I don't know where Caedon has taken Diera.*

But he put his hand on his amulet, and his courage rose.

He began to hike back down the steep hill that led away from the cliff where the farwydd of the Sea Child had her lair.

He was on foot now, his horse gone, all his weapons taken from him by those men.

He tried not to hate them. They'd only been trying to protect Diera. They were right to be suspicious. Suppose, as they thought, he'd been a decoy sent to delay them while Caedon took her.

And no one who could corroborate his story had been left alive except Wat and Kipp, far out of reach across the Northern Sea.

Now those men of Diera's must think I'm dead, thought Silence. He imagined their consternation as they retraced their steps up the path his horse had galloped down. He imagined them thinking he had disappeared into thin air.

But they looked like hunters. Trackers. They would have found the signs he'd stood on the cliff. They would have looked down to the lake below and thought no one could possibly have survived such a leap.

So, he thought. *They won't be after me. They think I'm dead. And actually, they're not far wrong.*

He nearly gave in to despair once more, when he realized how close he had come to finding Diera. How he maybe could have fought to keep her from being taken.

When he thought about that, he had to sit down on a boulder and wait until he gained the courage to keep going.

His Child helps him who helps himself, he thought grimly.

Then his thoughts wandered to those mysterious Three his farwydd had mentioned. *Who are They?* he wondered in confusion. He knew his farwydd had explained why They should care, but her explanation made no sense to him.

After three days of walking, drinking from streams and icy run-offs, swimming to refresh himself in mountain pools, Silence had come down from the high craggy country into gentler lands. At least the farwydd had given him plenty of cheese from her goats to take with him, so he wasn't starving.

From a ridge he saw far below him the glint of the sea. He could just make out tiny shapes of vessels, and their sails.

A port.

Silence knew about ports. He knew about their taverns and the information he could obtain in them. He was completely without coin, but he knew he could work as a laborer and make enough to keep himself while he scoured the taverns for the news he needed. And he'd be by the sea. That would sustain him as much as anything.

When he thought of Diera, though, his courage nearly failed him. *Caedon has condemned Diera to death*, he told himself, his heart pounding in his chest. *This town should be full of news about the capture of an important prisoner. An execution as important as that.*

He prayed to his Child he wouldn't get to Diera too late. As he and Wat had gotten too late to John.

When he came to the port and began his search, he discovered with relief that at least the execution was not to be carried out soon.

"There will be a trial, a public one," he heard people say. "She has been cast in prison," they said. "Caedon is putting her to the question."

The last chilled him to his bones. Would Caedon really torture the mother of his own child? he thought. Now he knew Caedon wasn't completely devoid of human feeling.

Devoid enough, he told himself, thinking of John. Thinking of Wat. He knew many men might treat a woman more softly than another man. Cadeon was not that kind.

"They say she was betrayed," one tavern muckspout proclaimed. "They say she was betrayed by a man who lured her protectors away from her."

Silence had to get a grip on himself before he rushed the man and beat his face to a pulp with his fists.

"No, man," another objected. "That's not the way of it at all. She was betrayed by one of her own household. A young girl. This young girl got word to the king, and then he knew where to find her."

What young girl, thought Silence blankly.

"She was richly rewarded for it, they say," said the man doing all the talking. "She's part of the king's household now."

The more the talk swirled around him, the more downhearted Silence grew. *But at least*, he thought, *Caedon isn't going to kill Diera. Not yet.*

Silence needed work to keep himself as he searched for more information. He found it as a sweeper of floors in the tavern, a hauler of ale barrels and sides of beef and pork. He was hardly the largest and burliest of men. But his life had made him strong.

He felt completely inconspicuous. Completely protected.

Being near the sea was soothing to him. He realized that whenever he was too far away from the sea, he felt bereft. In spite of his troubles and his fears about the dangers Diera faced, part of him felt serene, seeing the mighty breakers roll into shore, hearing the sigh and retreat of the waves, and then the cycle beginning again, and again, and eternally again.

Whatever came at him, he began to gain the confidence that he could meet it whole-heartedly.

So he was taken completely by surprise when the press gang came.

CHAPTER TWENTY-THREE

Impressed

The men of Caedon's press gang marched into the tavern's kitchen area and laid hands on Silence and one other tavern worker. Silence looked up in confusion at the big man who had him in hand.

"I've done nothing wrong," he told the man, who ignored him.

"You're grabbing my best workers," complained the tavern owner.

"Take it up with the king," said one of the press gang. The tavern owner cowered back.

"Want to file a complaint in the Hundreds court?" said their leader.

"No," he murmured. "I'm a loyal subject of His Majesty."

The leader lined Silence up with the others he and his crew had pressed that morning. "Let's go," he barked.

Silence glanced around for some way to slip off and hide, but there was none. He marched off with the others. *This is a fine kiddle of fish*, he thought.

They were herded on board a cog.

Almost everyone on the vessel huddled miserably on the deck, some spewing up their breakfasts, as they headed out into the choppy waters of the Narrows.

Not Silence, of course.

He leaned over the top strake of the cog looking out over the water, enjoying the brisk sea breeze. One of the mariners came by.

"Where are we going, good man?" Silence called out to him.

The mariner strolled over. "They haven't told any of you?"

"Not a thing," said Silence.

"Out to the Mid-Isle."

"The Mid-Isle?" said Silence blankly. "Why there?"

"Where have you been, man? We're fighting a war with one of the barons over that island."

"Baron Gilles?" asked Silence with a chill.

"No. One of those barons. I've forgotten which one," said the mariner. "Not that one, though." He went off to see about some matter involving the cog.

Well, thought Silence. *It would be pretty unlikely for Caedon to fight against Gilles.* As for himself, if he had to be under the control of one or the other of them, he supposed better Caedon than Gilles. It was a hard choice, though.

When they reached the island and Caedon's army's beach-head there, Silence found himself in a company of men under the command of an exasperated-looking grizzled old soldier.

"You've been impressed into the king's army. You should feel proud. I will teach you to fight. How many of you varlets have ever held a sword?" he barked.

Silence wasn't about to admit he could wield a sword, certainly not how well. His only hope, he thought, was not to come to the attention of Caedon at all, nor any of his officers.

He accepted a pike from the commanding officer's aide and listened obediently as he was told how to use it. Then he practiced with the others, trying to blend in and seem as awkward as the rest.

"What are we fighting over?" he asked the man next to him.

"Fishing rights," said the man.

Children preserve us, thought Silence.

"Follow me!" the officer bellowed. Silence fell in with the others, an irregular, stumbling little cohort trailing after him up the beach and into some dunes.

He lined them all up. He pointed with his sword over the dunes. "See those men over there?" he said.

They all nodded.

"When I give the word, you lot go running at that lot with your pikes. Try to kill them before they kill you. Understand?"

They all nodded. Silence saw some of them had turned as white as the snow cover of an Ice-realm winter.

Silence stood easily hefting his pike. He and his fellow raw recruits wore no armor. They stood bareheaded, barelegged, bare-armed, some of them barefoot, looking around the dunes, their eyes walling in fear.

After a long wait, as the springtide sun started heating the air and Silence felt himself begin to sweat uncomfortably, their group stood and watched as others around them were sent into battle and mowed down. Then their commander yelled their watchword, and Silence and the others ran in a ragged, yelling line toward the enemy to be mowed down in their turn.

Silence found himself in a striving, chaotic, screaming mass of men. He thrust with his pike, nimbly leapt aside as someone came at him with a club, and when a man just in front of him went down, a much more prosperous man in leather armor who might have actually intended to go for a soldier, he bent to the unfortunate fellow and grabbed the sword out of the dead hand.

Now he cut viciously through the melee.

I'm completely without protection, he thought. By then, he had fought his way over to a different group, better-armed. He looked around for his own officer, didn't see him, and started fighting beside these others. One glanced aside at him and tossed him a shield. Nodding his thanks, Silence hewed his way forward.

The battle lasted most of the day. Silence received a wound, but it was superficial. He didn't even remember being struck. He shrugged off another's offer of help. "Only a flesh wound," he murmured. He kept going.

As twilight came on them, he heard the horns of the retreat blasting over the field, and he fell back with the others to a camp alongside the shore. He dropped exhausted before one of the many fires and gratefully accepted ale and stew from half-grown boys circulating through the army.

He wanted to set aside the sword and shield. He didn't want to stand out. But he was afraid that if he did cast his arms aside, he might not have anything decent to fight with when dawn called them to another day of battle.

"You. Fellow. Over here." Someone summoned him from across the fire.

Silence got to his feet and stepped over to the man, who looked to be some kind of officer. Not his own. He didn't know what had happened to his own. Maybe killed. This man was armored, chain, not just leather.

"I was watching you," said this man to Silence.

Silence's heart sank.

"You fought well. What's your name?"

"Rafe Quarrel," he said. Rafe was a common enough name.

"Are you quarrelsome, then, Master Rafe?"

"Some have said so."

"As long as it's directed toward the enemy." He looked Silence up and down. "You have no armor."

Silence shook his head.

"See that man over there?"

Silence looked to where his finger pointed.

"Yes."

"Go over to him. He'll kit you out."

So by the end of the night, Silence had a leather helmet and cuirass, and leather greaves, too. With his sword and his battered shield, he thought he might survive the next day of fighting.

By dawn, though, the brief war was over. As carrion birds and scavenging animals settled over the piles of the dead and clawed each other for the best gobbets of meat and entrails, the generals drew up agreements for a cessation of arms. All the men stayed in camp for a sen'night while King Caedon and the Baron de Mornay ratified a treaty.

The next day, they were marched back to the ships, and soon Silence was disembarking in the port again.

He felt hopeful. Caedon hadn't noticed that one of his common soldiers was a man he very much wanted to imprison and kill. If he'd come to Gilles's notice, the mage had not done anything about it. Diera was still alive. Maybe they'd release him to go back to the tavern now.

But no.

He was an impressed man still. He was in Caedon's army still.

He was sent inland to a fort, and given a bunk in a barracks. *Here I am again*, thought Silence. *Different realm, same situation.*

Then he had to acknowledge, reluctantly, that his situation was not the same. He was a lot more exposed, this time, than he'd been in Hakkon's realm.

Later in that same turning of the moon, he and the others were called to the fort's outer bailey.

"Men," cried their commanding officer, a new one who strutted about in very shiny chain mail. "Line up. I will hand out rewards to those distinguishing themselves in the glorious war, fighting for our king."

The third name called was his.

"Master Rafe Quarrel."

Rafe stepped forward to receive a parchment proclaiming how impressive his king regarded his feats of battle.

And his armor was exchanged for chain.

And the arms master of the fort was duly impressed by Rafe's demonstration of knowhow with a sword and shield.

The whole situation, thought Rafe, was impressive all around.

Nine Spheres, he muttered to himself. *Now what?*

CHAPTER TWENTY-FOUR

An Exchange

As in all wars, the captured enemy were treated according to their status. Prisoners of name were held until ransomed by their families. Ordinary prisoners were sold into servitude, the way Silence and Kipp had been, years earlier. Nothing had changed about that. Either way, important prisoners or scum, the winning side made a handsome profit off their victory.

Even the losers benefitted in this way too, although their important prisoners were more likely to be used as negotiating counters rather than exchanged for the ransom. Common prisoners, by the treaty agreements, were more likely to be returned to their families. Not always, though. Sometimes the losers too sold off their common prisoners, if it was clear the men had no kin to care about them. It depended on what the losers thought they could get away with. War had its costs, but it was often profitable for both sides. And in the towns on both sides of the conflict, merchants saw their chance and raised prices.

The fort where Silence served, being closest to the coastal port where ships sailed for the Mid-Isle, held most of the important prisoners. They were kept in a large cage-like structure right out in the open, in the fort's outer bailey. The shame and degrading conditions, it was thought, would bring their families to terms more easily, resulting in a larger ransom.

Silence had to walk past this cage every day, and from time to time, he was set to guard it. He tried not to stare at the Baronies nobles inside it. Frequently, these prisoners tried to bribe the guards for privileges—special food, an extra blanket. Any guards found out aiding the prisoners were punished with scourgings, but good coin was worth the risk to many. War, what was it good for? Profit.

As the moon turned and turned about again, the stock of prisoners inside the cage steadily dwindled. Ransom was arranged, and the nobles and gentles among the prisoners walked free.

The common prisoners suffered a worse fate. They were kept in the fort's noisome dungeon. Silence dreaded the times he'd be assigned down there. The stench and misery reminded him too powerfully of his own experiences. Once, a party of guards was sent in to cull these prisoners—remove the bodies of those who had died before they could rot too badly and infect the others, and, worst of all, dispatch any prisoners judged too weak to stand or easily sell into bondage.

Silence shuddered at it, thinking how that could have been his own fate. He was glad he wasn't in the detail compelled to do such a thing. He wondered what he would have done if he had been. He agonized about how he should behave. He could sneak in and unlock the doors to their crowded stinking common cell. But where would the prisoners go then? They'd just be recaptured and probably beaten. Part of him hoped they'd be shipped off to their masters soon, so he wouldn't have to think about it. Part of him despised himself for this wish.

There were a few prisoners kept separately, not in the big common cell but in individual cells. They weren't nobles or gentles to be ransomed, but they weren't bondservants to be sold. They were somehow betwixt and between. One man, he heard, had been the master of the Mid-Isle's port. He was no noble, but he had a lot of knowledge that might be valuable to someone. Another was a celebrated physicker.

One day Silence was assigned to the dungeons. Thank the Child a culling had happened only days earlier, and he wouldn't have to be part of such a thing. But he was supposed to go into the big common cell and help choose ten of the strongest prisoners and take them out for someone to sell. Silence steeled himself to go in.

He was not in charge, thank the Child. He hung back and let the others do most of the work. He pretended to look busy when the leader of their group glanced in his direction, and he tried not to let the horror of the surroundings get to him. He tried to wall himself off from it.

The leader wasn't fooled. He summoned Silence over to him, to a corner of the room. "What's this, Master Rafe? Never seen the like of this before, have you? Sick to your dainty stomach, are you?"

Silence decided to be honest. "That's not the way of it, sir. I'm remembering my own time on the other end of it, when I too was a prisoner of war. It's hard for me, sir. Look here, sir." Silence did something he almost never did, especially not with strangers. He eased his leather armlet up and let the man have a look at his brand.

The man, who was not unfeeling, a baker in a former life, a man with a wife and children, put a sympathetic hand on Silence. "Ah, lad," he said. "I know you for a good soldier. Look, take a step outside for some air. Then head down to the special cells and inspect those. It's not as bad, down that row."

Silence nodded gratefully and got out into the dungeon's corridor.

The head jailer gave him a bunch of keys and pointed the way.

Silence went from cell to cell down the short corridor. There were ten cells. He entered each, checked on the prisoner inside. He tried to be kind. The prisoners cringed away from him. He recognized why.

In the third cell, the man inside was obviously sick and suffering. "Don't tell them," the man whispered. "They'll have me killed."

"I won't," Silence promised. He wondered if he could maybe find a healing potion and somehow get it to the man. He doubted he could.

The next cell housed a young man who moved to the far reach of his shackles, as far away as he could get, as Silence entered.

Silence wondered if anyone had beaten him or abused him in some way. Probably someone had.

"I'm here to check on you," Silence said to this dirty man crouching with his head down.

The man drew in a sharp breath and shook his head. "No," he said softly. "Not possible."

Silence looked harder in the dim light filtering in from the corridor. "What?" he said, bewildered. "Nine Spheres, Yann?"

"Master Rafe," said Yann carefully. "I'm not seeing things, am I? It's you?"

"Nine Spheres, Yann." Silence leapt to him, helped him to stand. "What in the Nine?"

"I'm a prisoner," said Yann with a slight smile. "And what are you in for? Good Lady, you're a guard?"

"Long story," said Silence. "How can I get you out of here, that's the thing."

"I doubt you can."

"What are you doing here? Tell me. We have time. No one is going to check. They sent me down here. I'm the person who's doing the checking." Silence felt he wasn't making any sense.

"I was in the war. I was taken," Yann said simply.

"Fighting on the other side? Against your father?"

"Yes," said Yann.

"Dark Ones take you, Yann. You're alive but now you're here. Why didn't you keep yourself safe." Silence gave Yann a little shake. "You're always walking into danger. I thought—we all thought—"

"Thought I was dead."

"Yes. Winter seas, and—how did you manage it, Yann? I'm so happy to see you!" Silence felt a burst of joy. All this time, he, like Wat and the others, had assumed Yann must be dead. He had had his hopes. But in the multitude of other matters, such as leaping from high cliffs and visiting his farwydd and getting impressed into Caedon's army, he had tucked this hope deep inside himself and hadn't let himself think about it much.

"I just—the Children stood with me."

"You're not even of the Sea Child," Silence marveled. "At least, I don't think you are."

"I don't know which Child watches over me. One of them does. Some of them must."

"Whichever one it is, I praise Her," said Silence. "I felt much to blame, when you disappeared like that. I felt I had driven you to despair, with the things I told you."

"Necessary things, Rafe. I needed to hear those things."

Not all of them, Silence thought. *You don't need to know about Diera. What could you do, if you did know?*

"But you didn't tell me everything, did you, Rafe." It was a statement, not a question. It was an accusation.

"I'm sorry," Silence whispered. "It was too hard."

"And now I know."

"How did you find out?" said Silence, wondering if they were even speaking of the same thing.

"My father told me."

"Why would he tell you, after such a long time keeping it from you?"

"He was furious with me. Furious at my betrayal. So he told me. He told me he had her in his power now, after long years of searching. He told me he was going to kill her."

So, thought Silence. *Yann does know.* "Yes," he said. He knew his voice was grim.

"He told me you had played him false with her."

Silence had to laugh. "Good one," he said.

Yann's eyes blazed in the dimness.

"That wasn't exactly the way of it, lad."

"What was the way of it, Master Rafe? And why are you some guard in my father's fort?"

"Too many questions. Not enough time to answer them all." *Where even to begin?* thought Silence. "Let me just tell you this. Diera, your mother, is my wife."

"You stole her affections from my father?"

"No. Dark Ones take it. It's too hard to explain, and the man's your father."

"I'm going to run mad with all these secrets," Yann muttered. "All these people keeping things from me that I need to know."

"Look. I'm not trying to. You love your father."

"My father and I—" Yann's expression became unreadable. "He has put me here," he said after a moment.

"Your father knows you're down here? Nine Spheres, how can he know that and let you rot here? Why isn't he demanding these stupid people free you?"

"He told me it was a good lesson to me, for my betrayal."

Silence passed a hand over his forehead. "Now you must tell me everything."

"Why must I do that, Master Rafe, when you only tell me bits and pieces? It's not a fair exchange."

"You must do it because your mother is in terrible danger. You must do it so I'll have a chance to help her."

"I don't even know her. She abandoned me. Apparently for you," he added, his eyes dangerous.

"That's what Caedon told you? Dark Ones take the man. No. He's lying to you, lad."

"Someone is," said Yann.

"Listen to me, Yann. Your mother doesn't even know you're alive. The day you were born, your father took you away from her. He told her you died of plague. Then he stashed you away in that little village."

"How do you know that?"

"I was there the day you were born. I was trying to get you both out of your father's hands. I failed."

"You're not telling me I actually may be your own son, are you?"

"No." Silence put his hand out to Yann, and Yann flinched back. "I wish you were."

"If I'm not your son, why would you care, back then?"

"I cared about her. Care about her. She had been through so much at your father's hands. I couldn't bear to watch her suffer."

"So you were married to her, and my father took her?"

"No, we married later. We both thought you were dead. Your father had told me the same thing about you, that you had died."

"And you believed him. You believed I had died of plague."

"No, but I believed you were dead. Your father said he had sent you to the Baron Gilles. Infants, children sent to the Baron."

Silence stopped, uncertain how to go on. "They never come back."

"I don't understand."

"It's too hard to understand," Silence agreed. "But here's one thing I know. I know your father knew that if he did send you to the baron, you would be killed. I know the reason your father kept you in that village all those years was exactly for that reason. So the baron wouldn't find you and kill you."

"So my father does love me. That's what you're saying."

"In his own way, he does. He must. He has taken an enormous risk, hiding you, and now that you are here in the world where he can't control you, Gilles de Rais is going to find out. I suspect your father will pay a terrible price for that."

"What do you mean, where he can't control me? He is controlling me," said Yann, spreading his hands wide to encompass the cell.

"By now, it's almost a certainty Gilles knows. Maybe your father thinks putting you here will protect you."

"So will Gilles try to kill me? What you're telling me makes no sense, but if he was cheated of my life, and if now he knows where I am, will he come after me and kill me?"

"You know," said Silence after a moment. "I don't think he will, not like that. You're in terrible danger. I am. Anyone in his way is in terrible danger, because he doesn't care whom he hurts as he goes after the one he wants. But now you're not the one he wants. He only wants them when they're children."

"So how can you say my father is in danger? Or you? You and he aren't children."

"No, but he took us both as children, and thinks he owns us, and now we have both thwarted him and cozened him. Now he's angry."

"You're speaking of him as if he's some all-powerful—"

"Mage," Silence filled in.

"Mages. That's only in stories."

"No. It's not," said Silence. "He sucks up the life force of others. Mine. Your father's. But the life forces that are his main food are children's. An endless supply of them. Easy prey."

"I may be having a nightmare," Yann muttered.

"Well, if you are, it's a bad one, and I need to figure out how to get you out of it," said Silence, making his voice practical. "So let's turn from these big hard-to-understand things to the immediate things. You say your father's the one who has locked you up here. That he knows you're here and wants you here. Let's start with that. We'll go back to the big things later, when we have more time."

"No," said Yann. "That's not the way this will go. Fair exchange. You ask me a question, then I ask you one." His mouth had set in a determined little line that Silence found very familiar. He felt dizzy.

"I go first," said Yann. "Why are you looking at me like that?"

"Because your expression reminds me so much of your mother's," said Silence, low. He looked up into Yann's eyes and smiled. "My turn. Why did you fight for the Baron de Mornay against your father in the Mid-Isle War?"

"Because he did something terrible to the girl I love."

"Elene?" Silence looked at him, startled.

"Yes. My turn. How do you know who Elene is?"

"I guessed."

"Not good enough. Tell me."

"Stars above. How to do that. I had escaped Gilles. He had me again, he and your father. I had lost my memory, it's complicated why. They were sending me out to collect children for Gilles, to test my loyalty."

"You're the one!" exclaimed Yann. "The one who came for little Gwyl, and then helped him instead!"

"With Elene's help. And then, when you began talking about her, I guessed the rest. I know the story of her family. I knew you must mean her."

"I love her. She disappeared. I fear my father did violence to her, or had someone do it for him. And he was already angry about—listen, Rafe, I didn't tell him, I swear it. I was so angry. I told him I had found Wat and had joined him. I did it to make him angry. I didn't tell him where Wat was, I swear I didn't."

"I'm guessing that did make your father angry. Very angry."

Yann nodded.

"Did you mention me?"

Yann shook his head no.

"Good. But it would have been better if Caedon thought he had killed Wat."

"I'm sorry," Yann whispered. He looked miserable.

"No need. By this time, Gilles surely knows. No doubt he has told your father. Probably about me, too. He knows things, Yann. He has his ways."

"How are you here, Master Rafe, in this fort? Aren't you in danger, here under my father's very nose?"

"I suppose. It's odd that Gilles hasn't tracked me here. I can think of that two ways. That Gilles really doesn't know I'm here, although that is hard to believe. Or that Gilles wants me here, as part of his plan to revenge himself against your father. I've thought for some time that you and I would never have met, Yann, if Gilles hadn't wanted it that way. Maybe that you wouldn't be here for me to conveniently find, if Gilles hadn't engineered it."

"That's a frightening thought. Is he so powerful?"

"Yes." Silence looked down at his shoes. "Where are we now, in our exchange of questions?"

"I don't know. I've forgotten."

"Any more questions?"

"If you and Diera love one another, why is it my father and Diera produced, you know, me?"

The question I've dreaded, thought Silence. "I'll give you the simplest, baldest answer, no matter the hurt, because we're running out of time. My officer at the fort is going to wonder why it's taking me so long, checking up on you lot." Silence drew a heavy breath. "Gilles wanted a child from Diera, who is part of the royal line. Don't ask me why. I don't know why. Gilles got your father to imprison Diera, drug her, and systematically rape her. Then she produced you. Then your father was supposed to send you to Gilles. Then—well, you know the rest."

There was a long silence.

"You must hate my father."

"Yes. I was charged with guarding Diera, and I had fallen in love with her, and I had no idea what your father was doing to her. I failed her. So yes, I do. I do hate your father. Now you know."

"Do you think he loved my mother? Do you think that's why he kept me? Do you think he's jealous of you?"

"Your father kept you because he loves you. Because you're his son, not because he loved Diera. He didn't. Gilles forced him to it. It must have been a big sacrifice for him. Your father doesn't like women," Silence said briskly. "He likes little boys, and if he can't have little boys, then little girls." Ignoring Yann's expression, he went on, "It's you yourself, Yann. He loved you. Loves you, I should say, because he still does, no matter what he thinks he's doing, leaving you here. Now you wait here, and I'm going to find a way to free you. Promise me. No desperate acts, like last time. Wat would have kept you safe, no matter how he felt."

"I'm to blame," said Yann. His expression was bleak.

Silence wondered if he had gone too far. But how to avoid it? "You're not to blame. I just want you to be prudent now."

"I shouldn't even be here in this world."

"Do you know how glad I am that you are?" Silence took Yann by both shoulders and looked into his eyes. "How glad I am you're not dead? How glad your mother will be, to find out you're not?"

"She could love me, after that?"

"I know she grieved, when Caedon told her you were dead. I know how much I came to value our friendship, when we met in the Ice-realm. Whether Gilles engineered it or not, do you know how glad I am? Stay here, Yann. Don't do anything rash. I'm going to get you out."

Yann nodded, his eyes dull.

"Besides," Silence said, "You must be desperate in here, without your harp."

Yann laughed a little at that. "Yes," he whispered. "It's true. I am."

CHAPTER TWENTY-FIVE

Cats and Dogs

L et's say a dog has cornered some small beast in the courtyard of the house and comes at it, meaning to tear it limb from limb. Let's say a cat has slunk in behind him and sees what he's about to do. But she wants that poor creature for herself, to play with and torment. Let's say she cozens that dog into turning his attention elsewhere. Then she seizes the creature and makes off with it, leaving the dog barking and furious behind her. And she looks behind her at that dog and smirks.

That's how Silence explained events to himself, as he lay in the power of Ailys the queen, wife of the deposed usurper king Audemar.

Silence didn't see it coming, the next blow the fates or the gods or whoever it was had in store for him. At the fort where he was stationed, he had left the dungeons determined to get Yann to safety. As he set foot in the outer bailey, he spotted the fort's commanding officer in talk with a cloaked, hooded man at the far end of it. The officer whirled around and motioned to some of the others, who rushed to Silence and seized him and marched him over.

The hooded man turned slowly around.

"Caedon," said Silence.

"Is that any way to address your king, varlet?" said the officer, dealing Silence a blow that sent him to his knees.

"Um," said Silence. "Hail, Your Majesty?"

"Better," said the officer.

"Thank you, good sir. I'll have a moment of private conversation with the prisoner," said Caedon.

"We'll wait just over there, Your Majesty, in case there's trouble." The officer and his men withdrew.

"So," said Caedon. "Here you are, Rafe. What do you have to say for yourself."

"What indeed," said Silence.

Caedon sighed. "I know what you've been up to. Gilles has told me every step you've taken, since you left to do an errand for me. Instead, you made off with my gold."

"And?"

"Now I have you. Now I will punish you."

"What about Gilles." *Which would be better,* thought Silence, *to end up in Gilles's hands or Caedon's?*

"Gilles has given me permission to punish you as you should be."

I suppose the man will try to kill me now, thought Silence. *Do the farwydd's words mean he can't do it, that I must finish my two tasks before I cross that river, or just that I must try even though I may fail?* He wasn't sure.

"What about your son?"

"What about him?" Caedon's eyes turned dangerous.

"You kept him from Gilles. What does Gilles think about that?"

"That's none of your concern," said Caedon.

"At least don't keep him locked up here in these vile conditions."

"None of this is your concern," said Caedon. "I refuse to rise to your bait, Rafe." He turned to the officer nearby. "Put him in my cart," he said, and Silence was chained and hustled off.

After a day and night of jolting across the countryside, and as the surrounding land grew hillier and more rugged, Silence had a good idea where Caedon must be taking him. That castle. Caedon didn't get into the cart. Silence was there alone. *He's keeping away from me because he doesn't trust what he'll do, around me*, thought Silence. *Somehow he really does think of me as his brother. His wayward brother.*

Now he lay in a cell of that castle, a cell just around the corner from the place he and Wat had failed to rescue John, the place from which he and Kipp had just barely managed to rescue Wat.

He lay there day after day, and still Caedon didn't come. *Leaving me here to think about how he'll torture me*, thought Silence, and couldn't help the sick fright that crept on him and held him sweating in his bonds. By now, he'd seen far too much of Caedon's methods.

Maybe a sen'night after he had been taken, Silence's suspense ended. He heard footsteps echoing toward him down the corridor to his cell, and he knew it wasn't the usual time the jailer brought him his noggin of water and some kind of vermin-infested meat.

The cell door opened. Caedon and the jailer stood regarding him. "Clean him up," Caedon told the jailer, "and have some men bring him up into the tower where I have my interrogation room." Caedon turned on his heel, his cloak swirling after him.

The jailer unchained Silence and hoisted him to his feet without a word. Silence was too weak to put up any resistance. The jailer walked him up to the outer bailey of the castle and behind the stable and mews. Silence looked over toward the stable longingly. Toward the hidden passageway out.

The jailer stood Silence against a wall and made him strip off his clothes. Some fellows came over with buckets of water and threw them over Silence, who cried out at the shock of it. *But it feels good, too,* he thought. *It feels good not to be so dirty.*

The jailer tossed him a rough pair of trousers, and he drew them on. Then the jailer took him into the castle's nearest mural tower and up a spiraling set of stairs to the top.

Caedon waited for him there, beside a post in the room, and a table with some leather straps laid across it. He dismissed the jailer.

"You know what to do," Caedon said to Silence.

Silence looked back at him, baffled.

"Dark Ones and unknown gods," Caedon spat. "You really don't remember?"

Silence shook his head no.

"You're lying." He took a menacing step toward Silence.

"Just tell me what you want, Caedon," said Silence, weary. "Tell me before I fall down. I'm so weak I can barely stand up."

Caedon's face went impassive, but Silence saw a flicker of some excitement in his strange amber eyes. "Go over there and stand against the post."

Silence did it.

"Do I have to bind you?"

"I don't know. Do you? Are you about to gouge out my eye or cut off my arm?"

Caedon moved very close. Much too close. "No," he murmured. He set his hands on Silence's shoulders and leaned his body against Silence's, while Silence tried to flinch away from him. "Hold still," he said. His mouth moved to Silence's ear.

And then, with a sickening lurch, Silence did remember.

And then Caedon had insinuated himself into Silence, through his ear, and a deeply cold poison began spreading and licking and eating itself into Silence's brain.

Soft music was playing somewhere. Silence groaned and stirred.

"He's coming to himself," said a voice. "Shall we summon her?"

Whatever they were muttering about, Silence didn't want to know about it. He burrowed into the furs of the soft bed where he lay.

Some time later, *quite some time later*, Silence thought, he blinked against the light streaming in on him from a high window and tried to sit up.

An arm supported him. Someone held a cup to his lips, and he drank. His lips felt dry and bitten.

"There now. Feeling better, Master Rafe?"

"Yes," he croaked. But very gradually he was feeling worse, because the memory of what Caedon had done to him, what in fact he always did, came seeping in.

How could I not have remembered that, he thought. He knew Caedon and Gilles fed on those in their power. He knew they had fed on him. He just hadn't remembered how. He had remembered in an abstract way. Not the circumstances.

Now he did, and he wished he didn't. *They could just do it and leave me out of it*, he thought miserably. Do something irreversible to his brain, so he wouldn't have to know. An irrational thought, to be sure.

"Let's clean him up a bit," said one of the women attending him. Now he could look around, and he saw them there. Healers, he supposed.

They summoned a servant who took him away to bathe him and put him into fresh clothing. Light linen things. The servant shaved his chin and cheeks.

I've had a high fever, thought Silence.

When they returned him to his bed, he saw they had brought in fresh bedding. They eased him down into it, and Silence closed his eyes gratefully.

"No sleeping, now, Master Rafe," said one of his healers. "Her Majesty has been summoned. She'll be here soon."

Her Majesty, thought Silence blankly. With a jolt of joy, he thought, *Diera*. Then, almost immediately, a sullen blanketing of joy. *No. Not Diera. Ailys*. The castle was hers now. She stayed here. Some said Caedon kept her here, his mistress, after he'd routed her husband Audemar and had taken his throne. Silence knew better than that. Others said Caedon kept Ailys here as a prisoner. Silence doubted that one, too.

"Here's our patient sufferer, Your Majesty," said one of the healers as soon as these thoughts had paraded themselves through Silence's mind.

"Leave us. He's too weak to do me any harm," said a voice.

Silence didn't remember that voice. He must have heard it, some time in his youth.

There was a rustle as the healers departed, and a scraping as someone, *Ailys*, he thought, pulled a heavy wooden object near. *A chair*, he thought.

He pried his eyes open.

"So now, Master Rafe. Are you lucid?"

"I suppose so. Your Majesty," Silence added.

"Our king has captured you at last. He's very relieved."

"I suppose he must be," said Silence.

"But now I have found a way to come to your bedside."

Well, well, thought Silence. *Not part of Caedon's plan*. But then he remembered what Wat had told them all, when Dru had freed him from Ailys a number of years earlier. He remembered what she had done to Wat.

I'm not some fresh young lad, though, he thought. *I'm safe from her, at least in that way*.

"Look at you," Ailys murmured. "Always the most handsome lad in the castle, and now look."

Silence had to smile at this. Now look at him. Not that person any longer. But then he tensed, as Ailys put her hand on his head and fondled his hair. It was beginning to grow long again. *How many days have I lain here like this?* he wondered.

"You have gray in your hair, Master Rafe." Her hand trailed down to his ear, and he flinched reflexively away from that. Then her cool fingers were on his face, and she was tilting his chin toward her and making him look at her.

"You're just as young as when I last saw you," Silence blurted out.

She laughed. "Yes. A little something the good baron has granted me."

The baron, he thought. She must mean Gilles. He remembered the talk about Ailys, that she had learned witchcraft. He stared at her, remembering the angular, sharp-featured young noblewoman he had once seen about court, a lady with status far above his own. He didn't think he'd ever spoken to her. Whatever Gilles had done for her, he seemed—along with keeping her young—to have softened the angles. Widened the shrewd little eyes. *You might even call her beautiful now*, thought Silence.

"A good trade, wouldn't you say, Master Rafe? You who have always loved the ladies. Still the same Sea-Child eyes," she said, tracing a line along his brows with a fingertip. She drew back the bedding as Silence tensed. "And look at this. The last time I saw you, Caedon was keeping you weak. Look at the muscle you've built since then. Even after what Caedon just did to you."

"I'm old and battered, lady," said Silence dismissively. *Get away from me, Ailys,* he was thinking.

"I always thought I'd made the wrong choice, going after Caedon," she said. "It should have been you, Rafe."

That startled Silence. He knew she and Caedon were in league together, but a sexual liaison? It didn't seem likely. Caedon didn't like women.

"Caedon has turned out to be a disappointing and inattentive lover," she said, with a petulant moue of her full lips.

I'll just bet he has, thought Silence. He even felt a moment of pity for Caedon. What he must have had to do to himself, to make love to this terrible woman.

"I really thought my poor friend Lyn should have taken you for a lover," said Ailys. "If she only had. Life would have turned out differently for her, then. You would have understood. You would have been discreet. More's the pity she ran after that silly minstrel fellow."

Silence closed his eyes so Ailys wouldn't see the sudden rage in them. Lyn's love for John had gotten her killed. And the gossip was, Ailys had betrayed her.

"Did you know, I once tried to help John, to warn him that Caedon was about to take him?" Ailys sighed. "The message was misdelivered. He ignored it, maybe. I'm not sure what happened there, but he was a foolish one, a dreamer. Enough talk," said Ailys. "Down to business."

Children help me, thought Silence.

"Here," she said. She ran a fingernail hard down the scar that stretched from the hollow in Silence's neck to the pubis. Silence's eyes opened wide. Her hand lingered there, at the roots of him, but then she withdrew it. "You know what this is," she said.

"Yes," said Silence. "Vigilia did it."

"You know what it means."

"Yes. That I'm dead." Then he added, "Sort of."

"Listen, Rafe. You know what I like."

Silence was weltering in confusion now. But she didn't leave him in confusion long.

"I like above all else a trade."

"And you want me to trade you something?" Silence whispered.

"Yes."

"What do you want?" *Not me*, he thought in relief.

"I want that boy. I want Yann."

"No," said Silence.

"I want him for another purpose, not what you think. I'm not going to do anything to him."

"Like you didn't do anything—not really, or so you complained—to my friend Wat?"

"Young Walter." A reminiscent smile curved Ailys's lips. "Now there was a beautiful lad. Not so beautiful, I think, after Caedon got through with him. If only I could have kept him. You know the only reason I had him was so I could keep him safe."

Silence shook his head, hard. He had no idea, really, what Ailys thought she was doing with Wat. He doubted Wat did.

"We're straying from the subject," she said, her voice hard. "I want Yann."

"No," said Silence again. "No trade."

As if he hadn't spoken, Ailys continued. "This is what I want. I want to get him out of his father's hands. Then I'm going to tell Gilles where he is."

"No doubt Gilles already knows that."

"No doubt about it. But I'm going to set him free as a sign of my loyalty to Gilles, and then he'll give me more of what I want from him."

"No, I won't help you betray that boy. You'll just make it easy for Gilles to grab him."

"The son of your enemy? You're worried about that? You surprise me, Master Rafe."

"I don't go around betraying people, the way some do."

"I suppose you mean Lyn." Ailys's eyes turned moody. "Caedon forced me to it."

"He wouldn't have been able to do that if you hadn't put yourself under his control."

"How do you know that?" Ailys demanded.

It was just a lucky guess, but if Ailys wasn't simply lying, Silence thought that must have been the way of it.

"I know Caedon really well," he reminded her. "Besides. What about Artur?"

She laughed. "Clever Rafe. You have me there. I betrayed him, and those nasty children of his. I admit it. Now I've given you something, Master Know-it-all. What will you give me in return?"

"That's just common knowledge, what you did to Artur and his family," Silence scoffed. *Keep her talking*, he thought. "You didn't give me a thing."

"But give me this," she wheedled. "Show me how to free Yann. Why should you hesitate? You want that boy freed too, it seems. Once he's free, let Yann keep away from Gilles if he can. I won't help Gilles grab him. Then I'll give you something in return. What can I give you, that you'd treasure?"

Make no bargain with a witch, Silence counseled himself. *She's just toying with you. In the end, anything she gives you will turn out to be a sham. Or a snare. Or both.* But the word burst out of him before he could stop it. "Diera."

CHAPTER TWENTY-SIX

A Throw of the Solids

A s everyone knows, the Children play at solids with the lives of the puny creatures crawling underneath the Spheres. Many object that such play is not justice. Followers of the Lady Goddess argue so. They use that argument as the basis of their apostasy. They themselves think followers of the Children are the apostates.

But those who study the will of the Children argue that the toss of the solids is the wisest type of justice, at least among the Four, for balance. What the Three think about it all? Now that is the mystery. Wise graybeards have many an argument about that, mostly unsatisfying, because none of them can agree on who the Three are, or whether They really even exist.

Silence felt that accepting Ailys's bargain was a throw of the solids. He thought of the jewel-like solids in Caedon's possession. Caedon knew about the solids.

When Ailys released Silence from his cell, his first emotion was one of vast relief. His second, deep anxiety about how he'd ever get to Diera. Feeling a bit foolish, he visited a sortileger in the marketplace.

Ailys had given him some coin, and now he handed a piece of silver to the shabby man, barefoot and dressed in a dirty robe. *This is a waste of good coin*, thought Silence. *I'm an addlepate.*

But he followed the man into the tent that served as his booth in the little market area just outside the castle.

"Come inside, good master. The stones never lie. I will cast them for you, and you will see," said the man, indicating a place on the ground for Silence to sit. Silence crouched down, and the man whipped out a white cloth and snapped it down onto the ground before Silence. From a velvet bag that had seen much use—moths had been at it, too—the man drew out four carved small stones. A cube. A strange pointy stone. A stone of many facets, eight, it seemed. And one more, that looked smoother and rounder.

The solids, Silence breathed to himself.

"Here," the sortileger said in an important voice, "We have the stone of the Earth Child, as stable as the earth." He picked up the little cube first and brought it close to Silence to let him see. "Hold it, good master, and think what answer you wish to your question."

Silence took it, held it, handed it back.

"And this," said the man, handing Silence the spiky little tetrahedron of the Fire Child. "It pricks the hand, does it not? As fire pricks the skin if you get too close. And this." The eight-faceted stone, which was of the Child of Sky. "The sky all around us, in its many aspects." The man waved his hands vaguely around. "Finally, this." He handed Silence the nearly round stone, and as Silence held it, he could feel it was not round at all, but slightly pebbled. He looked closer. No, there were just so many facets, so tiny. He counted twenty. "The multifarious sea," whispered the man. "Oh, yes." He cast up his eyes, as if the music of the Spheres played in his ears. "This is yours, good master. Your own Child," he whispered.

Well, thought Silence. *Anyone can see that, just by looking at me.*

He tried to still his skepticism as the man threw the little carved stones onto the white cloth.

"The Earth in captivity," the man squeezed his eyes shut, gabbling fast. "The Earth taken and held. The Sky over all, mysterious, no one knows where She is. The Fire. It burns. It will burn everything to ash. But here. The Sea. The Sea. That's the key, for you. The Sea."

He opened his eyes, as if coming out of a trance.

"That's it?" said Silence. "That's the message?" He made a disgusted noise and began rising to his feet.

The scrawny sortileger rose too. "The stones tell true," he insisted.

Silence realized there was little point in getting angry with the fellow. He himself had wanted the solids thrown for him, and now, when it turned out to be a load of claptrap and flitter-tripe, he could hardly take it out on the sortileger.

"Never mind," he said, and drew his cloak about him. He'd better be on his way. What was he thinking, wasting time so close to Caedon when he should be on the road and well away.

The sortileger trailed him out of the tent. "Good master. Good master," he moaned. "The stones tell true."

"Perhaps they do," said Silence, trying to look kindly on the man.

"Here." The sortileger pressed a small object into Silence's hand. "You are in danger. Take it. Take it. Maybe it will offer some protection." And he ducked back into his tent.

Silence looked down into his palm. It was the little solid associated with the Child of Sea. He closed his palm over it, and then he tucked it into his belt pouch.

What did balance demand of him, he wondered. Was there any justice in accepting Ailys's bargain? Yann got his freedom. Silence got his, and a map of Diera's location thrown in. Ailys needed his help finding and freeing Yann, and he gave it, always worrying that Ailys would use his information for some ill purpose.

As soon as he was well enough, she had disguised Silence as a tradesman and had taken him to the gates of the castle.

"My thanks," he told her stiffly, looking up at her. She used the ruse of going out of the castle on a pleasure ride, so she was mounted on a very pretty tall brown rouncey.

"You still aren't sure what I'll get out of our bargain, are you? Caedon is going to be furious to lose you both. That will be my first benefit. I'll find it highly entertaining. My second benefit will be far more serious. Gilles will reward me richly for getting Yann away from his father."

"He won't harm Yann, will he? Take Yann for himself?"

"I doubt that very much. Yann is much too old to benefit him now, as I'm sure you realize. But Gilles is in a pique over it. He wants to see Caedon punished. I'm not sure about the role Yann will play in this punishment Gilles has in mind. Gilles doesn't confide in his lowly handmaiden." Ailys batted her eyelashes. "And I don't care. I just care that he sees I've done his bidding."

"What about me?"

"I've given you the map. Whether you'll actually find Diera there, whether she's actually alive, I don't know and I have little interest in knowing. There it is. Make of it what you will."

Silence bowed and went out of the gate. He wouldn't stand there arguing and speculating. He'd get himself away before Ailys had a chance to think better of it. Or before Caedon realized and rushed to forestall her.

As soon as Silence could without looking shifty, he slipped away into the woods, and then he made his way quickly toward the coast.

As he walked, he patted the icosahedron of the Child of Sea, a pebble in his belt pouch along with Ailys's folded-up little map. From time to time, he took the map out and examined it. He knew of this town, a walled town at the very top of the Sceptered Isle, the northmost tip. Caedon had Diera imprisoned there.

"Much good my map will do you," Ailys had said lazily. "The place where Caedon holds Diera is well-nigh impregnable. The other walls are heavily fortified. The fortress in the town is built against the sea wall. I thought you'd drive a hard bargain, Master Rafe. Instead, you want this nearly useless information. But I hope it pleases you."

"My freedom is worth a lot to me."

"Yes, that," she said. "I suppose I see that. It's important to you, getting away from Caedon." She had looked down at him speculatively from her tall horse. "It must be very unpleasant, what he does to you, although if you'd just cooperate, I'm sure you'd get great benefit. Really, darling man, if you didn't struggle so, it wouldn't even be so unpleasant. However, that's none of my concern, and releasing you a mere trifle to accomplish, with myself handsomely paid off. Caedon will be quite displeased, and he won't be able to do a thing about it. I'm high in Gilles's good graces at present." Then she had turned her horse's head and had ridden away from him.

What mischief Ailys was about to make out of the bargain she had struck remained unclear to Silence. And she hadn't let him see Yann.

"That's not part of our agreement," she had said firmly. "With my gold and your information about the location of his cell, I'll easily find him and free him. Then I'll send him across the Narrows or maybe—I don't know. Somewhere. You don't need to know any of that. I need to act fast, not wait around for your tender feelings to be soothed. By the time Caedon realizes what I've done, the two parts of my plan will be already accomplished. He'll be angry and frustrated." She began to giggle, a high-pitched, ugly sound. "But he won't be able to do a thing about it. No point in running to close the stable door after the horse has bolted. That will put a spoke in his wheel, haha. As for you, you'd best get moving. Even if he tries to find you again, you're running out of time, aren't you? Snip, snip, snip, isn't that the way of it?" She mimed his life's chord snipped in two, and began to giggle again.

Now Silence walked through the woods, that giggle echoing in his ears. Ailys's coin would help him on his way, but it was certainly not enough to buy or even hire a horse. It would take him a long time, on foot, to get to the town where Caedon had put Diera. All of his efforts might come to nothing. Ailys was right, Dark Ones take her. He was running out of time.

His thoughts of Yann unsettled him, too. He agonized over whether his bargain with Ailys would help the lad or actually harm him. Maybe Gilles could find Yann more easily, now he'd been released into the world. Suppose Caedon was right, that he was protecting Yann by keeping him in that cell. But surely Gilles could find him there, even there, should he want to. If he demanded Caedon hand Yann over to him, Caedon would have to do it, and Yann would be conveniently to hand. This way, maybe Yann had a chance to get clean away. Silence didn't believe what Ailys had said, that Gilles wasn't interested in grabbing him and damaging him.

He wished he had had a chance to warn Yann. Surely Yann must have realized something had gone wrong when Silence didn't return, as promised, to help him escape. Silence had to hope that was warning enough.

Maybe, after all this was over, he could find Yann and help him.

But when he thought such things, Silence shook his head, driving them away. There would be no *after*. Once his task was accomplished, that would be the end.

His farwydd had confirmed it. Nine Spheres, Ailys had confirmed it. Snip, snip, snip.

As he walked, he began devising a plan. He realized he'd have to get to Wat.

A cast of the solids for sure, if he took the time to get to Wat. How much time did Diera have, herself, he wondered. He'd need to ask around. Plan from there.

With Wat, though, maybe there would be a chance to get Diera away from Caedon. Without Wat, none.

Or, he thought, although he didn't want to. *Or just get to her, whether I get her out or not.*

He took the little stone, the solid of the Sea Child, from his belt pouch and began tossing it in the air and catching it as he strode down the forest path.

He stumbled on a root protruding into the path and went down hard. The stone went flying. He lay sprawled in the dirt, cursing himself. Then he wasted many minutes searching for the little object. When at last he found it, he put it back in the pouch and swore he'd not let it out of his grasp again.

After all his skepticism, he couldn't help feeling that nearly losing the stone was an ominous sign. He couldn't stop a chill settling on him as he walked.

Twilight was coming on. He looked up into the sky where he could just begin to glimpse the first stars starting to shine as they hung glittering from their golden chains.

The four solids, Earth, Fire, Sky, Sea. But people who knew about such things speculated maybe there was a fifth. The dodecahedron, the twelve-sided stone. The Old Ones claimed this solid was responsible for the arrangement of the stars in their constellations against the inside of the Spheres. Somehow, they claimed, that arrangement held the Spheres up. Silence craned his neck to peer at the stars as he walked. The balance underneath the Spheres, the stars arching over it.

He thought of the symbols members of The Rising carved on the lintels of their doors as a signal to others: the harbingers of the four Children—blackbird, fisher bird, firebird, ghost bird. And then, always, these panels had a band of stars.

Suppose, as the graybeards speculated, the stars were the abode of the mysterious Three, Their higher justice arching over the balance of the Children.

It was too much for Silence. It made his head begin to ache again. Instead, he started to plan. Practical things, not the matter of the stars.

How many men could Wat bring, if they mounted an assault on the town where Caedon held Diera? How many men were still scattered around the realm and would rally to Wat, if he came? The town could easily withstand a siege. What would it take to lure Caedon and his men out from behind those walls? Silence turned his mind to matters like that. And he concentrated on getting as fast as he could to Sir Hugyn Crom, who would give him a ship.

CHAPTER TWENTY-SEVEN

Not only merely dead

On the shingle below the sea cliffs where the walled town perched, Silence waited for Wat's snake-ships, and his big knarr, to angle in and make anchor.

One last throw of the solids. One last chance to assemble an army of The Rising.

As Wat's men began straggling ashore, Silence thought in despair about the assembled men up the hill behind him. It wouldn't be enough.

Now a small boat separated itself from the knarr.

Shading his eyes, Silence could see Wat and Kipp in the prow. He rushed into the surf to help them to shore. He knew Kipp would be shaking with fright.

"There," he said to the two of them. "Dry land."

"Thank the Child," said Kipp fervently. Then the three of them embraced.

"How is it with you, brother?" said Silence to Wat. Wat was looking strong and hale.

"Fine. I'm thinking we're going to lose," he said bluntly.

"I'm thinking you're right."

"Should we even try it?" said Kipp, at Wat's shoulder. He steadied Wat across the stony beach. They began to toil upward toward the little camp where the assembled men waited.

"Yes," said Wat.

"Are you remembering that day, brother," said Silence, low.

"Yes," said Wat. "There was no way to succeed, that day. But Avery had to try it. One chance to get Diera out. And we did it."

"At terrible cost," said Silence.

"Yes. You of all of us know how terrible. But now we must try again. And Caedon is there, behind those walls. He arrived a sen'night ago, so our scouts have told me."

By now they were at the top of the cliffs, and Kipp helped guide Wat into the tent set up for him.

Silence followed.

"How many men do we have?" said Wat.

"Not enough. When you've rested, come out to greet them."

When Wat did, the soldiers of The Rising thronged about him, clashing their swords against their shields and yelling out savagely, their eyes shining.

"Are you with me?" Wat called out.

Silence always marveled at this. Wat was a quiet man. But in circumstances like this one, something else caught him up.

"We're with you!" the men shouted.

"Shall we get our queen out of Caedon's filthy hands?"

"Diera. . .Diera. . . Diera. . ." the men chanted.

Silence, Wat, and Kipp withdrew to Wat's tent to arm themselves. Wat had brought a chest full of magnificent armor.

"My pirates lifted this from some of Hakkon's ships," Wat said with a grin.

They all put on conical steel helmets, chainmail hauberks, steel greaves and gauntlets. Silence had mourned the loss of his sword with the martlet on the pommel, Caedon's gift. But he found a sword as fine in the chest, and a good round shield bound with iron.

Besides, carrying Caedon's sword into battle against him felt like a curse.

I'm becoming a superstitious old crone, thought Silence, discovering that he was fingering the little icosahedron, the stone of the Sea Child.

The object that gave him the most comfort, though, was his martlet amulet. It had stayed with him through everything. Even Caedon, doing his worst on Silence, had not taken it from him.

Kipp had his axe at his belt, and his pike. Someone at the flap of Wat's tent motioned to Kipp, and he stepped outside. When he came back in, he was holding two soldiers by the elbows, quick-marching them toward Silence. Kipp thrust the two at Silence. "General," he said.

Silence had to suppress a grin. *General!*

"Here are two who have somat to say to you."

"My lord," said one of the men, and knelt to Silence. After a moment, so did the other one.

Silence stood looking puzzled from one to the other. Then he recognized them. "Nev," he said. "Elstan."

The two looked aside at each other and hung their heads. "Lord," said Nev. "We didn't realize. We are to blame."

Silence groaned inwardly. If only they'd believed him. If only they'd been able to get Diera away from Caedon when he came for her after someone in her very household betrayed her to him. But that was all over now.

Silence stared down at the trembling men, looking up fearfully at him from under their brows. Thinking of the day he'd evaded them by making an impossible dive from an impossible height, he saw they were frightened by more than his status as a leader of the army. *What is this thing?* He could practically see them thinking it. *Is it a man? What will it do to us?*

"We beg forgiveness," said the one named Elstan, holding up his hands. "We didn't know."

"Noted," Silence said to them. "Get them out of here, Kipp."

Kipp hauled them up by the backs to their tunics and near-threw them out of the tent. He looked back at Silence, frowning.

"They couldn't have known, Kipp," said Silence. "Now they're here to fight. Let them. We need every man."

He turned back to his preparations. All of three of them—Silence, Wat, Kipp—had their spears—both angon for throwing and lugged spears for close-in work.

Armed now, the three of them went back to the assembled force.

"Men," Wat shouted out. "We get out there, we form up our battle line. But when they charge us, we set up our shield wall and use our pikes from behind it."

He threaded his way through the groups of soldiers to the men hauling the spears on carts, Kipp guiding him by an elbow. "Take these carts into the middle of the shield wall. Whenever one of us needs a new angon or one of the lugged spears, we'll drop back to pick one up. You men stand ready to supply them."

Now they all made their way to the town gates. The gates were shut tight against them.

"They know we're out here. They've heard we were coming," Silence said to Wat. "I'm going to walk out there and challenge them. The only way we have a chance is if we can lure Caedon's forces outside the town. There's no way we can wait them out in a siege. Walk with me, brother. You too, Kipp."

The three of them detached themselves from their battle line. They moved to the gates and stopped just beyond bowshot.

Kipp looked worried. "They can't reach us here with those bows of theirs? I heard Caedon has some kind of strange witch-bows."

"No, they can't," said Wat, after he made Kipp describe the terrain to him. "A really good shot could. Maybe I could have," he murmured.

Silence nudged him. "Boasting," he said.

Wat grinned sidelong at him.

"Do you want to shout our challenge?" said Silence.

"You do it. That's your wife in there."

Kipp looked over at Silence, startled.

Silence stepped forward a pace. "Caedon," he shouted. "You horse pricker. Come out from behind your walls. You sneaking usurper dog. You mere fellow."

A quiet settled over the field.

"He's not going to answer. They won't come out," said Kipp.

Silence had a moment of insight. "He will. This touches his pride. Wat and I, we've both thwarted him. He's done his worst to us, and here we are, outside his very gates."

They'd decided amongst themselves that Wat would stand with Silence now, for the challenge.

"I hope Caedon is looking out from one of those towers. I hope he spots me here," said Wat, in a near-snarl.

Once the battle began, "Assuming it does," said Silence, Kipp would lead Wat back within the protection of the shield wall by the carts of spears. Wat would direct the battle from there while Kipp fed him information and took it to Silence and the others.

"Listen, Wat," said Silence to him privately. "When Kipp tells you that you have to get out, you have to do it. Agreed? Don't stand there and be a martyr. You need to get back to the isle, if things go bad." *When they do,* Silence said to himself grimly. "If you're taken, Caedon won't play cat and mouse with you. He'll kill you outright, and The Rising can't afford that."

"What about you, brother." Wat's voice was quiet.

"If he takes me, then that's what has to happen. That's what has been decreed. You must not trouble yourself, if that happens."

"Word from your sarding Child, I suppose," Wat muttered.

"Think of it that way, if you must," said Silence. "It's something I have to do. I was brought back from that river to do it. Two tasks."

"One of them being me."

"Right."

"The other being Deira."

"Right."

"Diera," said Wat, and Silence had to remind himself that Diera was not only his own wife, but Wat's closest childhood friend and kinswoman. "Caedon is going to kill her, isn't he?"

"Unless we're very lucky, yes, he is. But I'll be there with her."

"Crazy talk, Rafe."

"It's the thing I have to do," said Silence, and Wat had to be content with that.

Now they stood underneath the sun beating them like a gong of bronze, and they waited for Caedon's answer.

The gates began to creak open. Caedon's men came pouring out. *Thank the Child the ground is too broken for mounted troops,* thought Silence.

"There's our answer," said Wat, listening.

Wat, Silence, and Kipp got back to their battle line, and Kipp took Wat behind the line to the spear carts, where the shield wall would enfold him and he could think about tactics.

Silence drew his sword and lifted it high.

As Caedon's men came pounding closer, he waited. He waited.

Then he brought his sword down in a decisive shearing, unleashing their forces.

He sheathed his sword, grabbing up his spear. A half-grown boy hovered beside him with extras.

The soldiers around him surged forward with ululating cries.

Silence's first cast of his angon missed its man, passing over the fellow's left shoulder. The boy tossed Silence another. He struck the onrushing man in the middle of the chest. The man fell with a thud, his arms and shield crashing about him.

Silence took a lugged spear from the boy and rushed on an opponent who had turned toward one of the Rising's men. Silence thrust it between the opponent's shoulder blades. With a grunt, he drove it straight through and out the chest, leaving the man to gush out his life into the dirt.

"Here, lord," said the boy, lobbing another of the angons at him. The boy turned to go back to the carts for more.

Silence stalked the field, lunging and jabbing at this man of Caedon's, and that. He saw his chance and tossed the angon at a running man, piercing him through the right shoulder and bringing him down. Another of The Rising finished him off.

Silence looked around for the boy and didn't see him. He drew his sword and chased down another of Caedon's men. He thrust through the man's right buttock and into the bladder under the bone. The man dropped screaming to his knees. Silence braced his foot against the downed man, heaving the sword out of the meat of him, kicked him over, and drove the point of his blade into the man's throat, ending him.

Someone came running at him, yelling, but Kipp appeared beside him, swinging berserk with his axe and taking the man out. With his pike, Silence ran another through the back of the neck, straight through past teeth and tongue. The man went down. The time of the battle went by in a haze of blood, the roar of screaming men, the stench of death.

"Kipp," Silence gasped. "Wat—"

"Draw back, lord," shouted Kipp into his ear. "Behind the shield wall."

They fought together back to the shield wall, where Kipp took up his position beside Wat again, and the boy stepped again to Silence's side with more spears.

We're losing, thought Silence. *We're fighting well, but we are too few, and we're losing.*

Through the long morning they fought from the protection of the shield wall. But at last Silence dropped back to where Kipp stood with Wat.

"It's time, Wat," he spoke into Wat's ear over the din.

"Brother," said Wat.

"It's time," Silence insisted. He embraced Wat.

They stood together for a long moment, holding onto each other.

"I'm not leaving you here," said Wat.

"You have to. You have to lead The Rising. And Wat—Mirin is out there somewhere. Your child is out there. They're not dead. You have to find them. You can't abandon them."

"I can't abandon you, Rafe."

"Wat. You're not abandoning me."

Wat just stood there stubbornly. "I'm not leaving you here to die. I'm not doing it. Do you realize this is the second time we've had this exact same exchange, me refusing to leave you to die, and you insisting I must?"

"It's a good thing I don't remember a lot of things, Wat," said Rafe, "because I don't remember that."

"It was after we'd buried Johnny."

Rafe pulled Wat close. "Listen, Wat," he whispered in his ear. "You're not leaving me here to die. I'm already dead."

He turned to Kipp. "Help him, Kipp. Some of you, go with Wat back to the ships. Save the ships," he called out, his voice ragged and hoarse. "Get to the isle. We others will hold them off."

"My lord," said Kipp, reaching out his hand to Silence.

Silence could see Kipp's heart was full. Silence took his hand and gripped it. "Child go with you," he said. "My good friend. You'll be with Wat. Already he loves you like a brother." They exchanged a profound look. "My friend," Silence said again. "My brother." He turned away, before he could choke up, and went on a run back to the fight, before the line could be overwhelmed.

Silence and a few of the rest fought bitterly, desperately, covering the retreat of Wat, Kipp, and the others back to the ships.

One by one, the little knot of men behind the shields were beaten down. They fought on.

Silence had been wounded, he wasn't sure where, but blood was dripping from some scalp wound into his eyes, and he tossed his helmet aside. He kept shaking his head, trying to clear his vision.

"That one," he heard someone just beside him. "The king wants that one alive."

And he was taken.

The men of Caedon marched him to the gates. Behind him, he heard his fellows being butchered.

I should be with them, Silence thought miserably.

What about your task, something inside him taunted.

To the Dark Ones with my task, he thought desperately, trying to wrest himself from the hands of those who held him, trying to force them to finish him.

Instead, one of them clubbed him on the head, and then they dragged him the rest of the way into the town.

He stood sagging between two of them as Caedon himself came striding up to them.

"Chain him up in one of the cells," said Caedon. He didn't address Silence. He didn't look at Silence.

Silence shook his head to clear it. "Afraid to look at me?" he said to Caedon. "Afraid I'll outwit you again?"

Caedon didn't rise to his bait. He walked off to the other side of the town's main square and stood talking to some of his officers. The men holding Silence hustled him away.

As Silence lay bleeding in the straw of his cell, he wondered. How in the Nine was this supposed to be fulfilling his task? Caedon would execute Diera, and he'd be down here, chained like an animal.

Well, he thought. *I did try.* The farwydd thought that might be enough, or so it seemed to him.

But I wanted to see her. I wanted to be with her, he cried out to his Child.

A voice was whispering, and Silence thought he was probably hearing things. He knew Caedon would execute him, as soon as he got around to it.

But the bleeding was copious. Maybe Caedon wouldn't get around to it soon enough. Maybe, Silence thought, he was fading from this life. Maybe he was hearing the whispers of those across that river.

"Rafe," the voice whispered. "Can you stand up? Try it, man."

"I'm chained to the wall," he whispered back.

"Wait right there."

As if I could do anything else, thought Silence. The whispering stopped. *Good. I can die in peace*, he thought.

But no. There came a grating, creaking sound. A sound of a lock being turned, a bar being withdrawn.

"Rafe. It's me."

"Yann?" said Silence, prying his eyes open with an effort. Dried blood had stuck one of them shut. "Dark Ones take you. You were supposed to get out of that castle and out of the realm."

"Instead, I tracked you here."

"And how did you get in here, after I made a bargain with a witch to get you away from your father? Let me guess. Once you were out, you got yourself back in. You turned yourself in to your father."

"The repentant son," said Yann, busy with Silence's chains. "There we go," he said at last. "Tricky locks." He hoisted Silence to his feet.

Yann handed him a leathern flask, and Silence downed it. Strong drink.

Silence felt revived. He wasn't about to move across the river, not yet. He was going to stay among the living, at least for a little while.

"How's the head?" said Yann.

"I think that knock on the head just stunned me. I think I'm fine."

Yann was busy about him, mopping up the blood and tying a bandage around his arm. "Nothing mortal," he said. "This is just a scratch. The scalp wound was doing all the bleeding, and it's nothing much. That's a good thing. I got myself in here to get you out."

"All for nothing, lad. I'm in here for a reason, although it looks like that is going to be thwarted. I need to get to Diera. I have to try. I doubt I'll be coming back out."

"Not all for nothing. Don't speak ill of my mother."

Silence and Yann stood smiling at each other. "Help me get to her. Then you get yourself out of here. I want you to promise me." At Yann's stubborn look, Silence said, "You don't understand. I'm a dead man, come back to do this one thing."

When Yann's eyes widened, Silence sighed. It seemed he'd had to go around from friend to friend, all day, trying to convince them of something the evidence of their own eyes denied.

As for Yann, the lad was turning from stubborn to skeptical to placating, the way you 'd look at a man run mad.

"No, really, Yann. Look here. See that scar? It's where Caedon's witch sliced me open to pack me with spices so my corpse wouldn't rot."

"I see," said Yann carefully.

Child take him, thought Silence. *He thinks I'm crazy*. "Yann. Don't you have your own task to do? Don't you have Elene to find?"

Yann nodded at last.

"So show me where they're keeping Diera. I'll do the rest. Then you get well away. Promise me."

"They're executing her in the morning," said Yann. "No one can get to her."

"I probably can't save her, but I'm going to try. Tell me where they're holding her."

"A guarded room. Door barred and guarded always."

"Are there windows into this room?"

"One, on the side that drops off to the sea."

Silence put his hand to his belt pouch, where the hard pebble of his stone lay under his hand. *The Sea. The Sea*, the sortileger had muttered.

"Yes. Perfect."

"Are you mad?"

"No. It just seems that way. Can you get me outside the walls?"

"Yes," said Yann eagerly. "That's what I came to do. Here," he said. "Here's the armor they took from you, when they threw you in the cell. Now I'm getting you out."

"Yann. Once you do that, I'm going back in."

"No."

"Yes. Help me, Yann. My Child commands me to do this. Thanks for the armor, but I don't need it. All I need is some rope."

CHAPTER TWENTY-EIGHT

A Tower

Silence had convinced Yann to leave the armor behind, although not his pack. He knew exactly what he needed to do.

He needed to be light, as light as possible. He'd hacked his trousers off at the knee with his knife. He had pulled on soft, close-fitting leather shoes from his pack. He had wrapped his hands in supple leather strips, as well, and he had tied his hair back off his face with a leather band. He didn't have his sword belted about him. It was too heavy. He left it with Yann, and all the rest of the armor. He didn't need it where he was going.

But he did have the knife, strapped to his leg, and over his left shoulder, he had coiled the length of stout rope Yann had found for him.

"This is probably goodbye, lad," he told Yann. They embraced.

"I pray to my Child, whoever She may be, that it's not."

Silence gave him a brief smile. It wasn't enough. He wanted to reach out to Yann, comfort him. But time was short, and he couldn't afford a close connection, grief over leaving a friend. It would draw him back to the world he felt himself leaving. It had been the same with Wat and Kipp. There was no time.

Reluctantly, Yann returned to the overhang of the trade gate of the city, where merchants came and went. He stood in the shadow of the gate, watching.

Silence lifted his hand in farewell.

Carefully now, he picked his way around to the far side of the town's wall, over the slippery rocks always dashed with spray from the sea. Along the way, he slipped out of his tunic and discarded it. His feet through the flexible leather gripped the stones. He balanced himself and tried to stay as closely pressed against the wall of the town as he could. Someone would have to be looking straight down from its windows to see him.

Every so often, he checked Ailys's map, and the hand-drawn map Yann had given him, both tucked into the waistband of his trousers.

After about a candle-measure of careful work, he came to the curve of a tower bulging out a little from the wall. He peered upward at a single narrow window. If the maps were accurate, that's where Caedon was keeping Diera.

Silence examined the big crumbling blocks of stone that constituted the mural tower embedded in the city wall. The massive stones at the base were striated with cracks where they fit together and where weathering had roughened and split some of the blocks.

The wall only looked to be vertical. It actually leaned slightly in from base to top. It was a formidable wall for defense, strong, built on a sheer cliff with the sea at its foot. As climbing challenges went, though, the wall was only a moderate one.

His boyhood expeditions to the mountains outside Gilles's estate had more than prepared him for a challenge like this one. And then, ironically at Caedon's directive, he had rediscovered the deeply embedded skill necessary to take it on.

Even more important, climbing the cliff in the Baronies had led him to the wellspring of his inmost self. That, no physical thing, was the resource he needed most for the work of this day.

Silence put his hand to his amulet. He touched it for courage—courage for what he'd discover at the top, not courage for the climb.

As he began to wedge his feet into the cracks of the big stones, lean his hips against the wall, reach out for handholds and places to wedge his hands, he saw, once more, how much his body remembered. How much his body joyed in the pull of muscle and sinew. The wound he'd gotten when he was captured bothered him hardly at all.

He worked very carefully. He didn't look down to the rocks and the sea below. He began to move up the wall, always upward.

Several times he found larger cracks where he could wedge himself and rest. After a few candle-measures of climbing, his head had come almost level with the sill of the narrow window, the window of the room the map designated as the place where Caedon was holding Diera.

He'd have to hurry. Daylight was waning.

He braced himself against the wall, drawing his breath hard, and tried to still himself enough to listen.

He heard voices.

He couldn't tell what they were saying. A man's and a woman's. They sounded like they were at the other end of the room, away from the window.

It was a risk, but with a final effort, he heaved himself to the rock ledge of the window, flattening himself back into the embrasure as much as he could.

Thank the Children. A thick cloth covering hung down over the window's opening, and he was concealed in its folds. Earlier he had noticed a kind of flapping and flickering at the window, and had hoped such a cloth would be there, but he hadn't been sure.

He crouched on the window ledge against the wall of the embrasure and hid behind the cloth.

Now he could hear better.

"Make yourself ready, lady," the man was saying.

Dark Ones take him, it's Caedon. Silence stifled the urge to leap from concealment and throttle the man.

He couldn't know if others were just outside. Surely they were. Surely there were guards. A rash move like leaping into the room could endanger Diera and any chance he might have to get her out.

For the woman's voice was Diera's.

His heart thumped in his chest, hearing it. He hadn't heard her voice for years, except in dreams, but when he heard it now, it arrowed straight to the core of him. It was hers. He remembered.

She made some quiet rejoinder.

"You'll be punished as the law decrees," Caedon was telling her. "You should spend the night in prayer to whatever gods you worship. At dawn, you'll die. See there. The game board tells the tale. Every night, I defeat you. This is the last night."

Silence listened. A door opened and closed. He heard the sound of a bar grating into its bracket.

Diera hadn't said a word after the indistinct reply she had made to Caedon.

He heard the slight movements she made beyond the curtain.

Now, he thought. *How do I get to her without frightening her? How do I keep her from crying out.*

He had to take the risk.

With one smooth movement, he rolled out of the window embrasure, leapt to her, clamped a hand over her mouth, and took her to the bed.

"Diera," he whispered in her ear. "Don't be afraid. It's Rafe."

She had struggled wildly, when he grabbed her. Now she lay still in his arms.

"I'm dreaming," she whispered. "You're dead."

"Maybe I am," he whispered back, "but I'm really here, and you're not dreaming."

She twisted around to face him. They lay on her bed face to face. He put out his hand and stroked her cheek. He was too moved to speak.

"Maybe they've already killed me, and I haven't realized it yet, and you've been sent here from the Land of the Dead to guide me over," she said.

Not far wrong, he thought.

"I'm here. My body is here in your arms, and your body is in mine. My love for you is near to choking me, Diera."

"You climbed in the window?" she said now. "But how? There's a sheer drop to the sea."

"I learned climbing as a boy. No one can keep me away from you."

"They'll kill me in the morning."

"I know, but maybe I can get you out."

She was shaking her head slowly. "I can't go up and down walls the way you do. The door is barred and guarded."

"I have a plan," he said. "It may not work."

"Shh," she said, and kissed him.

He kissed her deeply back. Staying quiet so no one outside in the corridor would hear, they explored each other urgently with their hands, their tongues, their lips.

They slipped out of their clothing and lay skin to skin. He tasted her and kissed her all over. Her back arched, and she moaned a little as he buried himself inside her and thrust desperately deeper. She entwined her legs about him to pull him deeper still.

Spent, they lay quietly together, stroking each other and murmuring words of love to each other.

A shaft of moonlight illuminated their bodies as it came into the room past a gap in the cloth hanging at the window.

She slipped from the bed to pull it wide, and came back to him. "I need to see you. I need to drink you in with my eyes. To make sure you're real."

"You can see for yourself. This is a body. A much older body than when you saw it last."

"And so is mine," she said with a smile, reaching out a loving hand to him.

In a while they embraced each other passionately again, more gently this time. More tenderly, with less panicked insistence.

They lay quiet. She traced the line of his scar down his torso. "What did they do to you, my darling?"

"Terrible things," he said, "but it will all come right. My Child has promised it. You'll see."

She kept running her fingers along the line of his scar. "And this," she said, catching at the little amulet on its thong about his neck. The martlet, the wanderer.

"And this." He folded her hands around it and folded his own hands around hers. He brought her hands to his lips and kissed them. *My wandering has neared its end*, he thought.

Then they slept a little in each other's arms.

As the moon was going down, Silence roused her. "We need to try my plan. We can't let dawn catch us."

He drew her to the window ledge. They stood together looking far down to the sea breaking in high waves against the fortified wall.

"I'm going out there onto the ledge. I'm going to swing out and climb the rest of the way to the top of this tower. Then—" he pointed to the coil of rope he'd dropped by the bed. "I'll lower a loop of this rope. Fasten it about yourself and push out of the window. Once you feel stable, lean back against the rope, hold onto it with both hands, ease your way off the ledge and brace your feet against the wall. I'll pull you up slowly. Just walk up the wall."

Her eyes had gotten wider and wider in the telling.

"Can you do it?"

"I'll fall," she breathed. Then she smiled a little. "If I fall, I'll die. But in only a few candle measures, I'm to be killed anyway. I'll try it."

"Listen, my dearest wife. My brave wife. I need to tell you something first."

"What is it."

"Remember your baby."

"My baby. He died." A shadow of sorrow passed across her face.

"He didn't die. Caedon lied to you. Your son has become a fine young man. His name is Yann."

Diera gasped and cried out.

Silence put his finger to her lip. They stood still, listening. There was no sound from outside the room.

"The guards will just think I'm frightened by thoughts of to-morrow," she whispered to Silence, when she could talk again.

"Now you see how much reason you have to try to live, Diera," he murmured to her. "I love you. You'll always have that. But if I'm not here with you, you'll have your son by your side."

"Why won't you be here with me, Rafe? I don't want your plan to work, if I can't have that."

"You must have courage. You must go on, if it comes to that."

"What will we do, when you draw me up on top of the tower?" she said.

What will we do indeed, he thought in despair. Maybe he could get her up there without dropping her. Maybe she could do it without panicking and falling. Maybe, once they were up there, they could find a safe way down and get away. But all of it was, he knew, completely unlikely.

"Rafe," she whispered. "You too have a son."

He stared at her in shock.

"The day you died, I knew it. No one had told you, I don't think. Remember Bertrys, my maid? Remember the girl Caedon made you—"

"Diera. There are things I don't remember. That blow to the head drove my memory out of it entirely. Your face. Your voice. They were the first to come back to me, when I began to remember. This woman you speak of. I don't remember her at all."

"She's the mother of your child, Rafe."

Silence saw how hard it was for her to say such words to him.

Now, in a rush, he recalled the time Caedon had sent him off to collect a boy for Gilles. He recalled Caedon's malicious tone, the strange malicious gleam in his eye. *Here's your task. Gilles and I will see if you perform it. It's a test, Rafe.*

That boy. The realization descended on him with the force of a blow. That was his son.

He recalled the terrible shriek of the boy's mother, when she caught sight of him, and suddenly he realized what it meant. There was no terror for her son. There was terror in her recognition. There he was at her doorstep, a dead man.

Silence felt himself fill with rage against her, against Caedon. A test of his memory, to see if he recalled this woman, this Bertrys. And a twisted little game Caedon was playing with him. *Bring Gilles a boy, so that he may toy with him and torment him and kill him. Gilles, a malevolent cat lying in wait for some soft quivering prey to stalk. Bring me your own boy. This will show that you truly do belong to Gilles. That you truly are his creature.*

He recalled the little boy. Gwyl. That was his name. A fine boy. Now rage gave way to love. Silence realized he didn't have time for the rage. He made room instead for the uprush of love he felt for this small boy he had saved. His son.

"I'm glad you don't remember Bertrys," Diera was murmuring. "What Caedon made you do was shameful. The day you drove me out of Treddian's castle, the day Avery and the others of The Rising—and you, Rafe—rescued me from Caedon's plans, and died for it, as I waited to get into the cart, Bertrys came to me and whispered her news in my ear. I can still see her triumphant smile. *Lady, I'm with child.* Later, I can't remember how or when, someone told me Bertrys had had a son. I always meant to find him. I never could." She stared into Rafe's eyes. "But you don't remember any of that."

Silence turned away from her uneasily.

"Rafe. I watched you die. I watched the light leave your eyes."

Silence nodded.

"So I'm dreaming. This is a vivid dream. Or I'm dead myself."

"No," he said. "Gilles de Rais, and Caedon his minion, and their witches got to me, and they stopped my journey."

"Your journey?"

"In a way, I am dead. I am," he insisted. "In a way, I'm not. I'm betwixt and between, Diera."

"I don't understand this." She got out of bed and pulled the nightrobe around her, shivering. "You're a ghost."

"Not exactly." He got up too then and began pulling on his hacked off trousers.

She looked at him sidelong. As their glances met, it rekindled all his desire for her.

"Not exactly," she whispered to him, and he saw an answering desire kindle in her own eyes.

She smiled and shrugged away from him. "No time," she said. She was drifting about the room as if she were already a ghost herself, her skin almost translucent in the moonlight. "Look," she said to Silence.

He looked where she pointed, to a small table. On it was a game board, the game Caedon loved so much.

In the puddle of moonlight from the window, the game board's squares gleamed black and green. One game piece, the queen, was on the board, and the queen was knocked over.

"You see I lost last night," she whispered, pointing to the fallen queen. "There's the sign of my submission to my victor."

"He plays his game with you? He always made me tip over my king. I think that's the thing you're supposed to do."

"He taught me, and every night he plays a game with me, and every night, he defeats me. And he taught me to do this." She fingered the little queen and smiled a little.

"Diera. Suppose we're all on a game board, a vast one, and the table is tilted so that all the pieces, sooner or later, get swept into the dark. Suppose there's no way to win, not on this board.

Suppose winning this game takes unnatural strength, and unnatural cunning, too. Suppose winning is not this definite thing, the queen cornered and fallen, or the king, or whatever game piece the victor demands. Suppose winning is a sliding point along a line that stretches from good to evil, and nobody knows where that point resides and so nobody ever knows if they've won or lost. But suppose this is not the only board. Not the only game."

Silence stepped to the board and picked up the little queen piece. He brought it to his lips and kissed it.

"We're wasting time. It's nearly dawn. Let's try your plan," she said. "I'll summon all my courage, and we'll try it."

Before they could, they heard tramping feet outside in the corridor, and voices.

"Too late," Diera cried. "Rafe, you must go." She pushed him toward the window.

The bar grated. The door burst open.

Caedon swept in at the head of a contingent of torch-bearing guards.

Diera stood in the center of the room, her nightrobe pulled around her, facing him with contempt.

Silence backed quietly to the window.

"Go," she said over her shoulder to Rafe.

"I don't think that will be the way of it, lady," said Caedon, motioning to one of his men, who strode to Silence.

Silence stepped up into the deep embrasure of the window before the man could lay hands on him.

"I'm taking you to your execution now, lady. You think I'd wait until dawn, once I knew this varlet had slipped out of my prison?" Caedon looked over coldly at Silence. "And you, Rafe. I'll make you watch, and then I'll see you hanged. Whatever botched job they did on you before, that day you should have died, I'll finish it."

Two of his men seized Diera. She struggled briefly, but then she stopped and stood quiet. The man coming at Silence paused and looked to Caedon for instruction.

"I know how you got yourself up the wall, Rafe. But don't think you'll be able to get back down. Don't worry," Caedon said to his men. "He won't jump. If he tries to climb down, shoot him." One of the guards unslung his bow and nocked it. "You think you're so clever. Either way will mean death," said Caedon to Rafe with a sneer.

"So why should I wait for you to mete it out, Caedon?" said Silence. "You, who tried to manipulate me into destroying my own son. And what about your son. He sees you for who you are. What will you do about that, Caedon? There's a trap you won't be able to weasel out of. You, who are trying to destroy the woman I love because you're incapable of love. You, who tried to destroy a son of mine, thinking it would be a good joke on me. You have to kill what you can't have, isn't that the way of it, Caedon?"

A look passed between them. Hatred. But something else. Silence had seen it before. He could never name it. Caedon motioned to his guard to step back.

Now he's going to do something to Diera that he thinks will force me to get down off the ledge and let him take me, thought Silence. *That's his next move in the game he thinks he's playing. But that's not the game, and that's not how this will go.*

Caedon raised his hand. "Listen, Diera."

Everyone in the room, Rafe included, stopped to listen. There was a distant murmur.

"People are gathering outside." Caedon smiled grimly at Diera, a smile that didn't reach his eyes. "They're waiting for dawn. The headsman is already there, Diera, and all the people in the city have assembled in the square below this tower to watch."

Caedon turned his eyes on Silence. "You had better do as I say." His voice was quiet, in command.

"Diera." Silence spoke to her past Caedon. "Look at me, dear one."

She turned in her captors' grasp to lock eyes with him.

"I'm going. I'm getting to that shore before you. Don't be afraid. I'll be waiting to guide you. Do you understand what I'm saying?"

She nodded at him mutely, her eyes wide.

"Foolish brother of mine," Caedon snarled at him. He'd lost his composure. "You think I'd have you killed? Gilles wants you. Get down off that ledge."

"Oh, this is all a bluff, is it? You're not my brother. You never have been. And you're the fool, if you think I don't know what you and that witch-woman did to me. If you think I don't understand what condition Gilles wants me in, when you take me to him."

Dawn was just beginning to tint the underside of the Spheres with rose and gold.

Silence looked over his shoulder to the sea. If he leaped far out from the wall, could he arrow down into the sea, the way he had to the lake? If the dive killed him, he'd get to that shore all the sooner.

He cast one backward glance at Diera, to lock her image inside him. He swiveled, rose to his toes.

Behind him, he heard Caedon keen out his name in a cry of anguish and sorrow.

He sprang powerfully up and dove out in a high arc from the window as Caedon's men exclaimed behind him.

As he entered the sea, the jolt was so massive he was sure it must have ended him. A thought rushed at him. The fall had killed him; he just didn't know it yet. But he found himself drifting, then pumping to the surface.

He struck out. He was floundering weakly. He gained strength and began to swim. He didn't look behind him. He struck out across the sea.

He swam for maybe a candle measure, maybe not that long before he felt himself chill and tire. He thought he'd probably sustained serious injuries, in the dive from such a height, and the chill of the sea was keeping the pain from him. But it didn't matter.

I need to get there before her, he thought. *I need to help her across.*

The drag on him was too much, irresistible. He slowed and the waves pulled him under. His hair floated free from its band. *Child knows I have tried*, he thought. His clenched hand opened, and the game piece, the queen, fell from it end over end into unfathomable depths. He felt in his waistband for the little solid of the Sea, brought it to his lips, kissed it, and let it drop as well. He skinned his trousers from him, kicked the soft leather shoes off and away. Let the leather strips binding his hands unwind and drift off from him.

Only the amulet about his neck. Only that he'd keep to the end.

Powerful currents began to tug at him. *I've lost*, he thought. He let the currents take him. His lungs burned. He couldn't hold his breath in any longer, so he let it all out in a long string of bubbles.

Briefly he struggled.

He felt himself numbing, growing peaceful, letting go. *Sea Child*, he thought. *I am yours now. It has taken me a while to get to you, but now I'm here.*

The cord with the little amulet of the martlet floated free of him. Floated away.

Maybe a moment.

Maybe an age.

He was breasting the waves, no longer dwindling down into green depths with their bursting pressure. He felt the bright sands of that shore slant upward under his feet ahead of him.

I haven't lost, he thought. *I've won.*

He turned, because all along, someone had been swimming, powerful and brave, just there beside him. He flung out his arm and gathered her to him. They stumbled ashore, helping each other. Laughing, dripping with water weeds, they struggled together out of the sea and onto the shore of that far land.

READER, Before you go!

The sweep of the nine novels in the Stormclouds/Harbingers series, and the two companion novels (Betwixt & Between) starts with the sighting of the comet of 976 CE, recorded in the British Isles. Except for that one reference, we know almost nothing about this hyperbolic comet, known as x976, but it did show up, and you can read about it in the historical record.

The events of the nine novels progress from the appearance of x976 to the famous sighting of Halley's Comet in 1066 CE. Halley's, one of the most-studied comets in human history, seemed to the people of the British Isles in 1066 to presage the regime change ushered in by the Norman Conquest, and it was observed in the Americas, too. These two comets frame my series of novels—with this difference, that the sightings of the two comets in my novels occur in the fantasy-verse, not in real-life history!

The nine books of the three interconnected series are all available in print or for Kindle through www.amazon.com. For more information about the novels in the series, and for a playlist that includes many of the songs the characters play and sing, go to my author web site, www.janemwiseman.com. To see the way people, places, and things may have looked in the Stormclouds/Harbingers world, go to my nine Pinterest boards: *Medieval Life—Gyrfalcon, Medieval Life—Shrike, Medieval Life—Stormbird* (for the **Stormclouds** series); *Medieval Life—10th Century* (about *Blackbird Rising*), *Medieval Life—Halcyon, Medieval*

Life—Firebird, Medieval Life—Ghost Bird (for the **Harbingers** series);. *Medieval Life—Martlet* and *Medieval Life—Nightingale* (for the **Betwixt & Between** companion series).

The "flavor" of the three series varies a bit. The novels of the **Stormclouds** and **Betwixt & Between** series are a bit darker and more adult, while the novels of the **Harbingers** series are a bit more YA/NA in flavor. Even though, chronologically, the **Stormclouds** novels come first, you may begin either with the **Stormclouds** novels or the **Harbingers** novels, and may want to read the **Betwixt & Between** novels last. A stand-alone novel, *Dark Ones Take It*, is true to its title. Pretty dark!

The Novels:

A Gyrfalcon for a King (Stormclouds, book 1) : King Ranulf is cursed, a curse of his own making, through his own misdeeds. Which of his sons will redeem him and which will be his undoing? Artur, the crown prince, scholarly and retiring? Audemar, the second son, conspiring to unseat him? Avery, the third son, alert to the dangers that surround the throne? Or John, Ranulf's bastard son—John the minstrel, John the mage.

The Call of the Shrike (Stormclouds, book 2) : Ranulf's true-born son Prince Avery and his bastard son John band together with three friends in the guerilla action they name The Rising. The young warriors of The Rising set out to right a great wrong that threatens the realm. They face a mighty enemy—not the enemy they thought they were fighting, but one more dangerous than they could ever have imagined.

Stormbird (Stormclouds, book 3) : The ragtag band of The Rising faces near-impossible odds in its quest for justice. How can the Six hope to prevail when they fight without resources; when they are picked off one by one? When they face an evil man backed by an unimaginably evil force? John's young brother Wat must take up his brother's fight, struggling against not only the powerful enemies of The Rising but his own self-doubts. Meanwhile, in the grasp of Caedon, their enemy, the Princess Diera and the man she loves must do the same.

Blackbird Rising (Harbingers, book 1):   An orphaned young girl, a band of spies and assassins, a sister lost, a queen found—in the midst of chaos and treachery, Mirin must somehow learn to trust. Only then can she fulfill the mission John the minstrel left her. Only then can she live up to the promise and the magic of her music.

Halcyon (Harbingers, book 2) : On the run, Mirin and Wat try to carve out a new life together. But when everything is taken from Mirin, she must find the strength to go on alone. Her music sustains her, and so does the mysterious power of the fisher-bird, the harbinger of her god.

Firebird (Harbingers, book 3) : Keera has one goal—avenging her parents—and boundless confidence. After all, she has her magic powers, and they are second to none. When she finds she must fight her battle with only her wits and her grit, how can she possibly prevail? But the girl has friends: an old mage who helps her, a young man with a twinkle in his eye who can't get her out of his mind—and a ghost.

Ghost Bird (Harbingers, book 4) : Keera and Gwyl voyage in Gwyl's dragon ship to the heart of a new continent. But their enemies from the world left behind are not done with them yet. The two of them have to fight for the life they want, pursued by a powerful evil, relentless and closing in. Lucky for them Keera is an ornithomancer like her mother, Mirin, and like her uncle, John—the kind of mage who calls upon the mysterious powers of birds.

The Martlet is a Wanderer (Betwixt & Between, book 1) : Who is Silence? He can't speak to tell anyone the role he played in the conspiracy called The Rising, and he can't remember it anyway. He knows only that he needs to find two people: a friend, and a woman who means more to him than life itself. How can he possibly carry out this mission? Especially since he might be dead. (The events of this novel take place in parallel with *Halcyon*.)

The Nightingale Holds Up the Sky *(Betwixt & Between , book 2)* : Say you've been kidnapped and dragged to the underworld. Say the man who loves you wanders the realm looking for you. Say he finds a way in. But suppose you don't want to be found. As for the fate of the realm in the grip of evil, the fate of the world underneath the Spheres; as for justice—what if you forge your own? (The events of this novel take place in parallel with *Halcyon, Firebird,* and *Ghost Bird*.)

And now: *Dark Ones Take It , being the origin story of Caedon and his brother Maeldoi.* Caedon and Maeldoi are gwrgi—creatures who look like the rest of us, except for their amber eyes. When they get into a rage, they transform. Like werewolves? Not exactly. To an out-of-control bestial form of themselves. As they reach manhood, the dangerous age, the brothers are separated. Caedon is adopted by Gilles de Rais, a powerful mage with powerful secrets, a sorcerer who values Caedon's rage and schemes how to use it. Maeldoi is taken off by his fellow gwrgi to be taught how to control the rage inside him. **Brother against brother.** When Caedon and Maeldoi meet again, the fate of the Spheres Themselves hangs in the balance.

About the Author

I hope you have enjoyed *The Martlet is a Wanderer*, Book I of Betwixt & Between, a mini-series of two novels that span the interval between the Stormclouds/Harbingers fantasy novels. Please leave a review of my novel on amazon.com and other web sites for readers and book lovers. I care about what my readers think! Please visit my author page on amazon.com and my author web site, www.janemwiseman.com. Follow my blog about speculative fiction, www.fantastes.com.

Jane Wiseman splits her time between Minneapolis and Albuquerque. She loves fantasy in all its forms, enjoys her family, reads all the time, and writes in many different modes. As for fantasy, she writes books that she would like to read. She also paints.

A NOTE OF ACKNOWLEDGMENT

Thanks to my wonderful daughter, Margaret Govoni, for your editing eye, especially in the early stages. You steered me away from many mishaps and missteps, Margaret. All the remaining ones are mine alone.

Many thanks to my friend Bob S., beta-reader extraordinaire.

Thanks for all the helpful suggestions I've gathered from a number of online Litreactor workshops, www.Litreactor.com and from other writing workshops, especially Tinker Mountain Writers:

www.hollins.edu/academics/workshops-online-writing-courses/tinker-mountain-writers-workshop-residential/

and the (sadly now defunct) Taos Summer Writers' Conference. The instructors' comments and suggestions were of course incredibly helpful, but I have valued beyond measure the comments and suggestions of my fellow workshop attendees. Thanks to all of you! You may not have been able to save me from all my writing sins, but you saved me from many. Thanks also to the Anam Cara Writer's and Artist's Retreat, www.anamcararetreat.com, on the Beara Peninsula of Ireland. What a peaceful and lovely place to write! Thanks, Sue!

And finally, thanks to all you Norrathians out there. You are my true battle buddies. You know who you are. You are my fantasy friends in the purest sense of all.

Thanks to these artists and sites

. . .for the public domain and royalty-free graphic design elements making up the cover art and the other design elements of the novel:

NOTES ON *The Martlet is a Wanderer*, from the author

This novel is a work of fantasy, not historical fiction. Just the same, it is indebted to history. For visual depictions of some of the scenes and ideas in this novel, visit my Pinterest board, Medieval Life—Martlet . For a full play list of songs from the Harbingers and Stormclouds series, visit my web site, www.janemwiseman.com.

THE TIME-PERIOD is roughly early medieval, in a realm vaguely resembling several of the Celtic, Anglo-Saxon, Viking, and Norman kingdoms and military groups vying for power in the 10th and early 11th century British Isles shortly before the Norman Conquest. There are hints of different ethnic groups and warring ethnic factions.

Twelve Realms:

> The Sceptered Isle stands in for the united Heptarchy (seven main kingdoms) of mainland Anglo-Saxon England, but also includes the northern part of the realm (Scotland), the Western Isle (Ireland) and the northern isles (islands off the coast of Scotland— Inner and Outer Hebrides, Orkney, and Shetland Islands). It does not include the area around Lunds-fort (London), however. Tambourne, its capital (with the king's citadel, Tam Fort), is very loosely based on medieval Tamworth, in Staffordshire.
>
> The Eastern Baronies stands in for a loose confederation of powerful feudal lords spreading across medieval France and parts of Germany. In my tale, the Eastern Baronies also own territory on the mainland of the Sceptered Isle—the land around Lunds-fort (London) and along the eastern edge of the mainland—in addition to their strongholds across the Narrows (the English Channel).
>
> The Southern Primacy stands in for medieval territories in Italy (as well as Portugal and Spain), the homeland to which the Old Ones (ancient Romans) pulled back as their empire dwindled.

The Lyre Lands stands in for the vestiges of ancient Greece and the lands rimming the Aegean in the medieval era, including that vast metropolis the Vikings knew as "the Great City," Constantinople (aka Byzantium, Istanbul).

The Realm of the Asp: the ancient Near and Middle East.

The Burnt Lands is a vague concept to people of the Sceptered Isle and similar northern realms. It stands in for North Africa and below, through Sub-Saharan Africa, but people in the northern realms know little of these lands.

The Ice-Realm stands in for medieval Norway and, in a loose sense, the other parts of Scandinavia.

The Fire Isle stands in for medieval Iceland.

The Mountain Fastnesses :the Alpine regions of Europe.

The Trade Road Fortifications: the old Silk Road of the late ancient world through the Renaissance, stretching along the Eurasian steppes.

The Silk Lands : China and southeast Asia.

The Forgotten Kingdom: the Indian subcontinent. No one in the world of Ranulf and his descendants knows much about this place.

ALSO:

The Unknown Lands (the Americas) across the Great Sea stretching to the west. Travelers have come back with tales of these lands but no one knows whether they really exist.

THE CONCEPT OF TWO COMPETING RELIGIOUS GROUPS , worshippers of the Lady Goddess vs. worshippers of an elemental universe controlled by earth, sea, fire, and sky, is fantasy but based on some actual bits of information about belief systems in post-Roman Britain and medieval beliefs in general, especially medieval ideas about the body and healing. (Present-day astrologers have their own settled ideas about these matters. I know nothing about their ideas and don't pretend to.) People in the fantasy world of this novel have a vague sense that there were even older gods than these, although they don't know much about them.

THE OVERALL CONCEPT OF THE UNIVERSE is Pythagorean: nine revolving transparent crystalline spheres carry the heavenly bodies (sun, moon, stars, planets) around the earth at their center. As the spheres revolve, they sing—although only those pure enough can hear this music of the spheres. This idea from the ancient classical Near East and then Rome (mentioned by Cicero in *De Republica*, and also by the philosopher of late antiquity, Boethius) was widespread in the medieval period and made its way into medieval Christianity and became important in the Renaissance, especially through the so-called Dream of Scipio in the re-discovered 6th part of Cicero's book—obviously long before anyone knew anything about the way the actual physical universe works. The Greek philosopher Empedocles envisioned this universe held up by the principle of harmony, produced when strife and serenity are held in balance.

THE COG, the workhorse ship of the middle ages, would not have had an enclosed cargo hold until after the time period of my novel. However, my novel is set in fantasyland, so my cogs do. Here's more about what they looked like and how they were sailed:
https://www.youtube.com/watch?v=JLT3cwVJn0Y
http://nautarch.tamu.edu/class/316/cog/

GILLES DE RAIS is an actual historical figure. A member of the French aristocracy, he supported Joan of Arc during the Hundred Years War between France and England, and fought at her side. Despite that heroic part of his life, he dabbled in the occult, thought of himself as a sorcerer, and confessed to being one of the most prolific serial killers in human history. His victims were almost all children. (The WiKippedia description alone is much more horrifying than anything I've written here.) Most historians believe Gilles was guilty of these crimes, although various conspiracy theorists have raised doubts. The real Gilles de Rais lived long after the time-period of this novel, but my fantasy version of Gilles de Rais lived many lives before he came to the attention of history, and many lives after. Could he be living another of his lives still? I'm not saying!

PSYCHOGENIC MUTISM and related disorders: A great deal of controversy swirls about this term and associated terms. What, aside from neurological damage, might cause such disorders? Here is a selection of references, in case you are interested (note that I am by no means a medical expert):
https://www.researchgate.net/publication/280242064 Speech and voice disorders in patients with psychogenic movement disorders
https://www.ncbi.nlm.nih.gov/pmc/articles/PMC3137816/
https://journalofethics.ama-assn.org/article/recognizing-and-treating-conversion-disorder/2008-03
http://www.onnovdhart.nl/wp-content/uploads/2008/09/somatoform ww1.pdf

CASTLES AND FORTS in the actual 10th century British Isles had long been built on the plans of the old hill forts and brochs that had served as fortifications for centuries. But by this time, Norman-style castles were becoming more common, fitting our popular conception of the medieval castle. My fantasy forts and castles are more like those.

VAMPIRISM is a complicated topic, and it's not just about fanged, blood-sucking, black-clad people who can transform into bats and are chased by buff young California girls or hunters with fake Dutch accents. So-called "psychic vampirism" is described in this article:
https://www.researchgate.net/publication/283273380 The Psychic Vampire and Vampyre Subculture
My fantasy version of Gilles is probably more akin to the medieval notion of the incubus or other types of parasitic demons than about vampires as usually depicted in popular culture, and he is also a necromancer.

THE MARTLET is an iconic depiction of the common swift, used as a mark of cadence for a fourth son in heraldry. The heraldic depiction of the martlet shows a small bird with folded wings. In place of feet, it has bundles of feathers, signifying that (in medieval bird lore) swifts never land but live their whole lives on the wing. Some think the association of younger sons of the nobility with the martlet icon represented their landless state—they had no place to call home, the way swifts, not having feet, can never land. Real swifts often nest in crevices of cliff sides.

COMBAT SKILLS IN THE 10TH/11TH CENTURIES: This is a complicated technical subject. Some of my details are authentic. Others are fantasy or are drawn from later centuries. I'm taking a certain amount of fantasy license here, readers. Thanks to the YouTube channel Modern History,
https://www.youtube.com/playlist?list=PLEdnpoTDGX7LE454gNUJrm2pMD3 wpLOVY,
and to web sites such as The Arma, especially
http://www.thearma.org/essays/StancesIntro.htm#.XOTYeIhKhPY
and the site's great collection of swordsmanship manuals,
http://www.thearma.org/manuals.htm#.XOsQsYhKhPY;
among others. Anything I've gotten wrong is not because of these sites! Anything I've gotten right probably is.

And here is Giocomo di Grassi on rapier and dagger fights, a treatise he wrote in 1570 and which served as a main text on the use of weapons for Tudor England (later than my time period, true):
http://www.cs.unc.edu/~hudson/digrassi/

THE PLATONIC SOLIDS are a very ancient mechanism for understanding the universe, reaching back further than the Greek philosopher Plato (born around 428 BCE, or maybe a bit later; died around 348 BCE), who described them (hence the name). *The Stanford Encyclopedia of Philosophy* gives the philosophical background in its discussion of Plato's dialogue, *Timaeus* (see section 8, "Physics"):
https://plato.stanford.edu/entries/plato-timaeus/
For a readily available translation, see:
http://classics.mit.edu/Plato/timaeus.html
Euclid (maybe born around 325 BCE) described them, too, in Book XIII of his *Elements*:
https://mathcs.clarku.edu/~djoyce/java/elements/bookXIII/bookXIII.html
The math education web site MathWorld gives a mathematical explanation (far over my head):
http://mathworld.wolfram.com/PlatonicSolid.html
But the solids have been used in fortune-telling and games of chance and other gaming (think of the many-sided dice of Dungeons & Dragons, for example) since time immemorial. There are four of these geometrical solids: a cube (six faces), to the ancient world representing the element earth; a tetrahedron (four faces), to the ancient world representing fire; an octahedron (eight faces) representing air; and an icosahedron (twenty faces) representing water. There was also a fifth solid that Plato and Aristotle described very mysteriously: the twelve-sided dodecahedron, which they thought might have something to do with the composition of the heavens.
Some believe Neolithic objects discovered in Scotland may be evidence that people were thinking about the properties of the solids as far back as prehistoric times. There is quite a lot of skepticism about that from reliable sources, however:
https://studylib.net/doc/7289332/the-macplatonic-solids--mathematics-in-ne-olithic-scotland

MACHIAVELLI'S *THE PRINCE* is the book Gilles de Rais brought back from his travels to a different plane and had Caedon transcribe. Somehow, completely improbably, the version Gilles managed to bring back was W. K. Marriott's 1908 translation into English. A better version for English readers is probably the

Russell Price translation in the Cambridge Texts in the History of Political Thought series, 1988.

ROCK CLIMBING is a strenuous sport, especially so-called crack climbing. I have used a few details from that sport, I hope accurately. Here is an interesting discussion of the sport's techniques: https://hikethepla.net/11-tips-to-learn-how-to-crack-climb/ But that's with equipment. See also this article about free soloing, which is what Silence is doing:
https://www.liveabout.com/dangerous-allure-of-free-solo-climbing-755444
Don't try this at home. (Remember, Silence has no fear of it because he is essentially already dead.)

"YOUR MOM" INSULTS have featured prominently in the obscenity vocabularies of many cultures since time immemorial. See
https://www.theguardian.com/football/2006/jul/12/worldcup2006.sport

NJARDARHEIMR is not an actual Viking Age village but a so-called "living museum" in Norway built in 2017 to introduce tourists to Viking life. Visit Njardarheimr! (I hope that mollifies the management, and that they take my allusion as a true sign of admiration, not as making light of their important enterprise.)
https://www.visitnorway.com/listings/viking-village-njardarheimr/200194/

CHESS was an important game in Europe from about the 10th century on, probably brought by the Vikings up the river trade routes from Constantinople ("The Great City"). Here's a quick account:
https://www.mark-weeks.com/aboutcom/aa06e13.htm

CLIFF DIVING: Except for very accomplished stunt and high divers, this endeavor is best accomplished by a leap with the feet pointed straight down: https://adventure.howstuffworks.com/outdoor-activities/water-sports/cliff-diving4.htm. Even then, it's a highly dangerous activity that should be reserved (unless they're characters in a fantasy novel, and only then if the Sea Child protects them!) for trained athletes. Even more dangerous are actual dives head-down, especially from great heights or into pools of unknown depths. Don't try this at home, either.

DROWNPROOFING is a technique taught to members of the U.S. Navy and Marines to stay in the water under adverse conditions without drowning. It is easier for a person with a "floater" body type than for a "sinker." During that training, trainees practice with hands and feet bound—difficult but certainly not impossible. This blog post describes one trainee's experience: http://www.stephentemplin.com/blog/seal-training-9-drownproofing

IMPRESSMENT: Throughout medieval and Renaissance Europe and into the 19th century, "impressing" men into the lowest ranks of an army or navy was the way a military force enrolled many of its common soldiers and sailors. Press gangs roamed harbors and taverns looking for vagrants and other men who wouldn't have powerful family members to protest when they were taken and forcibly made part of an army or navy. In the British Isles, the practice went back to the 13th century (a bit later than my fantasy era), and even though impressment in the British Isles has been most closely associated with the Royal Navy, it was also a practice in the army. For example, in Shakespeare's *Henry IV part 1*, the scammer Falstaff impresses a lot of beggarly people into his company of soldiers, pocketing the coin he had been given to pay them.

THE BATTLE SCENE TOWARD THE END OF THIS NOVEL is based in part on Book V of Homer's *Iliad*.

APOLOGIES for my petty thefts from, modifications of, and irreverent references to William Shakespeare; to W. K. Marriott's 1908 translation of Niccolò Machiavelli's early 16th century political treatise, *The Prince*; and to Homer's *Iliad*—with a little nod (who can resist?) to *Monty Python and the Holy Grail*. Lawyers! I say "theft," but I am making a joke. The literary figure of speech I am really using is "allusion," and my novels are at least partly a kind of literary mash-up.

And a final thank-you to Warren Robinett, the inventor of the easter egg.

The Nightingale Holds Up the Sky:
Betwixt & Between, Book II

the companion books to the Harbingers/Stormclouds fantasy novels

Prologue

Ailys, do this for me," said Caedon. He hesitated for just a moment before he spoke, such a small hesitation he doubted she'd notice his uncertainty. If she did, though, she'd start immediately planning how to use it against him. He knew this. He knew Ailys too well. Perhaps he shouldn't reveal so much, to such a person.

But no. He had to speak. He had to enlist her in his plans, as unpleasant as he always found her.

"Why should I do a thing for you, Caedon? You're such a liar. You promised me power, and look what I've got. Nothing." Ailys's voice rose to its usual whine.

Be easy, Caedon told himself. *It will be fine. She isn't aware of any worrying of mine.* He thought of a sleek cat worrying at the corpse of some dead animal, and shivered. If any worrying of some helpless victim was to be done, Ailys would do the worrying. But then he shook the thought away. *She has one thing before her eyes, ever. Herself. Here she goes,* he thought, *doing what Ailys always does.*

"You're queen. I don't call that nothing." He tried taking a reasonable tone with her.

It didn't work.

"A mere name. A mere sop." Her eyes narrowed angrily.

"You do have power. Gilles has given you powers," Caedon argued.

"Yes. Mine are the rival of Labinia's now. They rival her sister Vigilia's. And soon, Gilles promises me, I'll be more powerful than those two. Morgan herself will teach me."

"You see? That would never have happened if not for me. How can you say I've given you nothing I promised."

"Gilles is the one who has given my powers to me. Not you."

"If not for me, you wouldn't have even known about Gilles. Not Gilles the way he truly is. You would only have seen what the world sees, a powerful noble."

She gave him a grudging smile. "What about those horrible men you made me marry." Her lips pursed up in disgust. "Artur. What a bore. And then that pig Audemar."

"But they're gone. You remain. You're queen."

"Artur is dead," she said with a certain satisfaction. "We made certain of that, hey? But Audemar. Where is he? Is he dead too?"

"I'm not sure," said Caedon carefully. "But he's gone. That's the main thing. Leaving you with all this." He spread his arms wide.

"Look around this castle and tell me something, Caedon. Am I actually imprisoned here?"

"Of course not," he said, trying to give her a sincere smile.

"I hear you're going around calling yourself king."

"But I am king. I defeated Audemar. Wherever he may be, dead, alive, who knows? But one thing is certain: he's finished. Then, with the defeat of The Rising, the last threat, weak though it was. . . ." He swallowed hard and made himself go on. "Soon I'll have Diera in my grasp. She's nothing, of course. Less than nothing. A woman can't be monarch. I'll have her executed to make sure no one thinks otherwise."

"They're calling her queen, not me," Ailys said, her voice turning vicious. "Not in my hearing, of course. But I have my sources. And why, pray tell me," she rounded on Caedon, "can't a woman be monarch? If I'm not a monarch, and I'm not married to a king, what kind of queen am I? Are you thinking you'll have me executed as well?"

"Certainly not. We're allies." He tried an ingratiating smile.

"You promised I wouldn't have to marry you."

"I meant that promise." Now Caedon didn't have to pretend to be sincere.

"But you're planning to marry. Won't that make your consort the queen?"

"I suppose, in a nominal sort of way."

"So where does that leave me?" Ailys demanded.

"How about Queen Dowager?"

Ailys turned an icy stare on him. "That makes me sound old."

"Well, then," said Caedon, shrugging and throwing his arms wide. "What can I give you, Ailys? I need your help." He was taking a risk for sure, trusting her. But what could he do? He did need her help. He was desperate. Best not to let her see that, of course.

He had watched her carefully as she moved to the deep embrasure of a window in her private quarters in the castle and stood looking out at the high country surrounding it. The castle used to be Treddian's. The hapless addlepate, he was dead. Audemar had caught him supporting Caedon and had him executed as a traitor—one of Audemar's last futile acts against Caedon.

Now Treddian's widow and daughters were neatly packed away into the countryside somewhere. A good thing, because Caedon needed something handsome to give Ailys, once he had defeated Audemar and driven him into hiding. Treddian's castle was just the thing.

Ailys liked big things. Big gems. Big castles. He flinched away from the other big thing she liked. The castle, though. Now it belonged to Ailys.

But she was right. In a way, she was stuck here. Not exactly imprisoned, but not really free to roam about his realm. Certainly not free to exercise any sort of power in it.

His realm. It was his, now. Just as Gilles had promised him it would be. How far he'd come, from that penniless half-savage lad Gilles had taken to foster and tutor. Gilles had seen what was in him. Gilles had seen past Caedon's successful older brother. Only Gilles knew Caedon's true worth.

And he himself. He'd known it in himself.

Still, if Gilles hadn't given Caedon the means to exercise what he knew, he'd still be scratching and scrabbling, at best, for a handhold in the world of powerful men. At worst, he'd be squatting in some cave. Either way, always looked down on because of his kind. Always overshadowed by his older brother. Caedon knew he owed Gilles everything.

But then there was this one small matter Caedon had withheld from Gilles, in spite of all he owed his master and overlord. The small matter of Caedon being a father. The small matter of his failure to send his son to Gilles, as he was supposed to do. The small matter of his protecting the boy from Gilles and his appetites.

Caedon tried not to think about it, in case Gilles was focusing his attention on Caedon just now. If he were, he'd know Caedon's secret. Caedon felt himself breaking into a sweat at the thought.

"What's wrong with you? You look like the Dark Ones are after you." Ailys had swiveled around and trained her shrewd little eyes on Caedon. He stared back at her, wondering if she meant what she said as a simple insult, nothing more.

He got a grip on himself. Ailys was only a weak woman, and now her natural assets, such as they were, had begun to fade. Ailys's eyes had always been just a minim too close together, and now they had puffy little pockets underneath them. And her jawline was beginning, ever so slightly, to sag.

"The Dark Ones." Caedon tried to laugh. "No, I doubt they're after me. But I do have a small problem I'd like your help solving. I'd value your advice, Ailys."

"Now we come to it," she said sourly. "Not what you can do for me. What I can do for you."

Caedon drew in a breath. He took the leap. "I have a son."

Ailys laughed. "A bastard boy. That's a problem? Many powerful men have their bastards. Many ordinary men, too. What do you want me to do, help him to a position in my household? Done. I thought you were going to ask me to take on some unpleasant task, as you always have before."

"I'd never place a young man in your household, Ailys," said Caedon with a wry smile. He thought about the many Ailys had gotten within reach of her claws, and what she had done to them. Some of them from powerful families. That young prince of the Ice-realm, for example.

Ansgar. A very handy young man, as it turned out. Just when he'd needed such a man, there Ansgar was, easily bought. Easily wrested away from Ailys's influence. Now Ansgar owed his high position as king to Caedon, and someday, Caedon planned to call in that debt.

Then Caedon remembered something he'd nearly forgotten about Ailys.

Wat, he thought. She had had Wat in here helpless, until the ill-fated Earl Drustan got him away from her, shortly before Caedon had definitively, brutally taken care of his problem with the earl. Lucky Wat. If you could call such a life lucky, after what Caedon had done to him. He wasn't dead, though. He still lived underneath the Spheres, unlike all the other leaders of The Rising. But Wat wouldn't be lucky long.

Dark Ones take Rafe, Caedon snarled to himself, *thwarting my plans for Wat.*

But thinking of Rafe caused a pang of pain so severe to drill through him that he thought he wouldn't be able to catch his breath.

Ailys came up close to Caedon. She stared at him, her gaze fascinated. "What's wrong with you?" Then her eyes turned crafty. She began to toy with the neck of his tunic, as he made himself turn his thoughts from Rafe and stand there in front of Ailys without cringing away from her. "Odd you should say that, Caedon." Ailys's mouth was still flapping. Caedon tried to concentrate on what she was saying. "Odd that you'd imply no young lad is safe around me," she said, and smirked. "Many would say the same about you."

"What of it?" Caedon was irritated now. That was good. It steered his thoughts away from Rafe, and his grief. Because he did need Ailys's aid, and he had to be clear-headed if he were to get it without putting himself in danger. He shrugged out of her grasp. "Are we going to stand here trading insults, or are you going to help me?"

"Oh, very well," she said sulkily. "What do you need from me, and what do I get out of it?"

"I'll give you a place on my high council." *There*, he thought. *That brings a flush to her cheeks. She wants that.*

"Hmm," she said. "Maybe. If you throw in a fuck for old times' sake." Then she laughed raucously at Caedon's expression. "Never mind the fuck. I don't want you, either. Not any more."

She thought about it. "Very well. A place on the high council. That's something I do value. I accept. Depending on what you want, of course. Do I have the power to do this thing you want so badly?"

"I think so," he said carefully, recovering from Ailys's malicious little joke at his expense. He groaned inwardly at the effort he had once forced himself to summon up in order to satisfy her insatiable cravings.

"Well, tell me, then. I have things to do. Windows to gaze out. Servants to scold. Stable boys to corrupt."

"Listen, Ailys. I have enemies."

"No!" she said.

Ignoring her tone, he forged on. "Some of them have threatened magicks on my boy."

"Really? And Gilles doesn't know about them, and hasn't snuffed them out?"

"They're stealthy, Ailys, these enemies of mine. I'm sure Gilles will take care of them, or give me the means to do it, when he gets around to it, but they are mere hedge-mages, hardly worth his attention. Meantime, they'll go after Yann."

"Yann. That's his name?"

He nodded.

"Well, you're an odd one." Ailys regarded him with a frank smile, a genuine one. "You named him Yann, did you?" she murmured.

"Never mind that. Gilles has taught you some shielding powers, I believe."

"Yes."

"Could you cast one on him?"

"I'm pretty sure I could. I'd have to keep renewing it, though. These things start fading, after a season or so."

"If I brought him to you, say, several times a year? You could keep him pretty well shielded?"

"Yes. It's a small price to pay for a place on the high council."

"And Ailys. I don't want people knowing he's my son."

"Certainly. Might complicate things with that young girl you're about to take to wife."

"Oh, her," said Caedon dismissively. "She's of little moment. It's those mages. I know you'll have him well shielded, but I don't want any of those varlets finding out, in a roundabout way, and hanging around on the off chance they can damage him in between refreshers."

"I understand. Very wise."

"And he'll be with me at court, in some discreet position. You and I can watch over him." Caedon worried he was showing a bit too much of his troubled mind to Ailys. He worried Ailys might be getting suspicious.

But then, Ailys was fairly stupid, for all the powers she'd been granted. She'd have her little post. She'd never guess she wouldn't have any real power. She'd be occupied and happy, no longer the troublesome whiner she had proved to be, and she'd throw up that shielding spell, and he and Yann would be safe. It was, he said to himself, using a phrase of Gilles's, a win-win-win.

"I almost feel like the lad's mother," said Ailys, marveling. "Who is the lucky lady?"

"Oh. No one."

"Never figured you for the fatherly type, Caedon," she said, as he turned to leave her. She ushered him to the spiraling stairs that would take him to the castle's outer bailey and his horse.

Neither did I, he thought with surprise. Then he had another thought. He looked back at her. "Ailys, there's something else."

"What now?" she muttered.

"There's a girl involved."

"Not that unusual for a lad of what, around eighteen or nineteen. Unless he has your proclivities, of course."

"Nineteen. I want her gone, Ailys. The boy doesn't know his own mind."

"Shielding the boy might take some doing. But disappearing some little vixen. Very well. That will be the easy part. Consider her gone," said Ailys.

www.ingramcontent.com/pod-product-compliance
Lightning Source LLC
Chambersburg PA
CBHW021215260626
47172CB00002B/433